The Divine Arsonist

The Divine Arsonist

A Tale of Awakening

by Jacob Nordby

Awakened Life Publications
Boise, ID

Acknowledgments

I am deeply grateful for the many teachers, guides and helpers I have encountered. Without them, this book would not have been written. Several dear friends read the rough manuscript and offered critical encouragement: Mark, Shari, David, Craig, Roxanne, Lisa, Autumn and my mother, Corry.

My wife, Jennifer, held space for me to fall apart, find myself, write this book and do seemingly endless inner work.

I am grateful for the inspired help of independent editor, Autumn Antal. Her tenacity, patience and deep understanding of this book's spirit gave me great peace during the process.

Thanks to fellow author, Craig Hart, for formatting the book and providing much needed companionship along the way. www.CraigHartOnline.com

Thayne Rigby designed the cover, my website and is a friend I talk with almost every day. www.antishrillwebdesign.com

There are times on Earth when extraordinary consciousness invades everyday life. There are times on Earth when unseen forces make a calamity of the status quo. There are times on Earth when it seems as though a divine arsonist has set fire to the world as we know it.

— We live in such times.

Chapter One

"How are you feeling about this? You need to consider that before you make a decision," the stranger said.

I sat and looked at him across the campfire flames. In the mountain darkness, he seemed to flicker in and out of existence with the dancing firelight. Far away down the valley, an owl hooted. Suddenly the sound was over our heads in the tall pine tree. Another owl had answered the call. "Who," the owl asked persistently, "who, who?"

Yes, who indeed? Who was I? Who was living this night and who was this visitor sharing wine with me now under the stars?

The strange man sat still and looked into the fire. He appeared just a few hours ago and made me a most unusual proposition, but there was no urgency or nervousness in his manner. He was at rest and waiting for my reply, while at the same time, he gave me the sense that I could delay for decades before I answered if need be.

I, on the other hand, felt anything but restful. My central nervous system was sending out the kind of alarms that signal the fear of impending death. It was that same feeling of anticipation in the last seconds before a sky dive, or just after you've strapped in for the most insane roller coaster ride at an amusement park. I was sure that my mind was about to be blown.

I could not reconcile these physical sensations with my understanding of the man's words. Although what he said was not normal, it should not have triggered this powerful squeeze in my solar plexus. Something very big must be just below the surface, something that was not obvious to my conscious mind. It was as if I had crept onto the roof of a skyscraper. As if I were lying on my belly with my nose over the edge, watching the tiny people and cars moving seventy-nine stories below. Obviously, I would not fall. Yet I knew with deep inevitability, this time I would not be able to resist. Against all reason, I knew that I would leap, screaming and flailing into the unknown.

I rallied my senses and drew in a deep breath. The visitor's eyes met mine and he raised his eyebrows.

"I don't know how I feel," I said.

"You do," he told me, "but you don't want to admit to being afraid."

He was right. I knew better than to be afraid. I had cultivated a life of fearless behavior. Hadn't I? Fear was for lesser men and I had determined long ago not to be one of them.

"You should be afraid," he said. "Well, actually you shouldn't, but it is quite normal."

"That's it, though," I said. "I don't shrink from challenges. I meet life head on. I believe in the power of belief."

He fixed his powerful gaze on me. I felt locked in place.

"You are living a life you think you should live," he said. "You've built a castle in your mind and believe you're safe within its walls. If you come with me, I will take you to places so far away that you may never be able to return. If you do return, you will find your castle is no more. That's why you feel afraid."

"So you're asking me to change my whole life," I said.

"I'm asking you to let me show you things you've always suspected. Once you see them, once you experience them, once you know them with all your senses, then yes, you may have a hard time going back to what you currently call your life," he said.

~~~

The day a cosmic rock cracked the windshield of life as I knew it began like any other…

It happened on a bright autumn afternoon in mid-October. I was at my desk in a rare moment of stillness. Life was busy so life was good. I was an entrepreneur happily engaged in the pursuit of winning the "Big Game of Business."

I leaned back into the leather chair and rested my neck, something I seldom did in this office and closed my eyes. It felt great just to find a minute of quiet. My life was filled with meetings and telephone calls and debt payments and P&L sheets. I was a proud Super Servant to my clients and staff. I had studied intensely to become a man of value in every way.

Perhaps that's why I was so tired that day. It had been years since I had really slept well. I was famous among my friends and associates for waking up at 3:30 A.M. to devour books, write business plans and dream up exciting schemes.

A soft *"ding"* from the computer automatically brought my head upright. My eyes blinked open and took a few seconds to focus. I was like Pavlov's dog with my Outlook email notifications. It was now a conditioned response. I had a new message in my inbox. Must check it. Always.

This one was from my friend, Luke. He rarely sent me notes and when he did, they were straight from the heart. I double clicked and the new window opened.

>>*Hey, read this today while I sat by a lake up in the Wasatch Front. Thought you'd like it, wild man!*

"I went to the woods because I wished to live deliberately, to front only the essential facts of life, and see if I could not learn what it had to teach, and not, when I came to die, discover that I had not lived. I did not wish to live what was

not life, living is so dear; nor did I wish to practice resignation, unless it was quite necessary. I wanted to live deep and suck out all the marrow of life, to live so sturdily and Spartan-like as to put to rout all that was not life, to cut a broad swath and shave close, to drive life into a corner, and reduce it to its lowest terms."
— *Henry David Thoreau*

Love you buddy. Later.

Luke
P.S. Call me!

Something about that quote reverberated through my body like a deep gong. *Boomsheee!* I read it again. Then again.

"I went to the woods...to live deliberately, to front only the essential facts of life and see if I could not learn what it had to teach...to live deep and suck out all the marrow of life..."

It reminded me of one of my favorite movie scenes from *Dead Poets' Society* when Robin Williams leans in and whispers in a ghostly voice over his students' shoulders, *"Carpe...Carpe Diem...seize the day, boys! Make your lives extraordinary."*

I rubbed my eyes and rolled my neck. I could feel the accumulated weariness after a week of stress that often showed up as a headache by Friday afternoon.

Maybe today was a good time for a run to the cabin. I opened my calendar. It was hard to believe, but I didn't have much going on the rest of the day. I glanced out the window. The sun was shining and the orange leaves on the vine maple were being played by the breeze.

The phone intercom lit up and Sheila, my assistant, said, "Hey, I have a referral on the line. They want to meet today."

I closed my eyes and sighed. *Ah, yes. But the business needs me.*

"Um, okay. I can see them at 4 o'clock," I said. My finger hovered over the intercom button to switch it off. The gong sounded again inside me and I felt dizzy for a moment.

"No. Wait, Sheila. I need to get out of here today. Have one of the other guys meet them or see if they can be here on Monday," I said.

She was silent for a couple of seconds. I could hear her tapping on her keyboard.

"All right," she said finally, "I'll figure something out."

I felt guilty. *The company could use the extra revenue. What am I doing?*

I looked up when Sheila appeared in the doorway a few seconds later. She came in and leaned against the wall. She ran both hands through her dark hair and then crossed her arms.

"Are you doing okay today?" she said.

"Sure, what do you mean?"

"Oh, I don't know. You've been moody the last few days and it's not like you to turn down an appointment. Just checking to make sure everything's okay with you," she said.

I breathed deep and let my eyes wander over my desktop. Stacks. I was a stacker. I knew where everything was, but the volume of stuff that I had to keep track of always overwhelmed my ability to file it. That habit drove my neatnik partners crazy at times.

I looked back up at Sheila who was smiling a little.

"Yeah, I'm okay just kind of fried right now," I said. "It's been a long week. I don't usually do this, but I'm going to take off early. Maybe head up to the cabin and get some quiet...or something."

That's good," she said, "I worry about you sometimes."

"How do you mean?"

"Oh, you know...all of this," she gestured around the office, "It's all so important but I suspect you're a lot closer to red-lining than you know most of the time."

I was already closing down my programs and clicking the lid shut on the laptop.

"Well, I appreciate your concern," I said. "It's all part of the game. Ride hard, get there fast."

Sheila shrugged and uncrossed her arms.

"Get where fast? Never mind, let's just take some care with that," she said. "We don't need you burning out. I've got it covered the rest of the day. Everything will be fine. It's Friday."

She turned to leave.

"Thank you. You know the cabin has a phone if you need me. I'll take my laptop and check email from up there, too," I said.

She was shaking her head and waving her hands in the air as she left my office.

"Crazy people," I heard her mutter.

Her question lingered in the air, *"Get where fast?"*

You know. There.

I felt the silent gong crash in my gut again.

As soon as my car cleared the parking lot of the office complex, I knew that my historic decision to take off early on a Friday was good. Early autumn almost anywhere in the world is a wonderful season, but here in the high desert of Idaho it carries a special kind of magic. The backbone of dry summer heat broke in early September this year, after nearly three months of record-breaking high temperatures. Everyone was pitifully grateful for a week or two of clouds and rain.

Now, the weather had cleared and the wide sky was a deep-blue bowl held up by the golden hills that surround Boise. If you hiked up to the plateau known as Tablerock just outside the city, you could look down and survey the entire Treasure Valley. From there you could see why, according to legend, the early French explorers excitedly cried out *"Les bois, les bois!"* "The trees, the trees!" as they first glimpsed this view. The entire valley is surrounded by drab tan and gray sagebrush desert as far as the eye can see. The Boise River bisects the capitol city to create a willowy oasis along its banks, spread like a soft green carpet across the shallow floodplain. At this time of year, most of the maples were already showing tinges of orange and many cottonwoods were donning their golden fall cloaks.

My car windows were down and I could smell the smoke that the old farmers sent up as they burned the weeds in their irrigation ditches. The family farms were rapidly disappearing around the edges of town as new subdivisions full of miniature mansions sprouted like acres of asphalt-shingled mushrooms. Here and there, though, a stubborn holdout would forgo the big payoff for selling his land and maintain his pasture with several sheep, a steer and a couple of horses. I liked those old curmudgeons, many of them were descendants of early Basque settlers. I often felt that the urban sprawl was too quickly erasing important history and replacing it with the shallow veneer of modern luxury.

I plotted my next steps as I drove the short distance to my home. Arrangements must be made. My wife, Jennifer, understanding woman that she was, would need to be notified and perhaps cajoled just a bit. Our three children kept both of us busy all week, but my schedule often gave me an excuse to pass the mundane burdens off on her. I hoped that she wouldn't feel bad about my decision to get away without warning her first.

I would pack lightly, but I still needed to change clothes and grab a few things from the store on my way out of town.

Really, that was about it. I felt light and excited as the plan came together.

I hadn't done something like this for far too long. It felt like cutting class and catching a matinee, a freedom I envied of the "B" or "C" students in school but never indulged in myself. I was and always have been an "A" student. "A" students did not goof off. They achieved.

I fished out my wireless earpiece and voice-dialed Jennifer.

"Hey, baby," I said when she picked up.

"Oh, hey," she said.

"You doing all right?"

She blew out her breath, "Well, it's been quite a day."

This did not portend well for my easy escape to the mountains.

"What's going on?"

"Oh, you know, nothing too crazy. Lots of stuff with the kids. They have their fall yard sale at school and I promised to help this weekend. What's going on with you?"

I was relieved; this didn't sound like extraordinary stress, just the usual. I could probably trade some good-behavior credits and the promise of a date night in exchange for my solitary jaunt.

"Well," I said, "I am officially playing hooky today. Unless it's going to mess up your life a lot, I think I'll run up to the cabin for a night or two."

She didn't answer right away.

"Are you going up alone?" she asked finally.

"Yes, why?"

"Oh, well, no reason I guess. It's just not like you to take off by yourself. I thought maybe you were making it a buddy trip."

"Yeah. I can't exactly explain why, but I really need some quiet time right now," I said.

"That can't hurt," she said, "I've wanted to make you go off by yourself for awhile, but you never seem to take a real break from people."

"Well, all right then. So you're okay with things for a couple of days?"

"Yeah, I'll get pizza and a movie for the kids tonight. Maybe tomorrow we'll go to the park after the school yard sale. Just call me when you get up there so I know you're safe," she said.

This was too easy, but I had learned from years of sales experience that when someone gives you the buying signal—quit selling. Shut up and seal the deal. Press hard, third copy is yours. All of that.

"Okay," I said, "thanks for this. Let's do dinner together next week, just the two of us. Love you."

"I love you, too," she said.

And just like that, the final piece fell into place. I built my bridge to escape from the city. Now, off to see The Wizard.

~~~

Half an hour later, I was checking out of the grocery store with a few things. The cabin was a communal family lodge, so we maintained a full refrigerator. My basket held a few cans of soup, some eggs, a couple of bottles of a decent Merlot and a bag of fresh-ground coffee. At the last second, I tossed in a package of toilet paper as my nod to keeping the place stocked up.

Within ten minutes, I was crossing the bridge over the Boise River and following two-lane Highway 21. It winds through the old gold-mining territories surrounding Idaho City and terminates in Stanley, deep in the Sawtooth National Forest—one of North America's hidden alpine treasures.

I glanced to my left down the valley and watched the cluster of downtown high-rise buildings and the state capitol disappear behind the hills as the road turned north. To my right, the river flowed close to the road now. I passed several Spandex-suited bicyclists who leaned their helmets forward and pedaled hard into the stiff breeze blowing down the canyon.

This part of the forty-minute drive always filled me with anticipation. The high hills closed in behind me and the city disappeared. I was quickly surrounded by rough country. Even from the paved highway, I could still see traces of the original Oregon Trail cut into the sides of the canyon. It felt as if I were literally stepping backward in time. Here I was, speeding down a ribbon of asphalt in my tight little sportscar capsule. A single, sudden turn of the wheel could catapult me into a brushy ravine...where I might not be discovered for months. I loved the wild potential that lived here. Whenever I ventured outside the invisible walls of civilization, I felt unseen storm clouds of stress and fatigue vanish from my spirit.

In the new-found silence, I noticed that I had a CD playing with the volume turned down low. The music was like a tiny voice in the distance. I thumbed the volume switch on the steering wheel and Bob Dylan's harsh quaver boomed from the speakers,

you used to be so amused
at Napoleon in rags and the language that he used
go to him now, he calls you, you can't refuse
when you got nothin', you got nothin' to lose
you're invisible now, you got no secrets to conceal

how does it feel?
how does it feel?
to be on your own
no direction home
like a complete unknown
like a rolling stone?

His distinctive harmonica trailed off and the track ended. I often felt haunted by this song, but now the questions pounded the silent gong that had unsettled me all day.

How does it feel? Yes, how does it feel... An important question was being posed to me. I honestly had no idea what the answer should be.

Thirty-five minutes later, I turned off the gravel county road and drove up the sandy driveway. It wound gently between the tall, old-growth Ponderosa pine trees on our property. The recent rain and winds had showered the ground with long brown pine needles that crackled under my tires.

I stopped the car in front of the lodge. As I got out, I stretched my arms wide and breathed deep. I have lived all over the country and enjoyed most places, but this spot held special magic for me. The majesty of the views from atop our paradise knoll always stunned me. I turned around in a complete circle, the sun warm on my skin. We were surrounded by the higher hills and to the northeast, I could see the jagged Sawtooth Mountains. Our lodge stood on an open-topped hill that rolled down into a wooded meadow. In all, we owned twenty acres and I loved every square yard. During different times of the year a herd of elk and flocks of wild turkeys used our land as their bedroom. In the evening, we often heard them talking as they grazed and foraged close to the house.

I glanced at my watch. Despite sneaking out of the office early and making good time on my trip, it was already almost four o'clock. Up here, the sun would touch the top of the mountains in just a couple of hours. Once that happened, night fell fast. The temperature dropped ten degrees as soon as the sun set and it was already cooler here than down in the valley.

I loaded my grocery sacks and duffel bag into the house and walked around checking little details. Everything appeared to be in order. There were a few nearly dead wasps creeping up the inside of the windows. I could smell the funky odor of a dead mouse in one of the traps. This was all normal. I swept the wasps outside, emptied the mousetrap and started a pot of coffee brewing. This was my jittery time. It always hit me like this when I came here to the cabin. My body and soul sensed the need to fall into the natural rhythms of the place, but my mind yanked and pulled playing tug of war.

I felt like I needed to be doing something, sort of guilty. The quiet called to me, but I never felt like I had earned the right to stop. The silence itself was dangerous, a seductive siren who would lure me far off my course if I listened to her song.

I wandered out to the front porch and leaned against one of the rugged pillars. I closed my eyes and let the sun warm my face. Earthy sage and pine needle scents rose on a soft breeze.

Slow down. My mind caught up fragments of the Thoreau quote from the email I had received earlier.

"I went to the woods...to live deliberately, to front only the essential facts of life and see if I could not learn what it had to teach...to live deep and suck out all the marrow of life..."

Suck out all the marrow of life.

I went back inside to pour a cup of coffee.

Live deep

But I was doing that, wasn't I? I believed in the power of human potential. I even coined a slogan for my company, "A Passion for Extraordinary Service." I was stretched to capacity in my pursuit of the best kind of life. I took risks and carried terrific burdens in my journey toward success. Did Thoreau have other things in mind? I was beginning to think so.

The very idea that I might not be living up to an ideal made me uncomfortable. I was all about making the grade in every possible way.

The deep gong went off in my solar plexus again and I had to steady myself against the counter.

This has to stop.

Back outside and down the stairs, I unfolded a canvas camp chair by the fire pit. It was one of the deluxe models with its own built-in footrest. I turned it to face the remaining sunshine, sat down and leaned back with my coffee mug warming both hands. I relaxed and let my eyes focus miles deep into the bright-blue sky. A large black turkey vulture soared high across my field of vision and disappeared. I closed my eyes and breathed.

Chapter Two

I was splitting a fine cedar log with the hatchet.

Pop!

The gleaming metal edge sank into the wood and two clean halves flew apart. I put the hatchet down and shredded a few handfuls of the bark. I tore it into smaller strips and then worked the loose fibers until they formed a mass of rough woolly tinder. I placed this into the center of the fire pit and rocked back on my heels. A woody-spice aroma rose from the cut pieces. The smell conjured swirling primal memories of firesides that illuminated myriad lifetimes back to the mysterious void of prehistory.

A few more easy swings of the hatchet reduced one of the half rounds into thin wedges and then down to beautiful kindling splinters.

I took my time arranging the makings of my fire. The aromatic sticks formed a teepee around the tinder. It was good.

I struck a match and held the flame to the frayed cedar bark edges. Immediately, glowing yellow-orange fire fingers spread through the tinder and thin blue smoke curled up between the kindling.

I had fire!

I sat for a moment and watched the flames take hold and race up the dry wood.

The hungry infant fire spit and whined for more fuel, so I added a few of the larger pieces. These also gave themselves cheerfully to the blaze and I moved my face back from the rising heat.

I sat back on the ground and hugged my knees. The toes of my boots nearly touched the flames. Evening had fallen and the back half of my body was colder than the front. I was yin-yang. Dark-light. Cold-hot.

A small airplane sound caught my attention. I watched the tiny blinking lights track its progress over the dark ridgeline of the hills. The sun was well down but the moon and the first stars were not yet visible. From down in the valley, I could hear mongrel dogs barking back and forth to each other on the porches of their owners' ramshackle cabins.

The moment stretched out into silence.

"Hey!"

I jumped awake in the camp chair. Confused. My whole leg jerked back hard from a burning pain in the sole of my left foot. Coffee sloshed over the lip of the mug and spread in a dark lukewarm circle over the crotch of my jeans. *What the hell's going on?*

"Sorry to wake you up like that. Your toe was going up in flames," he said.

I shook my head and squinted across a real fire. A man was standing there holding several logs in his arms. He stooped and dropped them on the ground within the circle of light.

This was strange. My head felt ponderous and dizzy. I must have been asleep, but here was the same fire I had just built. In my dream.

"Who are you?" I asked.

He didn't appear threatening and I wasn't in a position to be aggressive. *Better go along and see what develops,* I thought.

He took his time about answering and squatted down to hold his hands out for warmth. He was dressed like a hiker. Expensive Merrell boots, olive-green canvas shirt, khaki cargo shorts. He wore a weathered bush hat made of leather. Three days' beard growth made his tan look swarthy.

"I was hiking along that ridge through the national forest land," he gestured, sweeping his hand to the east, "Wasn't sure where I was going. Came through here and found you sleeping in your chair."

"And the fire?" I said. The silent gong vibrated deep in my body again and a prickly feeling crawled between my shoulder blades.

He didn't answer and stared into the flames. *Sure of himself, this one. He wandered on to my land, walked up to my house and decided to light a fire while I slept a couple of feet away?* This seemed like more than just a case of confident behavior. He appeared sure that he was in the right place and on time for something. *For what?*

"I came a long way today," he said finally, "When I got here it was getting dark and chilly. I went ahead and started the fire. Didn't think you'd mind. I went to get some bigger wood and when I came back, you'd stuck your foot in the fire. That's when I yelled and you woke up."

I shook my head.

"Wait. Back up. I mean, it's fine that you lit the fire and I'm happy to meet you, but what...who are you?"

"You ready for this?" he said.

"Probably not," I said, "but that won't change anything, will it?"

He laughed aloud and his eyes met mine. Even in the deepening twilight, I could see that they were striking blue. He wasn't exactly handsome, but he exuded strength and charisma. When he stood up straight, he had the lithe powerful look of an athlete. You would notice him in a crowd.

"I'm Lucius," he said.

Not a surprise he has a strange name, I thought.

"Hi, Lucius, I'm Jacob."

We leaned forward and shook hands.

"Yes," he said.

Okay, time to get control of the situation.

"Lucius," I said, "look, I don't think we've ever met. I mix with lots of people but I never forget faces. You'd stand out anyway. So, maybe you could go ahead and enlighten me about what you're doing here?"

He laughed out loud again. His eyes and teeth flashed in the firelight.

"Enlighten you...sure," he said, "I know how you must be feeling. By the way, I'm not laughing at you. I just thought your choice of words was ironic."

He sobered and his heavy eyebrows drew together as he fixed me with his gaze again.

"There was no way for me to show up and make this seem normal. I could have been even more dramatic—really blown you away—but you're paying attention without that. Here's the bottom line. You and I have had an appointment for many years. We're both right on time. You probably don't remember agreeing to this, but I'll refresh your memory as we go along. Regardless of that, we have a lot to discuss. I'm aware this feels strange. In fact, I suspect that you've felt strange all day, maybe for months now. You have a choice to make," he shrugged, "I can easily just leave if you want me to. I'll disappear and you'll never see me again. You can get drunk and convince yourself that it was all a strange dream. Or, you can hear me out. If you have some food, why don't you bring it out here by the fire and we'll talk."

The gong crashed inside my body with a booming crescendo. I felt ancient stone wheels that held the temple gates closed slowly start to turn as an incantation was spoken. Moving, lining up and falling into place.

I was unable to move or speak for a moment. This stranger's words were improbable, but they made sense of the disturbing sensations that had brought me here today. The iron key had turned in the lock. I could feel the click run up my spine and tingle in my scalp.

"I'll go get some food," I said abruptly. It was all that would come out.

He nodded, "And I'll tend the fire."

Chapter Three

There was a loaf of French bread in the refrigerator, so I sliced a few pieces of it to broil while the soup heated. I liked to cook. In fact, back at the office, we had a full kitchen and it was common for me to make breakfast for everyone several days each week. It felt good to create a warm experience and, to be honest, I enjoyed the praise I got for doing it.

While the food cooked, I uncorked a bottle of the Merlot. I wondered if Lucius would share some. It didn't matter. I could certainly use a drink right now. Rummaging in the cupboard, I found the stemless wineglasses and placed two of them on the granite counter. I poured myself a glass and took a couple of long swallows.

The broiler glowed and the soup bubbled on the stovetop. I stirred, then leaned against the counter and shook my head.

I felt separated from my body. No, more like I was fractured and all my pieces were drifting apart from each other. One part of me could feel the cool glass in my hand, taste the complex fruit finish of the wine on the back of my tongue and smell the cooking food. The other less familiar part was hovering above my physical self in a neutral state of observation. The sense of duality was powerful and I was frozen in the moment.

I shook out of it as my internal timer blared a warning that the bread was about to burn. I yanked the oven door open and pulled the pan of garlic toast out of the broiler just in time. It was dark around the crusty edges but the butter and Parmesan cheese was golden brown on top. Perfect.

That was close, I thought, *I'm really a mess!*

I turned off the burner under the soup and filled two bowls. Fragrant steam rose and I sprinkled basil on top to perfect the presentation. I loaded TV trays with everything and balanced one in each hand while I navigated the stairs.

Lucius had discovered another camp chair and was sitting in it with his eyes closed when I arrived. He sat up, breathed in the mixed aromas and smiled.

"It appears that I chose well in coming here tonight. What are the chances that some guy hanging out in a cabin would unpack a gourmet meal in less than ten minutes? I expected to eat a hot dog," he said.

I chuckled and then lifted the bottle of wine and raised my eyebrows.

He nodded, so I poured him a glass and refilled my own. He accepted the wine and placed it on his tray. He spent a few seconds arranging the silverware and dishes, then he closed his eyes and began to rub his palms together gently above the food. He did this for a few seconds and opened his eyes to stare into the sky. He opened his hands and moved them with spread fingers around and down to the sides of the plate. It was as if he was creating an invisible dome over his meal. The steam from the bowl swirled and took on a magical glow in the firelight for just a moment. Then he picked up the bread, broke it and took a large bite.

I had already begun to eat, but when he began his odd little ritual, my spoon froze halfway into my mouth. He glanced over at me, chewing. I suddenly remembered what I was doing and fell to the business of eating.

"You seem confused," he said.

"Oh, no," I said, "Well, actually, what you did just reminded me of how I was taught to say a prayer before I ate. It's been a while is all. You did something extra, too."

"Ah," he said and ate a few more bites. The moment of silence stretched and I felt uncomfortable, as if I was waiting for an answer he thought he had already given.

He looked up again just as I turned back to my food.

"Ritual," he said, "You're surprised to observe mine. We'll talk about this much more."

"What, you mean your food blessing thing?" I said.

"No, we'll discuss ritual in general. It has been largely lost in human society, much to your detriment."

"Oh. But what was the thing with the food? That was just...different."

"Everything is energy," he said, "Food is a direct, powerful form of energy that we use to fuel our magical bodies. I pause for a moment before eating to feel gratitude and align myself with the energy of the food. That keeps me conscious of what I'm doing. When I hold out my hands with thanksgiving over the food, I am experiencing its pleasure and anticipating what I am about to put into my body. It's good to be mindful."

I let his words sink in while we both finished our bread and soup. *Magical bodies*, I thought and glanced down. My body wasn't something I enjoyed seeing in a mirror these days. When I married Jennifer almost fourteen years ago, I weighed one sixty-five, tight and lean. Now, although I hadn't been on a scale for months, I was probably seventy pounds heavier. I didn't feel magical. It was a nagging frustration. I couldn't seem to get off the roller coaster of fad diets. Then, there would be sporadic bursts of working out followed by months of indulgence. Lucius sat there looking like a goddamn mountain ninja—tan and sinewy. I envied him.

After a few minutes, we settled back in the chairs under the stars and sipped wine with the fire crackling between us.

The quiet night was punctuated by the sounds of small animals moving in the brush down the hillside. A breeze moved through our campsite and set the flames dancing. Sparks flew up into the darkness.

Lucius swallowed the last of his wine, placed the glass on his tray and leaned forward, elbows on knees. He stared into the fire and his eyes narrowed. He glanced over and noticed me watching him, then he gave a small shrug and clapped his hands together. A decision had been made.

"You'd like to know what I'm doing here, wouldn't you?" he said.

"I'm not sure. I have a feeling that I may not be ready for what you have to say."

He laughed then quickly his mood became serious.

"Yes. Your feeling is not only real, it's appropriate. I'd like to have a way to ease you into this, get you accustomed first. Things are speeding up though, so that isn't an option. You're going to have to trust me more than you normally should trust a stranger. It won't be easy at first."

I felt a chill and shifted closer to the fire. I leaned forward to face him.

"Look, everything that happened to get me here today and everything about tonight has been surreal. I feel like I'm dreaming right now. Whatever you have to say is going to fit right in with the overall weirdness, I'm sure."

He drew in his breath, held it and then let it out with a sigh.

"Here it is then. Your planet, all of humanity, is facing massive change. It's a birthing process. You've already begun to experience the early pains of this around the globe. The symptoms may look normal. Famine, war and oppression have been with the human race even before your history books were written. The difference now is that everything is speeding up and shifting much more rapidly. Know what I'm talking about?"

"Well," I said, "Yes. I mean, it does seem like there's a mad rush going on right now. Even in my life, things are moving so fast that I can't catch my breath. Is that what you mean?"

"That's a sensation and it's just one clue you've noticed so far. Everyone and all things are aware at different levels. You've been on the edge of waking up for some time, so you've probably had that acceleration feeling more than other people," he said. "Now that I bring your attention to it, can you think of other things you've seen or sensed?"

"Honestly? I've noticed that I'm tired. It's not that I just need some time off, either. I sometimes wake up in the middle of the night and feel terrified I won't be able to keep up much longer. There's nowhere for me to stop. I always thrived on hard work and challenge before. Now things are spinning faster and faster. I can't imagine what will happen if I lose my footing, but it feels as if I'm getting closer to losing it every day. It's an impossible situation."

He nodded.

"Yes. Can you think of another word for what you're feeling?"

I closed my eyes and said the first thing that came to mind, "I feel stuck."

"Ah," he said, "Well put. You are stuck. Most of the human race is stuck. Stuck, but moving at an ever-increasing speed. Headed for a crash. Before we talk about that, I need to caution you about something. You have identified your basic condition. As we examine this, you'll find yourself recoiling from the implications that emerge from the picture we'll paint of your life. It's going to be hard for you to believe. Don't worry about it right now, but remember I said this. It'll help you keep your bearings as we go."

Even as he spoke, I felt resistance to my own statement rise inside me like a solid object. *How could I say I was stuck? I lived a life most people envied. If I walked down the streets of Boise on any day of the week, I was certain to run into at least a dozen acquaintances who thought well of me. I played by the rules, worked hard and achieved a lot. I had a gorgeous office, a comfortable home and a great family. Yes, I was in debt, but so were most young entrepreneurs. I was on the right track. It was just a matter of time.*

I felt foolish and disgusted with myself for allowing the negativity to cross my lips.

Lucius fixed me with his stare.

"You see what I mean?" he said, "You spoke from your truth. Exactly what you felt. Now your ego-mind is busy trying to invalidate that and put you back in your place."

My eyes filled with tears and I turned my head to hide the emotion. A great sob rose up and sought to burst out, but I swallowed several times and took a long breath. I turned back to look at Lucius but my head felt pressurized, as if I had just stifled an enormous sneeze. I was dizzy.

Lucius was gazing at me with a look of such piercing compassion that I was undone in an instant. My whole frame convulsed and I pushed out my vocal sorrow so ferociously that I almost threw up.

I wanted to be self-conscious, to control this outburst in front of a stranger, but I could not. I surrendered to the tsunami of grief and pain. It didn't matter how I looked, this force had me in its grip. I was rolled over and over by it while hot tears and strings of mucus ran down my face. My diaphragm constricted repeatedly and I felt as if the bones of my chest would crack and burst open, revealing the dark vortex of grief inside me.

Minutes must have passed, but when I regained my composure I discovered that I was on the ground beside the fire, on all fours. I felt warmth from the flames on my face and pine needles under my fingers. My eyes and nose throbbed, swollen and raw.

Lucius knelt beside me with his hands held a few inches above my back. I heard him speak softly in what sounded like a foreign language. I didn't understand the words but they soothed my spirit, and I was able to sit up and take a long, ragged breath.

Lucius still knelt with his hands outstretched. Quiet now. He breathed deep and released it.

"All is well," he whispered, "All is well."

He opened his eyes and we both looked at each other. His face was sober. He nodded and strength returned to my legs. I struggled to the chair and leaned back. Exhausted.

With my eyes closed, I could hear him moving. He must have added wood to the fire because I heard fierce crackling and fresh warmth blossomed on my skin.

"Lucius," I said, still shaky but more tranquil than before, "what the hell was that?"

He didn't answer right away, so I opened my eyes. He was poking around in the coals with a stick.

"You experienced in your body what you talked about earlier and tried to rationalize. For once, you allowed the experience to be processed through your nervous system and bones and muscles. How was that for you?"

"It was…it hurt. I don't usually get out of control. I mean, I cry sometimes but not like that. I feel beat up."

"Yes," he said, "You spoke the truth before when you said you're stuck. You have no idea how deep that condition is within you. Because you have dammed up your feelings for so long, when a surge like you just experienced comes roaring out—it tears a path through years of clutter. That hurts. It's all right though, you'll feel better soon."

I nodded, "I already feel lighter. That was almost like therapy."

"Oh," he said, "It isn't almost like therapy. It is therapy and it's powerful, too. What I don't want you to do now though, is feel such relief that you lose sight of the bigger picture. It's too easy to blow off steam, get rid of the pressure and then return to what you call normal. Too easy to go on without seeing the mass of knots that have kept you tangled your whole life. What you just experienced is the merest whiff of what will come—if we continue together."

I felt another chill at his words and shivered.

"When you say that, I'm afraid. How did you make that happen a few minutes ago? What will our continuing on together entail?"

"First, fear is to be expected. You're peering into the unknown and humans dread that. I'm going to deal with the continuing on process later. As far as what I just did, that's a good question," he said.

"It's not that I did anything. The very fact that I'm here with you stirs up energy you aren't accustomed to feeling."

"What do you mean by that? The very fact you're here..." I said.

"I keep edging you closer to the truth," he said, "So here it is."

"I mentioned a while ago that your planet is under severe stress. The entire organism is experiencing the pressure of massive changes that are underway, but most people are only vaguely aware that anything is happening. A few tribes of people in places like Africa and Australia are sensitive to the vibrational shift. Wild creatures in nature feel it in their own way. What you call the civilized world though, is so insulated from reality that the message isn't getting through to those who need it most.

I occupy a different dimension most of the time, but I'm part of a group who you can call helpers. I am sent to find those who are ready in your world and help them to wake up."

"So you're an angel?"

"Mmm. Sort of, there are many of us here right now. In fact, down through history we have always held this space and been present. During times of extreme change, the veil that usually hides us gets thin. Then, we're visible and can communicate with humans. This time on Earth is critical, so my fellow helpers and I are moving fast. We only appear to people who are ready. I don't want you to get tangled up in a story of specialness, but you're one of a handful being visited like this now."

I started to speak, but he waved me off and continued.

"In the past, I would have befriended you in a normal way. You wouldn't have noticed anything unusual for years. I would have taken a lot of time to gain your trust, get to know you and move you into the process of awakening. Right now though, time grows short. Events and cycles are accelerating. This requires that I deliver my message in ways that don't allow for much buffering. You get the raw feed so to speak, the full dose.

This is rock-and-roll, buckle-your-seatbelt time. I wish it could be done another way, but it's too late for that now."

Irrational. Unbelievable. I was entertaining a visitor from another dimension. Wait until I try to explain this to anyone back in the city. Nevertheless, the deep silent gong that had reverberated within me all day long boomed again in confirmation. This strange man had much to say and instinct told me that I'd better listen—no matter how improbable the whole thing sounded.

Chapter Four

We sat silent for awhile, my senses felt magnified. The night was full of Earth-creature sounds. My eyes grew wide. Suddenly, I was swept up and standing on the spear-like point at the top of the world's tallest mountain. Below me, the rushing energies of every nation on Earth swirled and roared along in a ceaseless flood tide.

From my vantage point, balanced like a lone watchman in the night sky, the blackness of the entire outer universe became a living pressure. It held me in its magnetic grasp. For all the terrifying vastness pressing in, I was strangely comforted. I was safe—suspended in a powerful benevolent liquid. Like electric gelatin. The insanity of this sensation filled me with joy. Giddy, the laughing stars cheered me on while I attempted a pirouette.

Lucius cleared his throat, I jolted back into the sturdy camp chair. He glanced at me and I must have been grinning madly, because he chuckled.

"You okay?" he asked.

My voice cracked when I tried to speak. I swallowed and said, "I'm okay, but..."

"But what?" he said.

I tried to describe the fleeting experience and he nodded. Understanding.

"You just brushed the outer garments of *Who You Really Are* with your fingertips," he said. "I mean, earlier when you had the surge of emotion, it cleared channels of perception. It's common to see or feel things differently for awhile."

"So, is this the way you feel all the time?" I asked.

He laughed, "Oh, that's not even the beginning. Honestly, we don't have time to talk about these things. The Reality of Everything is so different from your normal perceptions that we could be sidetracked for years, for centuries, trying to describe the most mundane features of the universe. Because of our timetable, you're going to have to just strap in for the ride and learn through your body as we go. As one of your Presidents said, 'you ain't seen nothing yet!'"

I nodded because I couldn't think of anything relevant to say.

He leaned forward with fresh intensity on his face.

"As I was saying, you are here on Earth at a critical time. You and all your fellow humans chose to be here now so you could participate in the birthing of a new world. I'll reveal more about this later. I know it sounds strange. Just make note of it.

The current trouble is that most of the human race is disconnected from their true nature. They have forgotten Who They Really Are."

I raised my hand to interrupt him, "You keep saying 'Who You Really Are' as if there's a fact that I should already understand. If I'm not who I really am, then who really am I?"

"I'm getting there, hang with me," he said.

"As I was saying, the human project is in its final stages of forgetfulness. You have moved away from your natural powers and created a false reality that is complex and terrifying. For example, give me a few things that seem wrong about life on Earth right now."

"You mean...?"

"I mean, what comes to mind that is unjust, sad, depressing or completely out of balance?"

"Oh, well there are the obvious things like starving children, genocide, poverty, terrorism and drugs. But those have always been part of the human condition. They're deplorable, but they aren't new."

He bowed his head almost to his knees and shook it slowly. Suddenly, he was on his feet. Fists clenched, he leaned in close to my face. Our eyes locked and his gaze held a ferocity that frightened me.

When he spoke, his voice vibrated with passion, "Jacob, you listen to me. The time has come when the bloodshed and sorrow of life on your planet can no longer be ignored. You must not regard the pain and death of innocents as usual things. It is time that humanity awakens and remembers their purpose for being.

By the way, even though the atrocities you mention are terrible— what's behind them, what allows them to be commonplace in your societies concerns me more. Those are only symptoms of a larger disease."

He paused and straightened to his full height. The fire crackled and sent up sparks behind him. I sat waiting for him to continue.

"I chose to visit you on purpose. You live in America. You are following the great dream and working the system, but you're nagged by the knowledge there should be more to life. You have immersed yourself in the pursuit of wealth. You've built a prison of comfort and affluence. Sometimes imagining a simpler life moves you, but you're stuck. You can't see how this could ever come to pass because of your complacency, your position and your obligations. You can only hope somehow to outrun the monster you created. Only after you have piled up enough cash to pay all your debts and fuel your luxurious lifestyle—only then, will you turn to what you suspect is your true purpose.

I am here tonight to tell you that time has run out on your game. You have dodged the central question and remained asleep for as long as possible.

You've reached a decision point. One choice is to go back to your current reality and pretend that you met some lunatic up in the mountains. You'll forget me and go numb again with all your busyness.

The other path leads into the unknown. Into freedom. If you choose to follow me on it, you will discover Who You Really Are."

He stopped speaking abruptly and turned to stir the coals and add more wood to the fire. He sat back down in his chair and propped his boots on an upturned log.

A long moment passed. Then another. He seemed to have finished his speech, but there were many questions left dangling in the chilly mountain air.

The owl hooted in the pine tree overhead, I closed my eyes to consider this strange night and the unsought choices that were now in front of me.

Without warning, I was dragged down into a heavy sleep that swallowed me like dark velvet infinity.

Chapter Five

I opened my eyes. Confused.

Morning sunlight was bright on the coffee table and I struggled to focus my vision by squinting. Without moving, I began to assess my situation. I was warm and my face was resting on soft cushiony material. I closed my eyes and drifted for a while.

Thought fragments floated around in my brain. *Warm... Feels good... Wonder if... What time is... What?*

I must have slept again because the ringing phone lit up my system with adrenaline. I whirled in a tangle of blankets to a sitting position on the couch.

Awake. I looked around in a daze.

On my couch. The phone kept ringing.

Oh, yeah. At the cabin. By myself. I had to put both hands down on the cushions to steady myself. My head was spinning.

Where's...? I looked around. I was alone. The phone rang two more times and stopped.

I blinked my eyes.

I didn't want to move but it seemed right to get on my feet. Standing on shaky legs, I shuffled to the sliding door that led to the back, east-facing deck. The sunshine was brilliant and the cedar boards were warm under my bare feet. I crossed to the railing and leaned against it. I needed to pee and did so off the side of the porch. It was a caveman thing to do, but I always enjoyed this little freedom out here in the woods. The morning routine handled, I braced myself against the big pine beam that supported the balcony above me. My eyes were closed but the light glowed through my eyelids and felt good on my skin. I breathed the morning air. I could smell the mountain laurel and pine needles warming under the sun. Beautiful day.

Okay, my mind returned to its inquiry, *what happened last night?*

Oh, yes. Lucius. Where was Lucius?

The memory of my visitor of the night before woke me up completely. I was alarmed. He had asked me questions and there was something I needed to decide. I didn't remember making any commitments. *Had I?*

I walked quickly back inside and looked around. The house was quiet. I looked out the big front window to the fire pit below. *No one out there. Wait.* Only one camp chair sat by the cold ashes of last night's blaze. My chair.

I went to the kitchen. The empty wine bottle was standing on the counter top. A fly explored the dried residue at the rim. My bowl and glass were in the sink. The soup pan still sat on the stove with just a little congealed dinner left in the bottom.

So, it looks like I had dinner… All by myself.

I opened the dishwasher to check for other dishes. Maybe Lucius was extra tidy. Empty.

Immoderate panic seized my body and I struggled to breathe. *Stop. This is silly.*

I put my hand out against the refrigerator and its cool stainless steel surface steadied me. I'm okay. I'm okay. I'll figure this out.

The phone started ringing again. I took a deep breath and reached over to grab it off the wall.

"Hello?" I tried not to gasp for air.

"Are you okay?" my wife asked. She must be calling from the car. I could hear kid noise and the radio in the background.

"Um, yeah," I said. *Lying.* "How are you, dear?"

"Oh, I'm fine," she said, "You didn't call last night and then I had this strange dream. Just thought I'd check on you."

"Thanks. Sorry I forgot to call. I slept weird, too." *Should I tell her about Lucius? No. Better sort that out first for myself.*

"I miss you," she said, "The dream I had was of you leaving. It was bizarre because you weren't really gone, but you...changed. You were still you but also someone else."

"I didn't like it," she said.

My mind spun like a top, but I managed to find some comforting words.

"Well, I'm right here. It's a gorgeous day. I'm going to take a hike and then maybe a nap. Will you be all right?"

"Yeah," she said, "We're going a little early to the school yard sale. I think we might go to the park later. Oh, my mom's trying to beep in. I better go. Love you."

She was gone. I was relieved. Everything was normal on her end. The dream was a strange coincidence but she didn't sound too rattled by it. She must have been preoccupied enough to miss the strain in my voice. That was good. I hoped I could gain clarity before I returned home. *Glad I didn't try to explain anything to her yet.*

I stood there in the quiet kitchen for a few minutes. Through the window, I took in the mountain landscape basking gloriously in light. A hummingbird flashed into view and hovered for a couple of seconds. It seemed that she was trying to make eye contact with me from the other side of the glass. I smiled at her and nodded.

"Hi," I said. She opened her beak and laughed before disappearing with a hum of vibrant joy. *Talking to animals. Good. Perfectly normal, right?*

I looked around inside again. From where I stood, I could see evidence only of my presence in the house. One set of dinner dishes.

One empty wine bottle. No sound except the ambient house noises and a gentle wind breathing through the pine trees outside.

The floor was chilly underfoot, I went to the front door. The rough stone tile gave me a grounded sensation for the first time since I awoke.

The door was locked from the inside. *Never mind that right now.*

Out on to the front porch and down the stairs, the sun-warmed planks felt good.

I stopped behind my camp chair beside the fire pit and looked around. The coals from last night's blaze had burned down to feathery ashes in the breeze. My red canvas camp chair was sitting alone—exactly where I had unfolded it yesterday afternoon.

I squatted and touched the sandy ground with my fingertips. There were plenty of tracks here, but as I scrutinized them, they all appeared to be mine. *Inconclusive. You're no Indian scout.*

The other camp chairs were all stacked under the porch just as they always were. I walked over to look. A fine layer of undisturbed dust covered them. *Huh. The facts are piling up now, aren't they?*

A sharp *"caw, caw"* sounded behind me and I whirled and squinted from under my hand into the bright sky. A raven. From the corner of my eye, I could see the seat of my camp chair. Something was there. *A book? How did I miss that?*

Three quick steps and I had it in my hands. It was unusual. The binding and cover were made of supple leather. I turned it over to see the face. It was ornately hand-tooled and the title, *Emerson's Bible,* appeared burned in with a hot brand. I held it up close to my eyes and stared at the beautiful work. The borders were embellished with symbols, runes and ancient hieroglyphs. Most were unfamiliar to me, but I recognized a cross and the *yin yang* and Thor's hammer. Some of the markings looked like Chinese characters and others were sophisticated knots.

It was warm from sitting in the sunlight. I loved books but handling this one gave me a special thrill. It was alive in my palms. It was tied shut with a ribbon of butter-soft leather. I tugged at one of the ends and the bow slipped loose.

The cover fell open and a folded piece of notebook paper fell out into the ashes. I tossed the book on the chair and dropped to my knees to rescue the note. Just as I reached for it, a draft stirred the ashes and revived a small ember. The paper fluttered and its edge caught on the glowing coal. I was moving in a nightmare. Never fast enough. In slow motion, I leaned forward and grabbed the smoldering paper just as a flame sprang up on the spiral binding shreds clinging to its edge.

I clapped my hands together over the small fire to crush it. My palms were scorched, but when I opened them to look, no real damage had been done. I unfolded the sheet of paper and blew away the ashes. The note was handwritten in blue ink with neat letters. All capitals.

I sat down to read:

JACOB,

THANKS FOR DINNER. I'M GLAD WE COULD FINALLY MEET IN PERSON.

I KNOW YOU HAVE A LOT TO CONSIDER.

HERE'S THE NUB. IF YOU DECIDE TO ACCEPT MY INVITATION, MEET ME BACK HERE NEXT WEEK. WEAR YOUR BEST CLOTHES. I NEED YOU TO MEET SOME IMPORTANT PEOPLE IF YOU CHOOSE TO FOLLOW THIS PATH. I'LL WAIT FOR YOU UNTIL 5:30 NEXT SATURDAY AFTERNOON. IF YOU ARE NOT HERE BY THEN, I WILL KNOW YOUR DECISION AND YOU'LL NEVER SEE ME AGAIN.

*I'LL EXPLAIN ABOUT EMERSON'S BIBLE IF WE
MEET UP NEXT WEEK. SHOULD YOU DECIDE NOT
TO COME, BURN THIS BOOK. YOU WON'T NEED IT
IN THAT CASE. OTHERWISE, BRING IT WITH YOU.
IT WILL BE USEFUL ON YOUR JOURNEY. ALSO—
THIS IS IMPORTANT—SHOW IT TO NO ONE.*

UNTIL THEN, OR NOT.

LUCIUS

*P.S. ALSO BRING A FEW OF YOUR OWN FAVORITE
BOOKS. THE ONES THAT HAVE HAD THE MOST
INFLUENCE ON YOUR LIFE SO FAR.*

So.

I wasn't going crazy. Well, maybe I was, but at least I wasn't hallucinating about the visit from Lucius last night. Here was tangible proof. I folded the note and tucked it into my shirt pocket. The book lay shut on my lap. I crossed my hands over it, palms down and sat. The day was blue, gold and green. Silent, too. It seemed like every bird, dog and tree, even the wind, was holding its breath for a moment. Then, far out across the valley, the raven called. The harsh sound carried to me before I could see the bird that made it.

Then it soared into view. Beating its wings in time with my heart, it came to within fifty yards of the lodge and began to circle our hilltop. Counterclockwise. I sat and it disappeared behind me. Back around again. And again. The raven described three complete circles before it swooped down and landed on the path near my chair. I had never paid much attention to this particular type of bird before, these noisy feathered rats. This one commanded my gaze. Sunbeams gleamed in blue-black shimmers off its wings and it hopped a few feet closer. It cocked its head rapidly in a pattern of improbable angles as if to be sure that it saw me with both eyes to imprint my alien form in its memory. Mission accomplished. It blinked and nodded farewell before springing into flight.

"Caw, caw!" it said. I was sure it looked back as it flew away from me.

I nodded my silent agreement.

Caw, caw, caw...

The book was open on my lap and I picked it up. *What's in here?* I held the spine in my left hand and used my right fingers to flutter through the pages quickly. There was little text and a lot of empty space in the first third of the book. The rest of the pages were blank. Returning to the first page, under a faded black and white copy of a daguerreotype image, was an inscription that read:

> "*I went to the woods because I wished to live deliberately, to front only the essential facts of life, and see if I could not learn what it had to teach, and not, when I came to die, discover that I had not lived. I did not wish to live what was not life, living is so dear; nor did I wish to practice resignation, unless it was quite necessary. I wanted to live deep and suck out all the marrow of life, to live so sturdily and Spartan-like as to put to rout all that was not life, to cut a broad swath and shave close, to drive life into a corner, and reduce it to its lowest terms.*" — Henry David Thoreau

The antique picture was of the stalwart, whiskered philosopher himself. It honestly came as no great shock to me, reading that quote. The last twenty-four hours had held so many coincidences and otherworldly surprises that this synchronicity was perfectly congruent. I shook my head and accepted it with barely a trace of resistance.

Well, I'm here in the woods now, I thought, *Thoreau would be so proud.*

Turning a few pages, I saw but did not read more quotes with many empty lines beneath them. This must be a journal of some kind. Lucius said that it would be "*...useful on your journey.*" I would hold him to his promise to explain next week.

So, you've decided to go already? an internal voice asked.

Who knows? I need to think about it, I thought.

"I'm going crazy," I muttered.

The rest of that day is hard to remember. I sat in the chair for hours in a hypnotic daze. The sun was warm. I dozed on and off. From time to time animals ventured out of the brush and crossed in front of me. I sat still as a stone, so they must not have experienced their usual fear of humans. I could only muster the energy to watch them from between heavy eyelids. A large elk, a coyote, two jack rabbits and a family of wild turkeys all took turns staring at me curiously then disappearing into the woods.

Finally in the late afternoon, just before the sun disappeared, pain in my stiff muscles and the chilly temperature roused me. I dragged myself inside to discover that I was ravenous but lacked the motivation or focus to cook. I made do with a glass of water and two or three handfuls of granola from the cupboard. Although I had slept most of the day, deep fatigue wrapped me up once more. I barely got out of my clothes and into one of the beds before somersaulting into the black universe of dreams.

Chapter Six

I opened my eyes Sunday morning without drama. If my waking memory was accurate, there were no ghost visitors or disturbing visions during the night.

Clouds had moved in overnight. The gray light was sullen and misty rain was blowing against the windows. The tops of the mountains stood shrouded in fog. Faint, as if thick gauze swirled in the folds of the valley. Usually when this happened, I would light up the fireplace, start a movie and enjoy the feeling of silent isolation. Today was different. It was cold in the lodge. I felt anxious and irritated. The clock on the microwave read 7:43. It was early, but I had nothing left to do here. Time to go.

Packing and cleaning took about twenty minutes. I had spent very little time indoors, so my visit created none of the usual weekend havoc. I found my keys and pushed the little remote starter button on the fob.

Outside, the car turned over and then hummed smooth as oil. The lock-up process was simple. I set the thermostat, turned off the lights and activated the alarm system. Our cabin was at the end of a long private road and we had full-time neighbors who loved patrolling the woods with guns. These deterrents had still not prevented some local thieves from breaking in last year and literally stealing the new carpet right off the floor. I had to submit multiple pictures, a lengthy explanation and the official sheriff's report to our skeptical insurance claims adjuster to cover the damage.

"They stole WHAT?" he said after I finished telling him how I discovered the living room furniture pushed out of the way and the carpet gone.

"Yeah," I said, "just the carpet. It was cut clean out, but they left the padding. Nothing else is missing either...it's weird."

"Weird," he agreed, "Well, since you aren't claiming that they swiped your antique shotguns and a sack of Krugerrands, we won't do a major investigation. Get an alarm system, okay? I'll have a hard time paying for new carpet more than once."

I smiled and shook my head as I punched in the security code on my way out the door. Some redneck's hound dog, down in the collection of converted school buses and single-wide trailers known as Clear Creek subdivision, was probably scratching fleas in wall-to-wall luxury.

It wasn't raining hard but the steps down to my car were slick. Blinking against the cold droplets in my face, I tossed the duffel bag into the back seat and got behind the wheel. Turning on the heater and wiping the chilly moisture on my pants legs, I was grateful for the already-warm engine. The windshield had fogged, so I sat there mulling things over for a few minutes while it cleared.

I drove back in silence. *Emerson's Bible* sat on the passenger seat and I glanced at it now and then. Once I reached over and touched the leather cover. It was the only tangible remnant of my strange weekend. If it hadn't been sitting there where I could verify its existence, I would probably do what Lucius suggested and forget the whole experience. I'd write it off as the combined effect of stress, fatigue and alcohol mixed with mountain solitude like some surreal cocktail.

Yet, there the book sat while I drove. My emotions were quiet but thoughts flew back and forth as rapidly as the windshield wipers.

What will I do? If I go for it and meet Lucius again, what will actually happen? He said I might have a hard time returning to what I call my normal life. What was that all about? I mean, am I ready to leave my life behind me? What does that really mean?

Again, I felt myself leaning out over a terrifying height. All these questions settled in my gut and hardened into a solid, cold knot.

I arrived home and stopped in front of the house. Most of the drive was a blur and I sat there in the car feeling unprepared to rejoin the whirl of life. The dashboard clock read 8:54 A.M. Jennifer didn't expect me home yet. I shifted back into drive and rolled away from the house.

Maybe a latté will get me up to speed, I thought.

About four minutes later, I was standing in line at my favorite Starbucks. Even on the outskirts of a smaller city like Boise, the famous coffee chain had locations everywhere. This particular one was like my second office. I often held casual meetings, read the paper and networked with the regular crowd. I was a well-known figure here and Lisa, the head barista, smiled at me when I approached the counter. She liked the nickname I coined for her. She adopted it and had a special name tag engraved with "Coffee Ninja" that she was wearing now.

"Hey, you!" she said, "What can I get for you?"

Finally, something normal, I thought, right now I'll hang my hat on anything.

"A triple grande light foam latté, *por favor*," I said, "Extra hot."

"And, can I get a name for this order, sir?" she asked. Prim and proper.

"Xavier," I said. It was my little game to come up with weird names. It was my idea of fun to hear the baristas call them out over the noise in the crowded coffee shop.

She raised her eyebrows as if this were all new to her. "One triple grande light foam latté with extra steam coming up shortly. That'll be three seventy-eight, sir."

"How have you been?" I asked her, since there was nobody in line behind me.

She sighed and shrugged. "Oh, you know, it's all good. I've been here since 5:30. We had a big rush earlier. Must have been the rain. Everyone wanted their coffee today."

She glanced at me, "How are you doing? You aren't your usual dapper self. Have you been camping or something?"

I looked down at my clothes and ran a hand over my face. I was a little rough. Probably smelled bad, too.

"Yeah. Just pulled in from being up at our mountain place. Sorry to offend your delicate sensibilities."

She sniffed. "I'll let it slide this time, but let's observe proper dress code in the future, okay?"

Someone got behind me in line. Grinning, I nodded at Lisa and shuffled sideways so she could get back to work. She handed me the hot cup and smiled.

"Have a good day, Xavier," she said and leaned forward, "My advice? Take a shower. Your wife will thank me."

I found a dark leather chair in one corner and sat sipping coffee for awhile. I had brought the book in with me and I held it, unopened, on my lap. I wasn't ready to dive back into it just then, but it was comforting to have it close.

An hour passed. I was isolated inside the busy shop. Usually, I wandered around finding acquaintances and chatting with strangers. Today, I kept popping outside the social bubble and sat like a silent observer while it all happened around me.

My phone vibrated and broke what could have turned into another daylong reverie. It was a text message from Jennifer.

"Let me know when UR back in town. Meet up 4 lunch w/kids?"

I sipped my now-cold coffee and typed with my right thumb, "OK. *Early one? Where?*"

A few seconds later, it buzzed again.

"*Will get the gang moving. Cracker Barrel in 20 min?*"

"*Perfect,*" I hit send.

I got up and left without my usual round of farewells and handshakes.

Cracker Barrel was only about three miles away. I got there quickly and secured a table for five near the big fireplace. The breakfast crowd was gone and the Sunday lunch rush hadn't started yet. It was quiet in the restaurant and I enjoyed watching the fire chew on big oak logs in the grate.

Fire. I suddenly saw myself sitting in a red canvas chair by the campfire and Lucius leaning forward, gesturing with his hands as he talked. I shook my head. *Need to stay in the real world for awhile.*

Just then, with a rush of feet and coats, my family arrived. I stood and held out my arms.

"Hello, my beautifuls!" I said.

Jennifer stopped a few feet away and let the kids mob me.

"Daddy!" our six-year-old twins, Jay and Megan yelled in unison. I squatted and they both grabbed me around the neck. Jay, one minute older than his sister, had sandy hair and strong shoulders. He was aggressive and competent. I always called Megan my elf princess. She had a mass of red-gold curls, large luminous eyes and freckles on her nose. She was tiny and felt fragile when I wrapped my arm around her.

Our oldest son at ten, Nathan stood waiting for his turn. I let go the twins and gave him a hug. He was getting tall, this one. He would pass my five feet ten inches by the time he was a sophomore in high school. Must be the genes from my wife's side. Short, stalwart Norwegians and some mixture of other northern Europeans populated my own ancestry. He was sensitive and intelligent.

Nathan's advanced vocabulary by age two had earned the nickname of "Little Professor."

"Hi, Dad," he said. Then he wrinkled his nose and sniffed conspicuously. "You smell like smoke!"

"Well, I should," I said, "I just spent two days by a campfire."

Jennifer watched all of us and smiled. Our eyes met. She was beautiful and reserved. We married when she was only eighteen by a month and I was just over twenty. That was almost fourteen years ago. We had grown up together. A lot of water over the dam between us, but mostly smooth sailing these days.

I leaned forward to kiss her and she squeezed me a little tighter than usual.

"I missed you," she whispered in my ear, "glad you're back."

I held her for a few seconds and then we found places around the table.

Back home after lunch, I spent a few hours puttering around in aimless circles. After a long, hot shower, I sank into the leather couch to watch football. Jenn curled up at the other end under a blanket and dozed. The kids entertained themselves in far reaches of the house. It was a perfect day to fade into a numb zone of drowsy disconnect. I couldn't do that though. Every time I would try to immerse myself in the game, my mind wandered off and began gnawing on questions that brought me no comfort.

The television's incessant voice became unbearable. I touched the mute button and sat barely watching the moving figures on the screen.

Jennifer hadn't asked about my trip. She probably assumed that it was uneventful. What was there to talk about?

She hadn't seen *Emerson's Bible* yet, but if I actually accepted the invitation from Lucius to meet at the end of next week, I'd owe her some kind of explanation.

What could I tell her? A visitor from a different dimension showed up at the cabin...he said that I had some sort of date with destiny...he gave me a

book that was going to be a key to my personal transformation...my life
would probably never be the same...I was supposed to go back to the cabin
next weekend dressed in a suit...I had no idea what would happen next or
even if I'd be back any time soon.

Spilling a story like that on my wife would require courage and a
reckless panache that I was certain I didn't possess. I got up and
wandered into my office. My computer never left its bag up at the
cabin. Email was probably piling up. I stared at the leather case with
distaste. I had stepped out of the mad rush on Friday and now had no
desire to rejoin the rat race.

That's what I get for playing hooky, I thought.

The same whole-body weariness that prompted my escape from
the office a couple of days ago returned. Irritated and dissatisfied
without knowing why, I fiddled with the window blinds and looked
outside. The sky had cleared and the afternoon looked brighter.

My phone buzzed with another incoming text message. This time
it was my friend, Mike.

"Cigars?" He had been a lawyer in a past life and his messages
were often curt.

I wrote back, *"Perfect! Leaving now. OK?"*

A second later, buzz...*"Confirmed."*

I pulled on a zip-up fleece jacket and peeked in the den to check
on Jenn. She was sleeping soundly. I found one of the twins and
instructed them that "when Mommy wakes up let her know that I'll
be back in awhile. Oh, and try to be quiet so she can sleep."

Mike and I sat in lawn chairs on his back deck under a tall
propane heater, the kind they use on restaurant patios to keep away
the chill. We enjoyed smoking cigars together. He had an extensive
selection in the humidor and knowledge to match. We were both in
the mortgage lending business and often compared notes or
commiserated with each other on the state of industry affairs. He was
older than I, and had put on extra life mileage with a ten-year legal
career before he launched a series of successful brokerages. Now he

consulted and coached small business owners toward what he called "entrepreneurial fulfillment." I often asked for his advice, not just because of his business acumen either. Mike was a lifelong student of achievement. He coined a phrase that I hoped would end up in my own eulogy someday. It was printed across the back of his business cards. "*Living Inspired & Fully Engaged.*" I got a lot out of our friendship and hoped that I could leak the story of my weekend to him and get his objective advice.

"So," he said and paused to tap the ash from the end of his hand-rolled Opus X. "You went to the cabin without me."

"I...turned out I needed some solitude," I said, bracing for an onslaught of friendly sarcasm. Mike had visited the mountain lodge many times with me and I knew he'd be disappointed to miss a getaway.

He just grinned and leaned back to blow a plume of smoke into the weak sunshine.

I leaned my elbows on my knees.

"It was a quick trip," I said, "I took off early Friday. Almost didn't happen."

He held up his ever-present BlackBerry, "Funny. Damn thing never even rang. Huh. Wonder if it was broken on Friday when you tried to call?" He shook it and held it up to his ear.

We both chuckled and then smoked in silence for a while. Finally, the urgency of the story within me could wait no longer and I decided to wade in before the conversation changed direction.

"So," I began, "This is going to be kind of weird..."

He raised one eyebrow, "Sounds normal coming from you so far. Carry on. I'll be the judge of weird."

"No, seriously. Something happened at the cabin. I can't wrap my head around it and I'm afraid that anyone who hears this will think I'm nuts. Hell, maybe I *am* nuts." I was transported back to the sensations of my bizarre weekend for a moment. *Fear, exaltation, confusion.*

I rallied and Mike was regarding me in silence. His expression said tell me more. He was a good listener.

So I told him. Everything. It all poured out of me. I found myself digressing into emotional descriptions that forced the tears in my eyes to spill down my cheeks. He didn't interrupt. Just sat there quietly drawing on his cigar and letting the smoke drift away on the chilly breeze. His eyes were very still and wise while he listened.

My disjointed tale ended. "Now I have this book I can't show anyone and a choice to make that seems like it will change my whole life one way or the other. I didn't ask for any of this, but I can't ignore it either. I have this...knowing...that whatever is going on is real and it feels very important."

Mike's expression was inscrutable. He just sat there holding his cigar loosely in his fingers and looked at me. I wiped my face on my sleeve and drew on my own cigar a few times. It had gone out while I talked. I gently knocked off the ash and relit it. It helped to do something with my hands. Mike had not spoken a word yet.

Finally, he cleared his throat and rubbed his chin. "Well, you know what Yogi Berra would have said right now, don't you?"

I shook my head no.

He grinned, "When you come to a fork in the road, take it!"

He must have worried that I might be offended by his humorous response because he quickly continued, "But really, I have no idea how to answer. Coming from almost anyone but you, I'd say, 'take the crack pipe out of your mouth and get back to reality.' This sounds like Art Bell stuff, but you're not one to make things up. One big lesson I've learned over the years is to trust those things you called *knowings* a minute ago. If it's that real and solid inside you, you should pay attention. So, what's your gut telling you about this choice?"

I shook my head. "I know that I should meet Lucius next weekend. I *know* that, but the things I *don't* know argue against a leap of blind faith."

"Things you don't know like...?"

"Well, my wife and kids. What will I tell them? I don't know how long I'll be gone. And the business. These people, my partners and staff, they depend on me. We're going through a tough time right now. If I don't stay on my game, I'm not sure it will all hold together. We have debts and leases and..."

Mike held up his hand. "Hang on. I didn't say that everything would be neat and tidy. I said you should pay attention to your intuitions. You want to know why?"

I nodded.

"A Chicago journalist, Sydney Harris, once wrote *'Regret for the things we did can be tempered by time; it is regret for the things we did not do that is inconsolable.'*"

"So, you're saying I should do this thing?" I said.

"Oh, no," he said, "You don't get to put this on me! I'm saying that you need to look deep into your heart and mind. Make your decision based upon things other than all the pressures that would normally keep your head down and doing what you've always done. This feels like an important time for you and I think you're the only one who can choose. Just be sure you do this one for yourself, not for anyone else."

I felt resistance inflate like a steel balloon in my chest. "Mike, you know that's not how I do things. It's the needs of the group...my team, my family, they always come first. I'm not very good at making choices that'll create hardship for other people."

"Yep!" he said, drawing the word out deliberately, "That's exactly what I mean. May I be completely honest with you?"

I nodded.

"No, I mean really, painfully honest?"

I raised my eyebrows. "Sure, Mike."

"Jacob, I've known you for a few years. We're friends. I've hung around your office and watched you in action. You're a wonderful guy. You care about people and they love you for it. To be perfectly frank though, I think you're stuck. You've built a business that looks great from the outside, but I'm an insider. I know that things are a mess. Everything depends on you, at least you think it does. In fact, your wonderful guyness is kind of a trap. You're stuck in it and so is everyone else around you. In our many conversations over lots of cigars, I see how much you long to take off in your life. You have things to share with the world. I've read some stuff you've written. Listen, you want more but you think you have to earn your freedom to pursue it."

I felt a choking pressure in my throat. I interrupted, "But I *do* have to earn my freedom! It's not fair to these other people if I led them into a..."

Mike held up his hand again. "Let me finish. I can't tell you exactly how to work this all out. All I know is what you just told me lines up with everything I've been feeling about you for awhile now. As your friend and as a fellow entrepreneur, I've observed your growing disconnect and unhappiness with your business. I wasn't sure how to broach the subject with you, because I know that your whole life is tied up in what you've built. It's not easy for me to tell you that despite your passion and hard work, you've actually sort of painted yourself into a corner."

He paused to take a quick puff on his cigar. I waited. I had a sensation of disoriented nausea rolling around in my guts.

Mike squinted thoughtfully into the distance and blew out a stream of smoke.

"Look," he said, "If you hired me as a consultant, I would ask you a whole bunch of questions. I'd learn all the things I already know about your business. We'd talk finances and management. I'd ask you about your process and your vision for the future of your company. I'd charge you a lot of money. Then, after all of that if it turned out that things were in crisis mode, I would get you alone and ask you one more question. The big one.

I would look you straight in the eye and say, '*Mr. President, you have big problems on your hands, but I can help you fix them. I just need to know one thing. Do you have a burning desire and the absolute, one hundred percent commitment to make the changes and tough choices it will take for your company to survive?'* If you didn't instantly respond in the affirmative, I would act like a doctor delivering the bad news about terminal cancer. — Then it's just a matter of time."

He looked over at me.

"Pretty heavy, huh?"

"Well, yeah," I said, "But I'm not sure what you're saying to me. I'm supposed to shut my company down?"

He was shaking his head.

"No, no, no!" he said, "I'm saying that over time you have revealed enough so that I know your heart's deepest desire isn't to captain the company you set out to build. I don't think it's just tough times in the industry either. I believe that you have worn yourself out and that the freedom you hoped to achieve by chasing down the American dream now just seems like some kind of sick fairy tale.

You aren't rich, although most people probably think you are. You aren't really your own boss. Now the juice you always got from being a super servant to everyone in sight is starting to run out, too. You're frazzled and exhausted but you don't think you really deserve a break until you take care of everything and everyone else. Again, I'm being brutally honest here. Can you handle it, or have I gone too far?"

I sighed, feeling sad.

"I can handle it. I just don't know how it really helps. My decision seems to have gone from should I take a little stab at a weird adventure to should I wreck my entire life and the lives of everyone who depends on me?"

Mike tossed his cigar down in the white and gold ceramic Tommy Bahama ashtray that sat on a small table between us and stood up.

"Jacob, hear me clearly on this, please. As your friend, I know you are not and have not been happy for some time. I don't know where your weird adventure, as you call it, will take you, but I am begging you now to decide what to do based on what you know is right.

Whichever way you choose to go, don't do this for anyone but yourself. Follow your heart. Please. That's all I ask."

I didn't say anything for a second. He held up a finger.

"Oh, and one more thing. Maybe, just maybe, it's time you figured out that other people could make it without you. Your playing God in everyone's life might not be good for you or for them."

I felt bruised and stunned by the reflection he held up before me. I wanted to be angry, to mount a defense but I couldn't. Mike had given me the gift of some painful insights. I would love to pretend they didn't strike me dead center, but like darts, they hit the bull's eye of a Jacob-shaped target.

I stood up. Mike stepped over and put his hand on my shoulder. Our eyes met. He shook me gently.

"I love you, man. You know that, right?"

I nodded. He patted me on the back.

"Okay, call me later this week?"

I nodded again and walked toward my car in silence.

As I drove home, a question kept surfacing.

If I'm in denial about my career, what other messes have been swept under the rug in my life?

Chapter Seven

The next several days were a tedious blur. I buried myself in work and tried to pretend that I was not rattled by the events of the previous weekend.

I met with clients, answered phone calls, checked my email and returned voicemail messages. I was doing it all like a joyless robot. Going through the motions.

The conversations with Lucius and later with Mike had opened some sort of window. Now, like a prisoner who smells fresh air and freedom for the first time in many years, I was miserable in my accustomed routine. Until today, the pressures and difficulties of my work just seemed like part of the entrepreneurial trade-off. When you captain a ship, sometimes there's a storm. Pretty simple. Stressful but normal, just table-stakes to play in the big game.

Not anymore, though. I felt like Jonathan Swift's character, Gulliver. I was trapped and tied down by a million tiny ropes. I felt restricted and imprisoned by the very structures that I had helped to create. Even more troublesome, I could not imagine a scenario that would cut me loose without also capsizing the ship for everyone on board. My metaphors were being scrambled, but I didn't care.

My partners were pre-occupied with their own business. They didn't seem to notice the way I withdrew from the social flow inside the office.

Sheila tried to corner me a few times and drill down for an explanation, but I was evasive and always found a way to change the subject.

Evenings at home provided no refuge from my irritated restlessness, either. I would sit at the dinner table and force a smile while my family chattered about school and video games and the toys they wanted for Christmas.

"It's only a two and a half months away, Dad," Nathan would say. I would rally and nod, pretending that I was engaged in the conversation.

At night after the children were tucked in, Jennifer would talk about the small dramas going on between her friends and travel plans for the holidays. I made an effort to emit interested noises and keep the appropriate facial expression, but it was often futile. My mind would sneak away to open the closets of shadowy questions that I didn't want to acknowledge.

"Are you even listening to me?" she said on Wednesday night as we sat in bed.

My head jerked as my eyes refocused on my wife's face. She looked a little irritated.

"Huh? Oh, I'm sorry. I think I must be getting sleepy," I said.

She shook her head with frustration, made comical by the large curlers she had rolled into her hair. I must have grinned and this further exacerbated the situation.

"What? You're laughing at me?" The slippery slope appeared before me. I was never very good at avoiding this kind of thing.

"Hey, hey...what's going on?" I said and reached over to caress her back.

She moved her shoulder away from my hand.

"You've been ignoring me all week," she said, "Tonight I'm trying to ask about it and now you think it's funny."

"I'm sorry," I said, "I really didn't hear that part."

"Yeah," she said, "I noticed. I said that you've been acting like you're on a different planet for a few days. What's going on?"

Surely, this isn't the time and place to spill the Lucius story, I thought.

I stalled. *Answer a question with a question…*

"How do you mean 'a different planet'?" I said.

She sighed with frustration.

"How many ways could I mean that? You've been distant and moody. You come home from work and barely say a word all evening. You've been grinding your teeth and muttering in your sleep."

"Oh, that planet." I glanced over at Jennifer. She was sitting with her arms crossed in the universal spousal symbol of discontent. My reply must have sounded flippant. That strategy never seemed to work out well, but I had often tried it, just the same.

"I've had a lot to think about," I said, "things have been…complicated."

"Complicated how?" she said. This seemed promising. Her demeanor had softened and turned a bit sympathetic. She had turned her head and was looking at me full on.

Do I take the plunge now?

I breathed in deep and let it out slowly. *Where should I start?*

"Something happened up at the cabin," I began. Her eyebrows drew together in the first stages of alarm.

I told her the story in sketch form first. She needed to know more, so I answered her questions as best I could. After the basic shape of the whole picture had emerged, we both fell silent for awhile. Jennifer looked thoughtful. A few seconds passed. She reached for my hand and held it.

"So, what are you going to do?" she said.

"Well, ask me again this time tomorrow and you might get a different answer. Right now, I keep vacillating between *'yes'* and *'hell no, I must be crazy'*," I said.

A clever thought occurred to me then. "What do you think I should do? I mean, you're affected by this in a big way."

She raised her eyes until they met mine directly. Suddenly, tears sprang up and spilled over her eyelashes. Her face crumpled and she bent her head.

"I think you know that this has to be your decision," she said. Her voice was thick with a sob she was working to suppress.

I leaned over and folded her in my arms. Her whole body convulsed and she struggled to regain composure. I stroked her hair and she pushed her forehead down against my shoulder.

"It's all right," I said, "I've felt the same way all week long."

A couple of minutes passed and she pulled away from me and sat straight. She used the edge of the sheet to wipe her eyes.

"I don't know what to think about this. You've never done anything really strange before, so it's hard to imagine that you're making it up. It's just so...weird," she said.

"I know," I said, "If I hadn't personally experienced all of it, there's no way I'd believe me, either. It all happened, though. That's what keeps pushing me to take this step into thin air. I have an internal... something...that tells me that I've been waiting my whole life for this. As Lucius hinted, it feels like I'm finally keeping an appointment I don't remember making, but it's right there on my calendar, all the same."

"Tell me again what's the grand plan behind all this. Why right now and why did he pick you?"

"Well, he kept saying, 'you need to discover Who You Really Are.' He said that the world is approaching a time of crisis. That a lot of us are being sort of awakened or activated, or something. Honestly, I get a little fuzzy on the exact wording he used, but the general feeling is that some people are ready to wake up and discover their purpose for being here. He said that I am stuck, in fact, that almost all human beings are. Apparently, those of us who pay attention to this call will add our awareness to a rising tide. He said it was kind of like inertia or momentum. Once the ball gets rolling, things will start moving a lot faster. People will start getting unstuck all over the place and the world we live in will change. To heal."

"That sounds kind of..."

"Crazy?" I said.

"Well, yeah."

"I know. Believe me, I know how it sounds."

"So, what are you going to do?"

"I feel, even more now that I've told you about it, that I better go see what this is about. I guess I can always hit the stop button if things get too bizarre." Even as I said words meant to comfort my wife, I knew that the gears of fate were again grinding into motion. There would be no emergency brake to pull after I left town for my meeting with Lucius in a few days. She must have felt this, too, because her eyes welled up with tears again and she just nodded silently.

We didn't talk more that night. We turned off the lights and lay awake with our backs to each other while the growing questions between us hovered over our bed like dark shadows.

Back in my office on Thursday morning, I had a quiet conference with Sheila to set the stage for my leave of absence. She was very competent and I had several junior consultants who could handle the clients I would normally see. She was to ride herd on them and try to maintain the equilibrium until I came back. The added responsibility didn't seem to intimidate her. If anything, she'd probably run things more efficiently without me around to muddy the waters. I didn't tell her The Story. Just claimed a bad case of burnout. She had already planted that seed, so it wasn't much of a stretch.

The big hurdle for me was to break the news to my partners. I had rehearsed and revised my explanation to them a dozen times. It still didn't feel very convincing. The trouble was that even without the excuse of a strange summons from the Universe, I just didn't take a break very often. I wasn't sure they were going to believe me when I said that I needed some unexpected time off.

My conversation with Mike kept replaying itself in my head. *What was the last thing he said? Oh, right "maybe, just maybe, it's time you figured out that other people can make it without you. Your playing God in everyone's life might not be good for you or for them."*

Playing God? I don't do that. I know better. Well, I do like to help people. It makes me feel important and it makes them happy. I like to make sure that people are happy and cared for. That's not wrong. You can have anything in life you want if you help enough other people get what they want, right? I looked around my office. Could they really make it without me? A tumble of panic started up inside my rib cage and I wondered if the fear originated in concern for the people who depended upon me, or was it some deeper dread attached to part of me I couldn't see?

If all went according to plan, I would not come back in the next day, so I felt obligated to leave my office in some degree of order. I had decided to spend Friday with my wife and children. As if to punish this indulgence, the phone kept ringing and email notifications constantly popped up on my screen as I plowed through the stacks on my desk. I ignored the interruptions, although the glowing red voicemail light on the back of the handset reminded me that I was an indispensable gear in our operation. Remarkably, I was angered by this obligation. This was new. Usually I responded with enthusiasm when people needed me. Today, though, my mind sifted back through years of recorded messages.

"Call me ASAP…"

I need to hear something from you…"

Jacob, if this doesn't happen on time…"

On and on and on. The messages were all urgent and important. I held people's happiness and comfort in my hands. It was all personal to me. I suddenly got this image of myself like the picture on the front of the DVD case for the movie *Office Space*. I was a man smothered in yellow sticky notes. Every one of them cemented to my soul with super glue. Each of them carried an urgent demand for my attention and they were all slowly sucking my life dry. It didn't seem to matter how I diligently handled every single issue. In that brief moment, I knew with certainty that I was drowning in a never-ending river of duty to people who would forget I even existed as soon as we finished with their transaction. Somehow, in my *"Passion for Extraordinary Service,"* I had conjured a flood of needs that threatened to suffocate me.

I shook my head. *Need to focus. Where's all this negativity coming from?*

After working for a few hours, I looked around and was pleased to see a clean desk. For the moment, every pressing situation was handled. My email inbox was clean. I had set an auto-response directing people to Sheila while I was absent. My voicemail greeting said, *"Thanks for calling. You've reached Jacob. Please listen carefully. I will be out of the office and unavailable for awhile. Don't leave a message here, press zero and ask for Sheila. She'll answer your questions or schedule a consultation. Thanks again and make it a great day!"*

"Make it a great day." That was my signature voicemail farewell. It had been for years. It was strange to hear myself say that I would be *"out of the office and unavailable."* With the exception of a couple of long weekend getaways with Jennifer, I had been always been available all the time for longer than I could really remember.

Bob Dylan's voice whispered inside my head:

how does it feel?
to be on your own
no direction home
like a complete unknown
like a rolling stone

An Outlook calendar event appeared on my screen with a little chiming sound. Subject line: "Partner Meeting: Conference Room." Ready or not. It was time.

I was first in the conference room. I took my usual chair at the head of the long table and arranged my bottle of water and a pen in front of me like a shield and sword. I glanced around the room. It was a beautiful space and seeing it again brought back a rush of memories. Our office building was an expression of my vision for the company as a whole. The very fact that we were finally able to build it, had been a major milestone. In one corner stood the shovel we used at a small groundbreaking party. I had a picture hanging somewhere of our whole gang standing out in the cold holding up plastic goblets of champagne while I chipped out a frozen divot of dirt. High times!

The conference room ceiling was coffered with hand-polished, knotty alder timbers that gleamed in the soft light. This was The Board Room where I delighted in holding meetings. It was a rare person who was not impressed. I designed it that way. "This is your stage on which to play...use it to create a memorable experience for your clients," that was my mantra when I tried to infuse the staff with my passion.

The door opened and my two partners came in. They were busy. Finishing phone calls, tapping out text messages. Deep in their own work. Finally they found a seat and a moment of silence reigned. All eyes on me.

I looked around. These were my friends and comrades-at-arms. We had started the company a few years before with twenty thousand dollars of my saved cash and a couple of their credit cards. I was the Pied Piper and Chief Imagination Officer, but these fine people had helped me hammer out every key decision. I spun the dream-wheel and then we all put boots on the ground to execute the plan.

We had taken a serious leap of faith to build this office. It was multiple times larger than the first small space we rented. We had been solidly profitable in our first location. It had been my idea to go for it, to get aggressive and ramp up the operation. The way I read the future for the next five years, we should take advantage of the booming real estate market to build a company envied by competitors and loved by clients. Reality had been much less kind.

Just as we moved into our exquisite new space, the market reached its frothy top and started to subside. We had difficulty attracting the top sales people my plan called for and our revenue projections were in a constant state of revision. I took responsibility for this and found myself toiling under feelings of failure and stress. My golden dream had turned into a salt mine. No matter, though, I was strong and capable. This was all just a test of my resolve. All my books and teachers said so. Just keep going. Never give up.

John fidgeted his pen and cleared his throat. *Time to get this party started.*

"Thanks for joining me," I said.

They nodded. Waiting.

I wasn't sure how to start. *Ask a question. Make conversation.*

"How's everything going?" I looked at them each in turn.

Their eyes asked questions. They shifted in the leather chairs.

John spoke first. He was always the most direct.

"Um, everything's fine, but I have a lot to do. What's this about?" *Time to dive in.*

"Guys, this isn't like me, but I need a little time off. I'm going to leave tomorrow and be gone for a while." I wanted to give a plausible explanation, but there wasn't much else to say. Without telling the whole preposterous tale of my previous weekend, I didn't have a good excuse. No way that I could paint the full surreal picture for them. They already thought I was a wild-eyed dreamer at times.

David's eyebrows shot up and he leaned forward. "You're what?"

"I think I need some time to catch my breath or something."

They looked at each other and then down at the table. *Awkward.*

"Is there anything we need to know about this?" John said.

David's phone buzzed and he silenced it impatiently with a slap at the buttons. He shook his head.

"Jacob, I mean, we're all tired here. Things are pretty intense right now. How long are we talking?"

Acid boiled in my stomach. This was exactly what I hated to do. Any time I needed something for myself, I felt guilty, like a little boy begging for a favor. It wasn't fair! My face burned and my heart pounded.

When I replied, it was louder than I intended, "I'm not sure, David. I hate to be a burden but I'm sort of processing things at the moment and I need some time away to get through it."

John's face looked tight. "Anything we can do to help you 'process' whatever it is? We kind of need you back at full capacity as soon as possible," he said sarcastically.

"Look," I said, "This is unusual. I am aware that none of us has had a real break for the last couple of years. That's not good."

"We can't exactly afford vacations right now," David broke in, "We need all hands on deck if we're going to make it."

"I know we can't. Believe me, I know. I've got Sheila lined up to take care of my work for a little while and I'm confident that everything will keep moving just fine."

"How long are we talking for this...break? A few days? A few weeks?" John said.

"Honestly," *this is the hard part,* I thought, "I don't know."

They shook their heads, disgusted, and I could see jaw muscles clenching down on words they wanted to say. I once read that nonverbal cues and body language make up seventy percent of communication. Theirs were particularly eloquent. *Crossed arms. Contracted faces.*

I hurried to explain further. "I know this isn't my usual mode. I'm sorry to inconvenience you guys. I'll be back in the saddle as soon as possible."

We all sat in the uncomfortable silence. No one made eye contact. The meeting was clearly at an end when they pushed their chairs back and started for the door. John turned before he left the room and looked back.

"Do you suppose you'll be able to join us for the meeting with the bank next week?" he said. "It's kind of important if we're going to stay afloat." There was a brittle edge in his voice. He could not seem to believe that we were having this conversation.

"John, I hope so," I said, "I just don't know."

He pulled the door closed and I was alone sitting in the thundering silence. My breath rushed out and I fell forward to rest my forehead on the table between my arms. *Am I really doing this?*

Back in my office, I felt light. I had slashed through most of my self-created tether. It was time to pack up and go. I looked around. My desk was tidy. The trash can was empty. I loaded my laptop into its leather case, swung the strap up on my shoulder and turned to the door.

Still need to do something. What?

I put the computer bag down and stood there taking inventory. *Keys in my pocket. Cell phone in my hand. Wallet. Check.*

I turned my head and looked around for a clue. My walls sported nicely framed success posters. "Dare to Soar" one said. It had the picture of a bald eagle gliding through a blue sky. Right above my desk, there was my vision board. I created it after being inspired by watching "The Secret" movie. It had pictures of the finest things in life. Big house, luxury cars, sandy beach, Rolex watch. In the center, I had pasted a picture of my family. Above and to the left were the cut out words "Freedom" and "Time." There were pictures from a health magazine. A well-muscled torso with the words "Radiant Health" glued above it. Interesting. Some of the things had come into my life, but they had pushed out the less tangible ones. I had the house and car, but the debts that accompanied them had made radiant health and time with my family seem like distant goals. I was overweight and stressed and running ragged. *Maybe Lucius will help me figure out this puzzle*, I thought.

This train of thought triggered my memory. *Books! Lucius said to bring books.*

I stepped over to the bookcase and surveyed the titles. I started reading success literature as a young teenager. Zig Ziglar, Brian Tracy, Napoleon Hill, Charlie "Tremendous" Jones. I had quite a collection. Tony Robbins, James Allen, Jim Collins, Dale Carnegie. Some old, some new. I ran my fingertips over the spines of my friends. The ideas contained in these books had formed the foundation of my resolve to create the life of my dreams.

Which ones will Lucius approve of? I wondered.

I put Brian Tracy's, *The Psychology of Achievement*, Napoleon Hill's, *Think and Grow Rich* and *See You At The Top* by Zig Ziglar in a pile. So many great books. They had all been influential. I liked to think of the men and women who wrote them as my teachers. I put the small stack under my arm and turned to leave. Just then, the dark DVD case of *The Secret* caught my eye. I wedged it on top of the others. It had bridged the gap and delved into the spiritual metaphysical side of success.

Sheila appeared at the door just as I was leaving.

"Hey. You out now?"

I nodded.

"I'll walk you to your car."

I had decided to leave without any fanfare. No need to alarm the staff or fabricate an explanation for my sales team. Sheila would just let them know that I was going to be away for a while on a well-deserved vacation. We left through the kitchen and walked out to the patio. The sun was shining but a chilly wind blew down from the mountains. Sheila stopped and wrapped her arms around herself against the cold.

"Well, I hope you really get some rest," she said.

"Thank you, Sheila," I said, "I can't say how much I appreciate you stepping up like this for me."

She smiled, then reached one arm and squeezed me around the shoulders.

"Just get yourself sorted out and don't worry about us here. Everything will be all right, even with the Chief away."

I patted her on the back with my free hand and then moved toward the car.

"See you later," she called after me.

I smiled and waved. She couldn't see that sudden relief had exploded inside me. I felt buoyant and excited about my decision for the first time.

As I turned my steering wheel, I glanced at the image in the rear view mirror. My building appeared to be on fire, engulfed in a blaze of flames so bright that it hurt my eyes. I blinked and looked again. The impression vanished and what remained was the ordinary scene of a small office park. *That's weird! Must have been a trick of the sunlight.*

So why did the now-familiar silent gong send a vibrating crash through my body at that moment? *Boomsheee...*

On Friday, Jennifer had everyone up and dressed by eight-thirty. She had called the school and our children were going to skip a day so we could spend it together.

We started with a big breakfast downtown at Moon's Cafe. Our table was a glorious riot of sticky donuts, biscuits and gravy, and hot chocolate with whipped cream.

We held a vote and decided to watch an early screening of a new 3-D movie in the big multiplex.

The whole day went like that. One good thing after another. We laughed, ate, and bickered a little. In the late afternoon, everyone was exhausted. On a whim after lunch, we had driven the winding road up to Bogus Basin. We hiked as far up the snowless ski hill as possible before the twins mutinied and threatened to die rather than take another step. The view was spectacular from our vantage point at

6,900 feet. Far off, beyond the city that sprawled in the valley, the Owyhee Mountains spread across the horizon to the west. We took turns finding landmarks. The air down below was smudgy with pollution, but the wind blew clean and cold in our faces as we sat perched on top of the world.

On the way home later, warm silence reigned. Everyone was quietly absorbed in his or her own thoughts but we felt connected and peaceful. I kept turning to look at my family. These few slow moments were golden and I was conscious that my journey into the unknown might well disrupt this comfortable picture.

We came to a stop inside the garage. Three seconds of perfect stillness passed before everyone roused and the car became the eye of a noisy hurricane. As soon as we were inside the house, the children vanished into their various dens of entertainment and Jennifer stood with me in the quiet entranceway.

She smiled at me in the half-light and I reached to help with her coat. As she turned to slip from the sleeves, her body brushed against mine. Our eyes met with the silent understanding that comes from years of marriage. Her arms went around my neck and I pressed her tight to me. She radiated soft inviting warmth. I kissed the smooth skin behind her ear and she nodded against my neck. We hurried up the stairs to our bedroom and locked the door. While she undressed, I turned on quiet music and lit the flame in the gas fireplace that was her only demand for the master suite when we built the house. The firelight glowed and created an intimate envelope of warmth that welcomed us as she walked across the room and stepped into my arms.

She made love to me with an unusual urgency and afterward, she turned away and wrapped the sheet around herself. I placed my palm against her back and felt her body shaking. I moved close and touched her face. My fingers came away wet with tears. I pressed my forehead against the back of her neck and shook my head.

What is going to happen to us? I thought.

Chapter Eight

The office is on fire!

I stood on the little strip of grass outside the building watching helplessly as intense heat shattered the bronze-tinted glass on the side windows and flames roared through the ragged openings. Panic stricken, I whirled looking in a full circle for anything to stop the blaze.

Where were the emergency crews?

Out in the parking lot a small crowd was gathered. I squinted through the hot smoke that blew in my face. Oh, good! My staff was out. They were all pointing and waving their arms at me. I waved back.

"It's okay," I tried to yell, "I'll handle this!" My voice stuck in my throat and the sound came out as just a strangled whisper.

I turned back toward the burning building and felt a fierce searing sensation. A blast of superheated air whooshed out as the side exit door collapsed onto the patio.

Through the flames, I thought I saw someone struggling inside. I tried to take a step closer but the heat drove me back. Two figures appeared and I recognized my partners. They were trying to save the office. Running back and forth, they were desperately moving furniture around and stacking up boxes of important files.

"Stop!" I screamed, "Get out of there!" Again, the words were painful grunts that barely cleared my lips.

Everything was in slow motion. I began to spin in place, a human pinwheel. Some horrible knowledge stabbed into my mind and I looked down. In one hand, I was waving a flaming torch. As I spun, my clothes had caught fire. I tried to fall down, to throw away the burning wood but I was frozen.

My employees dashed over and formed a circle around me. They were staring with a strange mixture of terror and sadness and accusation.

Suddenly I knew why. I had burnt down my own building. I was the arsonist. It was so obvious.

The fire in my clothes began to scorch my skin. The smell of burning hair reached my nostrils and, in the distance, a fire engine siren screamed. Great grief and guilt ballooned inside, but I couldn't release the sobs imprisoned in my chest.

I awoke in my bed, trembling and panting hoarsely. I was sweating and tangled in the sheets but my body was frozen in place. It took more than ten seconds to catch my breath, unlock my muscles and realize that the experience was only a product of my own subconscious. A nightmare.

I loosened the bedclothes and sat up. Shaky. The alarm clock on the fireplace mantle said 8:12. Morning. Saturday morning. I took a deep breath.

The house was quiet. I tested my footing and walked into the bathroom. No Jennifer. I pulled on a pair of gym pants and walked downstairs. It was altogether silent. I looked around. The living room was unusually tidy for a Saturday morning. The kitchen counters were clean and everything was in perfect order. This was not the normal state of affairs for a weekend morning.

I spied a sheet of paper taped to the refrigerator. Moving closer, I could see my wife's handwriting:

Jacob,

I decided to take the kids out this morning for awhile. We'll be gone all day and then probably stay over at my friend's house tonight.

I love you but it's too hard to hang around all day and wait for you to leave.

Please be safe and call me if you can.

I believe in you but I'm afraid, too. Just do what you need to do and I'll be here when you come home.

Love and prayers,

Jennifer

Love and prayers. Yes, I need lots of both, I thought.

I showered and shaved while a pot of coffee brewed in the kitchen. With a towel around my waist, I peeked outside. It was another perfect fall day. I decided to get to the store early, come back and pack up.

Pack what, though? Lucius had given me no details about my journey. *I assume that we'll be at the cabin, but how long? He mentioned meeting some other people. Would I need to provide food? How many days of clean clothes should I bring?* Too many questions and they were not even the ones that concerned me most.

I dressed and left the house with a large travel mug of coffee in hand. After visiting the gas station, I drove around and wasted several hours. Around one-thirty, I met my friend, Thayne, for a spontaneous late lunch at our favorite Thai restaurant. He was a brilliant web artist and an amateur philosopher. We enjoyed long abstract discussions and often met Mike to solve the world's problems over cigars. Today, it was just the two of us and our conversation stayed on the surface. I was grateful for this. My last week had been intense and it was certain that the rest of my journey would be even more rigorous. It was good to chat about normal life, but at the same time I kept finding myself suspended over the table like a silent third party. Watching and listening. Detached.

We took our time over *tom kha gai*, spicy coconut soup, and I finally glanced at my watch. 3:35. Time to go. In fact, now I would have to hurry a little. Thayne shook my hand as we left.

"Enjoy your day, good sir," he said.

I smiled. "Thank you. I'll call you when I get back to town and we can catch up again." I had told him that I was taking a short leave of absence. He was a little surprised but encouraged me to "really rest up." That piece of advice seemed to be the first thing most people said when they heard the public version of my plans. Perhaps my ragged edges were showing more than I realized. We parted and I broke the speed limit all the way home. All the traffic lights were green, so I arrived in less than twelve minutes.

My energy shifted into a state of nervous excitement. At home, I tossed a couple pairs of jeans, some long sleeved shirts and sweaters into a duffel bag. Assuming we stayed near the cabin, there were plenty of jackets and gloves in case of colder weather. Down in my home office, I loaded the books Lucius had asked me to bring. As an afterthought, I included the old King James Version Bible that had been a gift from my parents on my fifteenth birthday. Lucius said to bring material that had been influential in my life. The Bible wasn't something I read often these days. Yet, there were still large sections of it burned into memory from my church-going childhood.

That was a whole lifetime ago, I thought as I pressed the worn black book into my pack. This copy had accompanied me through my late teen years and then moved from place to place as I married, started work as a young adult, and eventually launched my ambitious dream-turned-quagmire of a company. It was present on my philosophical journey away from the fundamentalist Christianity of my youth. Even now, in my state of religious limbo, it was a disturbing, sturdy block in the framework of my beliefs. I wasn't sure what to do with it, exactly, but it contained wisdom and undeniable truths that were difficult to banish. I didn't even want to banish them, but they no longer fit that well into my modern perspective.

My palm was flat against its cover. I could feel the book's energy, like a magnetic force field, and my internal resistance and attraction to it. I flipped it open quickly, not sure what I was doing. The worn binding opened at the first chapter of St. John's Gospel. My eyes caught on an underlined passage from the first verse, "*He was with God in the beginning... In him there was life, and that life was the light of all people. The Light shines in the darkness, and the darkness has not overpowered it.*"

Love it or hate it, this was not a book I could ignore. It had influenced my past deeply. Maybe Lucius would have some thoughts on how to deal with it. I closed it and zipped the duffel. Something was still incomplete. *What?* My nervous system sparked and the internal clock ticked loud. Time to go. *What am I missing?* I looked down at myself and ran a quick inventory.

Clothes! I was still wearing jeans and a long-sleeved T-shirt. "Dress in your best clothes," Lucius said. It was a weird demand, but so was everything else. I raced upstairs and hurried into a dark gray worsted wool suit. Brioni. Ridiculously expensive, I bought it after seeing Pierce Brosnan wear one in a James Bond film. I selected a white shirt with French cuffs and stepped into my shiny black shoes. In the full-length mirror, I grinned at my reflection while I tied a maroon tie. Good thing no one was around to see me heading out for a wilderness weekend dressed for dinner at the White House. The truth was, I loved this suit. It always made me feel powerful and important. It was like bespoke armor for the modern warrior. The clock said 4:13.

Downstairs, I grabbed a piece of paper and drew a big heart with a black marker. Inside the heart-shape, I wrote, "I LOVE YOU." It was all I could think to write.

4:15.

My keys were on top of the duffel bag by the front door. I looked around quickly. *Something still missing...out of time!* Out the door and halfway down the front walk to where I had parked my car, I realized what was nagging me. *Emerson's Bible.* I just didn't want to look at it all week. In fact, it was hidden in one of my desk drawers. I dropped my bag on the sidewalk and jogged back to the house. It took less than thirty seconds to find the book, lock the front door again and get behind the wheel. All loaded up.

I turned the key and my internal systems fired along with the engine. Everything was in place now. As the car rolled away from the curb, I felt my energy shift. I was moving. The decision had been made and now action confirmed it. It was like untying from the dock and pushing my canoe into a racing river. I felt fear, excitement and anticipation of the unknown. It all moved inside me as I accelerated through the subdivision and down the main street that led to the highway.

A time would come much later when I would look back on that moment and wonder if I could have driven into the mountains that day had I known everything that lay ahead.

Chapter Nine

I drove in silence. The scenery passed outside like a movie on fast-forward with the sound muted. Again, I felt strangely separated from my body. As an observer, I was in the back seat watching. The familiar physical sensations were distant, as if a remote receiver was transmitting them. In this state, I maneuvered. I could control my hands on the steering wheel, but didn't seem to be fully associated with them, either. *Like a ghost in the machine*, I thought.

This play of sensory dissonance was shattered by a siren behind me. I slammed back into physical awareness. My fingers tingled and my heart raced with adrenaline. I looked ahead; somehow, I was rounding the sweeping curve of Highway 21 where it skirts Lucky Peak dam. I couldn't remember making all the stops and turns to get there, but that wasn't important now. Red and blue lights flashed in the rearview mirror and I pulled over at the first turnout.

Think. What did I do? I could remember nothing about the last ten minutes. On autopilot, I reached into the glove compartment for my registration and proof of insurance. The policeman was certainly taking his time. I rolled my driver side window down and waited. The dashboard clock read 4:27. I hoped the officer would just give me a warning, or write me a ticket, or whatever he needed to do. Fast. I wasn't running late yet, but this was cutting it close. I began to regret my long lunch.

Gravel crunched beside the car and a pair of uniformed legs appeared at my open window. The patrolman bent down but I couldn't see his face past the brim of his hat. State Police.

"License and registration, sir." he said.

I handed them through the window. He took them from me and stood there for a minute. I kept looking straight ahead. My mouth felt dry. *Damn it! What did I do?*

"Do you know why I pulled you over, *sir*?" his voice contained a smile. He had over-emphasized the "sir," he was poking fun at me. I turned and the tall officer squatted so I could see his face. He was shaking his head, grinning at my distress.

"Dave?" I half yelled in surprise. It was my boyhood friend, David Simmons. I had attended his swearing-in as a State police officer a couple of years earlier in the rotunda of the capitol building. He patrolled a five hundred-mile square of wilderness highway that included this stretch. I rarely saw him up here but he sometimes stopped by our cabin. He'd write a note on the back of his business card and tuck it in the door frame. It was a small show of force in case the carpet thieves returned.

We looked at each other. He reached in to shake my hand.

"Actually, I don't know what I did," I confessed.

He made a show of peering in through my windows to look for contraband.

"You just seemed like a suspicious character," he said, "Actually, you drifted across the line a few times, but now that I've pulled you over, I see your suit's probable cause enough. You going to some kinda redneck Mafia funeral or what?"

Yeah, how do I explain this, I thought.

"Oh," I said, "I just left a wedding. I decided to get out of town right after and change clothes at the cabin." That was an easy lie.

"Huh," was all he said, "Well, I'm going to need you to go easy on the speed until you get where you're going, okay? I'll let you off with a warning this time, but stay in your lane."

In that moment, it didn't matter that he was my friend. Relief cascaded down my shoulders. My driving record was clear. Nice to keep it that way.

We chuckled and I thanked him. A blast of air rocked the car as a large Ford pickup blew around the curve. His brake lights lit up when the driver noticed the patrol car, but it was too late.

David tapped the edge of my window. "Duty calls! Be careful out there, man."

I kept the car in park while he roared away in a spray of gravel. Dust from his exit swirled around the windshield so I waited for it to clear before moving back on to the highway.

4:35. I wasn't tardy yet, but Lucius had asked me to return to the cabin no later than 5:30. He said he would wait for me until then but if I didn't show on time, he'd vanish forever. I was pushing things a little too close. Again.

As often happens in southwestern Idaho, the autumn weather had turned during the afternoon. Cold gray clouds had blown in across the Cascade mountain range from the coast of Washington. It wasn't raining, but that was probably next. In the higher elevations, we'd likely get snow before morning.

I drove with the headlights on. Not quite dark yet but the gloomy weather hastened twilight. We were in the midst of hunting season and most of the deer were hiding far back in the mountains. Even so, I was watchful.

The road narrowed to two lanes as I passed the cafe at the crest of the small summit known as Hilltop. It was the last place to get a cup of coffee between Boise and Idaho City. The parking lot was full of hunters' pickup trucks. The little restaurant was attached to a convenience store that specialized in cold beer, ice, bait and fishing tackle. You could buy ammunition and disposable cameras there, but you paid the price for not picking them up before you left town.

I crossed the high bridge over the almost-empty reservoir. Every spring, melting snow rushed through the creeks, fed into the branches of larger streams and filled this waterway. All summer, people navigated the narrow channel with small fishing vessels, wake-board boats and jet skis. In late September, the pent-up river finally drained away under the dam and into the irrigation canals that watered the valley's lawns and farms.

The highway snaked around the crumbling granite knees of the mountains, where they knelt down to drink at the water's edge. My agile little car gripped the curves with ease. I could have driven faster, but as I drew close to my appointment with Lucius, somberness settled over me and required a deliberate pace. Perhaps it was an effect of the cloudy afternoon, but whatever the cause, my mood was tinged with foreboding.

My mind fell into a cycle of reveries for the next several miles. Around and around. I replayed conversations, emotions, and strange dreams of the last seven days. My reason kept rebelling against what I was doing. *You're driving right this minute back into the mountains, wearing a suit. You're meeting someone who claims to be visiting you from another realm? Your whole life might change. You're going along with this scheme?*

I finally switched on the radio and let it cycle through the crackling channels. Only one country music station came through clear. Not my usual choice, but the words of the song it played captured my attention.

> "*I went sky diving, I went rocky mountain climbing,*
> "*I went two point seven seconds on a bull named Fu Man Chu.*
> "*And I loved deeper and I spoke sweeter,*
> "*And I gave forgiveness I'd been denying.*"

I turned up the volume...

An' he said: "Some day, I hope you get the chance,
"To live like you were dyin'."

Like tomorrow was a gift,
And you got eternity,
To think about what you'd do with it.
An' what did you do with it?

The music disappeared into a haze of static as the road curved between high canyon walls. I thumbed the button on my steering wheel to turn the radio off. *Live like you were dying...* I always preferred to live courageously and not think much about death. Death would come someday and I would deal with it. I was more concerned with chalking up a high score. My grand plan was to make a pile of money and then, armed with wealth and leisure, to devote myself to building a generous legacy. Whatever I was up to at present pointed in a different direction.

Grimes Creek runs directly into Highway 21 and rushes around a sharp bend as it joins More's Creek to form a larger stream that empties into Lucky Peak reservoir. Most of the roads in this rocky region follow these creeks. It's an acknowledgment of Mother Nature's superior wisdom in taking the path of least resistance. In my imaginative state that day, the highway's twists and turns made me feel like I was riding the back of a giant snake that would carry me far back into the mountains according to its own whim.

The clouds closed in and a fine, misty rain fell as I approached the left-turn for Grimes Creek road. The thermometer read thirty-nine degrees. It was getting cold. Overnight snow was likely.

4:57. I braked and waited for a car coming fast in the opposite lane. Its headlights glared on the wet pavement and it threw a spray of water against my windshield.

I was already coasting forward to make the turn and as soon as the lane cleared, I pressed the gas. My tires spun on the slick road and I never saw the vehicle that materialized around the bend. It was driving without headlights in the gloom and, when the impact came, I was astonished.

CRASH. I was flung hard against the seatbelt. My hands flew off the steering wheel and I opened my mouth to scream. Side curtain airbags exploded in the rear window. My entire car was lifted and whipped around in a circle, as if some clumsy giant-child was spinning me like a top. Sounds, lights, and grinding metal blended in a shocking collage that burst across the sky in my mind and hung there, suspended in stillness for a long moment.

A few dazed seconds later, I squinted and looked around. *I'm okay. No blood. Nothing hurts much.* I blinked and turned to look for the other car. Aside from the adrenaline still sparking through my system and muscles stiff with terror, I seemed to be injury-free. Through my windshield, I could see that my car was facing the wrong way. The highway was quiet. I glanced in the rear view. No sign of the other vehicle. I became aware of a cramp in my leg. The car was still in gear but I had my foot clamped on the brake. I shifted into Park, then thought better of it and eased off the brake and feathered the gas. The car moved, but a grating sound from the rear quarter panel told me that not all was well.

Still in shock, I navigated a slow three-point turn and pulled off the highway on the sandy turnout at Grimes Creek Road. I unbuckled and opened the door. *4:58 That all happened in less than a minute,* I thought. Chilly moist air and the sound of rushing water from the stream rallied me and I climbed out of the car. Leaning against the door frame, I was dazed. Fear drained away, leaving me shaky.

I shook my head and looked around. The dusk was quiet except for the water sounds and rain-patter. I shuffled back to the side of the highway and looked both ways. I could see red tail light shatters scattered on the road but there was no sign of another vehicle anywhere. Concentrating for a moment, I realized I had zero impression of the other car. Nothing. As if a ghostly freight train had exploded out of the night, smashed my vehicle and disappeared without a trace. *Probably can't use that explanation with the insurance company,* I thought. *Really, though, it was a hit and run. The other guy never slowed down at all.*

I walked back to my car and knelt down to inspect the damage. The fender behind the rear passenger tire was crushed. The trunk had sprung open and the bumper was almost touching the ground. I touched the crumpled sheet metal with my fingertips and flakes of paint stuck to them. Strange, I couldn't find any color from the other car. *Curiouser and curiouser.*

Numb fog hovered inside my brain. I took a few steps toward the creek and leaned against a pine tree. The breeze carried the smell of wet willow shoots and sagebrush growing on the alluvial flats across the water. I breathed deep. This cleared my head and triggered the ticking of my internal clock. *What time is it now?* I glanced down at the glowing dial of my stainless steel Rolex Submariner.

5:04. Still plenty of time if I could figure out a way to make the car drive-able. There was probably a bungee cord or some kind of strap in the trunk. Hell, I'd use my necktie if it came right down to it.

These practical thoughts steadied me. I closed my eyes and took a few more slow breaths.

In the same instant, a hand touched my shoulder and a man's voice said, "It's time to go now."

Electric surprise and fear jolted me. I whirled.

Lucius stood within arm's length, regarding me with steady eyes. Drops of rain hung from his leather hat brim but his clothes weren't wet.

"What? You're...how did you get here?" I said, my voice loud and harsh.

He raised his eyebrows. Why should his arrival occasion this reaction? The accustomed rules of travel through space and time seemed to be optional for him. He looked so thoroughly human that it was hard to remember that he was a transdimensional visitor.

"I was coming," I said, "I'm not late yet."

"Yes," he replied, "We need to go. Now. They're waiting for us."

"How will we go? Wait, where are we going? I thought we were using my cabin."

"No," he said, "We have a journey to make. Leave your car here. I have a truck." He pointed behind him. Sure enough. Beside my car was a large black Nissan Titan, that looked brand new. It was idling and the headlights shone through falling rain. I never heard it approach. The river gravel didn't crunch under his feet as he walked to where I stood. It was all very odd.

"I can't just leave my car," I said, "That would cause all sorts of panic. Someone will find it sitting here and connect the dots. They'll call the police to report the accident and that will create drama, especially if I'm not around to explain what happened."

"That's not important," he said, "But we can leave it at your cabin if you like, get it out of the way for a while." He walked over and pulled up hard on the dragging bumper. As on most modern cars, this one was a plastic cover more than a real bumper. He hit it with his fist. Twice. It popped back into place and stayed.

"Come on," he said, "This will work for now. Let's get going."

By the time I returned to the car and buckled in, he was already driving away. I followed his taillights and soon we left the pavement to climb the muddy roads toward my property. He drove fast, sure of his directions. The wet forest closed in on both sides like a dark tunnel.

When we reached my driveway, Lucius pulled over so I could pass. I climbed out in the rain to unlock the gate chain from its post and swing it open. Large cold drops ran down my neck before I could huddle back into the warm car. I stopped in front of the lodge and the big truck came alongside. The passenger window slid down and Lucius leaned over. I opened my door and stood up.

"Put your things in the back seat," he said, "We need to be off." He obviously wasn't going to waste time explaining. I handed my duffel bag through the window. Glancing around, I scooped up *Emerson's Bible* from the passenger seat and unplugged my cell phone charger from the socket. Probably wouldn't have any use for that, but better take it just in case. I shut the door and pushed the button on my key fob. The car alarm chirped twice and I climbed into the cab next to Lucius. He looked at me as I buckled my seatbelt.

"Ready?" he said.

I nodded. *Ready or not*, I thought.

Chapter Ten

We drove fast, retracing the route to Highway 21. The truck's cab was warm and I soon noticed a damp wool smell from my suit as it dried. I struggled out of the jacket and laid it over my duffel bag in the back. My state-dinner appearance had deteriorated. My hair was matted in wet strings on my forehead. Mud smeared my shoes and pant cuffs. I pulled the front of my shirt as straight as possible. I had managed to get a smudge on the wide part of my tie.

"I hope whoever we're going to see will forgive this mess," I said.

"Mess?" Lucius looked confused at first, "Oh, your clothes. I wouldn't worry about it."

He glanced over at me and noticed *Emerson's Bible* on my lap.

"So, what did you think about that?" he said, nodding at the book.

I loosened the leather tie and fanned the pages.

"Honestly, I didn't spend any time with it this week. It's beautiful, but I wasn't sure what to do with it. Was I supposed to have read it by now?"

He drove in silence for a few hundred yards before answering.

"I didn't expect you to do much. Did you even open it?"

"Well, sure. I read the Thoreau quote on the front page and saw some more of them scattered around. It looked like mostly blank pages. Like a journal?"

He nodded.

"Do you know much about Emerson?"

I shook my head, "Not much. I've read some of his quotes. He seems intriguing, though. I probably need get into his work, don't I?"

"Oh, intriguing isn't half the story," he said, "He was an important messenger who made a huge impact in the eighteen hundreds. He became known as the leader of the Transcendentalism movement in America. He hung out with people like Thoreau and Nathaniel Hawthorne and Samuel Coleridge. You might enjoy reading his essay titled *Nature* sometime. There's no hurry, though. Emerson himself would tell you to get rid of your mental baggage. It's not about piling up facts at this point.

"So, back to your book. Emerson said '*make your own Bible. Select and collect all the words and sentences that in all your reading have been to you like the blast of triumph out of Shakespeare, Seneca, Moses, John and Paul.*'

"As I said in the note I left, this is going to be a very useful friend for you. You'll know more when the time comes. Look through it a minute. Tell me what you notice."

I flipped it open about halfway through. This page had two quotes on it. I began reading out loud.

The breeze at dawn has secrets
to tell you; Don't go back to sleep.
You must ask for what you really
want; Don't go back to sleep.
People are going back and forth
across the doorsill where the two
worlds touch. The door is round
and open. Don't go back to sleep.'

"That's by Rumi," I said.

Lucius smiled, "Ah, Rumi. The old Persian! He has a lot to say. Have you read any of his poems?"

"No," I said. I was starting to feel inadequate, "I've read stacks of books about business and success. After I left the church I grew up in as a kid, I only focused on my career. I'm fascinated by these ideas, but it's been years since I tried to put any of the pieces together about religion and theology."

"Yeah," he said, "Don't worry too much about the pieces right now. Actually, tell me about yourself. Start from the beginning. What's the story of Jacob like?"

We had made it back to the highway. It was full dark and the rain fell heavily now. Lucius flipped the left-turn signal. We were headed north, away from Boise.

"Okay, but where are we going?" I said.

He turned his head to look both directions and then we were moving on to the highway. A green sign with reflective letters said "Idaho City: 10 miles."

"Oh, we still have a way to go," he said vaguely, "It'll take a while."

I unbuttoned my top shirt button and loosened my tie. As they dried out, my shoes began to feel tight. I untied the knots and got comfortable. The interior of the cab was finished with gray pebbled leather. It all smelled new.

I cleared my throat and looked at Lucius, "So, my story. Where do I start?"

"Wherever you like," he said, "Unless something else sticks out that you want to talk about. Tell me where you were born, who your parents are. That sort of thing."

My mind began sorting through folders of memories stuffed in mental cabinets.

~ *The Divine Arsonist* ~

"Well, let's see," I began, "I was born in Santa Rosa, California in seventy-three. My parents were hippies. In fact, I'm pretty sure I was conceived in a little coffee shack where they were living off the land on the Kona Coast in Hawai'i. They always told me and my brothers and sisters that they loved all the papayas and grapefruit and mangoes that grew wild near them. We finally pinned them down and made them admit that they also loved the marijuana hedge right out in their front yard. They hated to confess it because they took a hard right turn into Christianity after I was born. They liked to pretend they weren't hell-raisers back in the day."

"How many kids in your family?" he said.

"I'm the oldest of six," I said, "Four boys, two girls."

"The eldest son," he said, "What's that been like for you?"

"It was a lot of work, growing up," I said, "I felt, still do, huge responsibility for the whole family. It seems like I had the job of breaking ground for the others."

A few bits of memory swirled in my mind and I fell silent.

"I interrupted you," he said, "You were telling me about your hippie parents."

I sat quietly for a minute, thinking about them.

"It's hard to remember them that way. Actually, I can't. When I was six months old, they moved to Idaho. They had heard a myth that the government was giving away free land up by McCall if people would just go and homestead. Dad built a wooden camper shell for their old Dodge pickup. He covered it with cedar roofing shakes and they took off. They got to McCall in November, I think, and discovered there was no free land. They were California people and it got so cold they thought all three of us were going to freeze to death.

Some guy they met in a coffee shop took pity on them and hooked Dad up with a contact in Boise who might have a little work. We got down there and moved into a converted shed on the back of this person's property.

~ 94 ~

My father was good with wood. He started doing some carpentry, but work was spotty. He was a hippie and really wanted to live off the grid. In fact, down through my life, I see that desire never left him. He tried to fit in and take care of the family, but it never suited him very well."

I glanced at Lucius. He was listening, eyes on the road. He looked over and nodded for me to continue.

"Now that I think about it, Dad had a hard time with life in general. He's an individualist, a philosopher. The whole thing of having a steady job and sliding along comfortable never seemed to work for him. In fact, I never put all this together before, but what I just said colored my whole growing up experience. Dad didn't fit in and neither did we. I remember always feeling like other people lived inside a nice, safe bubble, but not us. We were poor but it was more than that. Mom found a way to keep us well dressed, so we kept up appearances, but we were standing outside looking in on a world other people lived in and we didn't."

This realization developed and emerged like a dark little balloon that floated around between us inside the cab. My face flushed.

Lucius looked at me. His eyes were kind and knowing.

"You're doing well, Jacob," he said, "That was a real gift, you know."

"What was?" I said.

"You were given the gift of not fitting in."

"I'm sure this is a bad question, but how is that a gift? I spent most of my life feeling awkward. It was painful."

"You'll learn much more about this later, but you will come to know that you were given the ability to see things differently from other people. The price you paid feels high, but you'll soon understand that it was worth every moment. By the way, most people don't realize that the most precious gifts in life come hidden inside of painful wrapping paper."

"I'm not sure what to say about that. I've spent almost two decades at seminars and reading books learning how to be a successful human. Are you saying I've been wasting my time?"

He chuckled, then turned serious.

"Nothing is wasted. Ever. All experiences have a purpose. Having said that, you've been working hard in your life to be someone other than who you really are. That has worn you out. It's time for you to come home to yourself and see how it all fits together."

"I'm sure you're saying something important, but it doesn't make a lot of sense. I'm sorry."

He shook his head, "Don't apologize. It will all become clear. Back to the gift, though. Almost no one can see outside the bubble they were born in, that's what I'm saying. Their apparent reality is everything they've ever known, their way of life, their beliefs, their assumptions. It's all a tightly woven illusion but they can't imagine life any other way. When someone is given the gift of not fitting in, they have the chance to see things as they really are. More often than not, though, they do what you've done all your life and work themselves to death to look normal."

"So, I've been doing it wrong?"

"It's not about right and wrong, Jacob. You've been doing it how you've been doing it. That is all. You will find that all your doing has led you to a place of decision. You can choose to keep discovering who you really aren't, or you can take the direct path home and experience who you really are."

"Circles," I said, "You're talking in circles. It makes me dizzy."

"Ha!" he laughed, "You just spoke more truth than you can possibly know."

The highway was lit by a couple of street lamps ahead of us. We were coming into Idaho City. The road signs read "Reduced Speed Ahead, 25 Miles Per Hour, Strictly Enforced," Lucius braked to a crawl. We passed a U.S. Post Office and a Mormon Church. They were by far, the most modern and well-maintained buildings in the little community. Back in the rough gold rush days, Idaho City had the largest population in the Northwest, even more than Portland. The miners lived in tents and tiny shacks while they worked the dredges in search of a fortune.

In fact, over two hundred fifty million dollars worth of gold was taken from the river beds and hills surrounding the town after the first big discovery in 1862. When the fever passed, the treasure seekers disappeared but left behind a landscape scarred by piles of river-rock tailings and semi-toxic placer ponds. By 1920, only one hundred and four people lived in the area. Now, the original wooden buildings on Main Street were home to a few dingy restaurants, some trinket shops and a combination taxidermy-vitamin store. My favorite was The Shady Lady. They claimed to be the location of a brothel once—now it's just a struggling café and gift shop. I liked the character of the old place and the comical, lascivious woman-of-the-night on the painted sign.

I pointed ahead to where a dirt side street turned left off the highway.

"My dad lives back in there," I said.

"Really?"

"Yes. He bought an old house a couple of years ago after he and mom divorced. The plan was to remodel it, but he started gutting the place and found out that it was built around a little shack. It's like his mission in life now to figure out how to make it live-able."

"Your father sounds interesting."

"Dad's very complex and intelligent, yes. He's an artist. He taught himself to carve violins. In fact, I play one that he made. It has beautiful mother-of-pearl inlay set in the back. I always wished that he could break free and share his gifts with the world. He has so much talent, but his inner barriers have kept him from..." I searched for the right word.

"Finding his music?" said Lucius.

"Yes. That's perfect. In fact, he was quite musical and even learned to play the violin himself. He bought dozens of classical records, Beethoven, Mozart and Vivaldi. I fell asleep almost every night listening to the music playing on the turntable when I was only four or five years old. He would sit and listen and sometimes cry. I remember that now."

There are no stop lights in Idaho City. We passed through it and the small town was swallowed in darkness behind us.

"You said something about Christianity earlier," said Lucius, "Care to tell me about that part?"

"It's a long story," I said.

"We have time. Do you feel some resistance about this?"

I drew a deep breath. Held it. Then blew it out.

"Maybe. I don't know."

"You said that your hippie parents took a hard right turn and became fundamentalists. How did that happen?"

"When I was just a baby, not long after we moved to Boise, my mother met a neighbor woman who invited her to church. Mom was raised Catholic but got caught up in the sixties wave. When she was seventeen, she hitch hiked to New York City from California, then took a one-way flight to Paris. She taught herself to speak French on the street in less than three months and then traveled around Europe. After she came home, she plowed right into the whole Haight Ashbury scene. In fact, she told me that she was thumbing a ride outside of San Francisco once and got picked up by Carlos Santana and his band on their way to a concert. Crazy times…

Anyway, after she met dad, they tried to connect the spiritual dots without all the religious baggage. He didn't grow up going to church and she was sick of her alcoholic parents and their hypocrisy. They dabbled with Eastern ideas, meditated, smoked lots of pot. Dad was more of a philosopher but my mother was all about action.

Not long before we all moved to Idaho, Mom went to a Pentecostal church, where they speak in tongues and roll around on the floor. She liked the vitality but she said some of it seemed phony.

As I said, they moved into this little house, actually it was a converted chicken shed, down in Boise not far from the river. After two or three weeks, a neighbor lady knocked at the door. Turns out she just had her fourth baby and noticed mom carrying me around in a backpack. They became friends and the lady invited my parents to church. Dad didn't go, but mom did."

I stopped talking and looked out the window. Lucius was quiet. To our right, I knew the stream flowed close against the road, but it was invisible in the darkness.

"So, what kind of church was this?"

"How much do you know about churches?" I said.

"Mmm...just assume I can follow along," he said. *A fine, evasive answer.*

"It was called Bible Missionary. It broke away from the Nazarene Church in the nineteen fifties. They got too liberal, the Nazarenes started allowing women to cut their hair and the big issue of the day was whether or not television should be allowed in the home. The Nazarenes said yes. The Bible Missionaries said no."

"So you grew up..."

"Yes, I grew up without television. No TV. No movies, no dancing, no bowling. We didn't wear short sleeves and the women all had to wear long dresses. My mother never cut her hair. We weren't allowed to wear any jewelry. Not even wedding rings. We went to church at least three times a week, sometimes every night during special meetings called revivals."

"That does sound extreme in modern America," he said.

"We were taught to see anyone who wasn't part of our group as *the world*," I told him, "Even most other church people, Baptists, Methodists, had enough wrong with their doctrines that we didn't associate with them. Catholics and Mormons were just going straight to hell, naturally."

He laughed aloud and slapped the steering wheel. It was funny. I hadn't told anyone this story for a long time. Explaining it to an outsider was always difficult unless they had experienced something similar.

"It wasn't just the dress code, though," I said, "We believed that man is sinful and could only be saved from hell by accepting forgiveness from Jesus Christ."

"That's in line with most Christian churches, isn't it?" he said.

"No, let me finish," I said, "My group took it a step further. They believed in something called a Second Work of Grace."

"A what?" he said.

"They also called it sanctification. Basically, if you allowed God to forgive your sins, then you were saved. This was like a first step on the path toward Heaven. It was an insurance policy against going to hell when you die. That was the first work."

"So then, sanctification did what?"

"That's more complicated. Are you sure I'm not boring you?"

He shook his head. "Go on."

"Sanctification was when you would go and pray for a long time. Usually this was done at an altar in front of everyone. It got noisy. Preachers and other people would scream and pray at the top of their lungs and pound you on the back."

"What were you hoping sanctification would do?" he said.

"You were trying to achieve total surrender to God's will. God was supposed to purge the sinful nature that all men are born with. Once this happened, you were supposed to be delivered from anger, lust, greed, envy. Things like that."

"That's ironic," he said.

"What's ironic?"

"No. Keep going. It's just interesting to hear you use the word surrender. What else? Did sanctification work?"

"That's the trouble. It was so nebulous. On one side, claimed that the Bible said you had to 'get it' if you wanted to escape hell. On the other side, it was difficult to know for sure when you got it."

He waved his hand. "Wait. This was going to happen all at once? Not over years?"

"Right. You were supposed to pray and wait and struggle until you were sure that it had happened to you. Some kind of a certainty would hit you. You got it and that was that."

"So what happened to you? Did you ever get it?"

I sighed, "I thought I did. You have to realize that this was very important in our group. I was the model oldest kid in my family, too. Good grades. Obedient. I desperately wanted to fit in and keep the authorities happy, too. When I learned that I needed to get sanctified, I went for it. It was confusing. I would have stood on my head for months if they told me to. I didn't want God mad at me and I didn't want people disappointed, either.

"I was such a good kid. I never really did the whole teenage thing. I was too busy walking my religious tightrope and suppressing wrong desires. It wasn't hard for me to look the part."

"That's fascinating, he said. What happened later? You obviously broke away at some point."

"Oh, I did," I said, "Wow. That was a terrible time." My mind sorted back through old files and opened the one containing memories from that period in history. The pain and confusion were thick.

"I can imagine," he said, "I'm surprised you left. What could have happened to break you free? I mean, when someone is really tied up needing other people's approval, it's almost impossible to step away without something major happening."

"What I said before...about fitting in? I found a way to fit in with this group. I went to the bible school and got top grades. I met Jennifer and we got married. Her father is a minister in that church. I became a song leader and a Sunday school teacher. They trusted me and needed me," I said.

"Which makes it even more surprising that you left," he said, "This wasn't just a light activity for you, was it?"

"No," I said, "That was who I was. In a group like that, it's not easy to just walk out. Everyone is under constant scrutiny. The congregations are small. Everybody's in everybody's business. I was one hundred percent immersed."

"So how...?" he asked.

"Something about my childhood," I said, "The mixture of being poor and always on the outside. Whatever it was, I had a burning desire to chase the American dream. I read piles of books about success and business. I took jobs in sales and worked up business plans.

"Anyway, at the same time I was being a Sunday school teacher, this other new person was emerging. I happened upon some books by Wayne Dyer that rocked me. They nailed me with questions that I couldn't answer. It was disturbing. My safe little world as an important church person started looking like a prison.

"Also, being in the business community, I started to spend time with people who claimed to be Christians. Turned out they were good people. Honest. Some of them were even a lot more friendly and Christ-like than the people in my church who had their black belt in purity."

My face was hot. I worked my jaw, that was clenched so tight I was sure my teeth would crack. *I'm angry*, I thought. *Why am I angry? This stuff was done years ago.* Lucius looked over.

"You're doing well. Do you know what this is called?"

"No, what?" I asked, fuming internally.

"Recapitulation." Lucius said.

"I've seen that word," I said, "But I don't really know what it means." I told him.

"Recapitulation. You move your attention back through your stored memories. Can you feel the energy?"

"Yes. It doesn't make any sense, either. I'm angry right now but all of this happened a long time ago. It's over," I said. My voice came out harsh and much louder than I intended.

"Let's examine that," he said, "Describe what you're feeling right now. Like a picture."

I closed my eyes. My breath came hard. Ragged and shaky.

I opened my eyes. My glare was intense with itchy heat. Words expanded in my chest and crowded each other in a suffocating rush to find expression through my mouth.

"I'm tied up with hot bungee cords," I said. I wrapped my arms around my chest and squeezed my ribcage with splayed fingers. "It's a spiderweb cocoon. I can barely move or breathe. It's not fair! I didn't ask for this. All these people standing around looking at me. They want me to be something I'm not anymore. I'm trapped. I'd rather choke to death than let them down. They need me to keep being what I've always been. They seem afraid. Like if I break free and leave them, it will open a door and let in a demon. They'll be in danger and it's all my fault."

My breath pushed out heavy as wet cement. I was nauseous. Lucius sensed my distress. He pulled over and stopped beside the road. I clawed at the door looking for the handle. Then I was out on my hands and knees in the rain. My gut heaved and a choking wave of anger washed out with the vomit. A painful animal growl ripped through my body. My spine arched and my fingers were stiff claws in the sharp wet gravel. I groaned and retched until nothing was left in me, only thin strings of mucus hung from my mouth.

Lucius knelt beside me. I heard him whisper strange words in a language I couldn't understand. His hands weren't touching me, he stroked the air a few inches above my back. *All is well*, he said, *all is well*. My muscles relaxed at once and I would have bloodied my face on the rocks if Lucius hadn't caught me. He lifted me to a sitting position and rested his fingers lightly on my shoulders.

"Can you get in the truck?" he asked, close to my ear, "Take your time, but you're getting soaked."

I nodded and he helped me to my feet. The rain soaked through my hair and trickled cold down my temples. I crawled into the truck and Lucius shut the door behind me. He went around to the driver's side and rummaged in the back seat.

"Here," he said. He had found a small white towel and held it out. I dried my face, then pressed the cloth against my eye sockets. It had a pleasant herb smell, lavender and something else. My lips felt raw and swollen. The wet knees of my suit pants stuck to my skin.

We were moving again. Lucius hummed a quiet tune in the darkness. Something nudged my leg and I looked down. Lucius held a water bottle for me to take. It was cool in my hands and when I took a sip, the water was sweet. Its freshness washed away the acid in my mouth.

"You're wondering why these sudden waves of emotion keep rolling you over? It's not normal and you're afraid you might be going crazy," he said.

I blinked and shook my head. *A mind reader. He just read my mind,* I thought.

"Yes," he said, "It's not hard to do."

I looked at him. "What?"

"Read your mind. It's not difficult. Humans have this ability but most are hypnotized by their own story. The story creates interference. Save this idea for later. Right now I want to talk about what's happening with you."

My purging experience was still vivid inside me. I was relieved but exhausted. Small electrical charges were arcing between my solar plexus and spine. I sat quiet, holding the water bottle between my knees and waited for him to continue.

"Like I said last week by your campfire, normally I would have taken much more time with you. I would have become your friend and we would have gradually stepped through doors of awakening. You will come to see that time is short. I must accelerate your progress. Your mind will never accept the truths I have for you. The only way is to expose you to powerful energy that will bypass your mind and go straight into your soul.

Like all humans, you have layers of misunderstanding and old errors wrapped around who you really are. These are like wounds hidden under your clothes. You carry them around and pretend they don't exist. Each of them drains your power and leaves you weak.

I have been sent to pull back the curtain to let fresh air and light shine in your life—so the lesions on your spirit can heal. You have work to do on Earth, but first you must see your illusions for what they are. That won't be easy. You are addicted to your story."

I leaned back in the seat. Lucius adjusted the buttons on the stereo and soft music filled the warm darkness.

"So, you're making these surges happen to me?" I said. When I looked over, Lucius was concentrating on the road ahead. The cobalt-blue light of the dashboard glowed on the lower half of his face leaving his eyes hidden in shadows.

"Let's just say that my energy touches your latent emotions. Together they create a kind of harmonic buildup that explodes like fireworks in your nerves. Your other responses are just the result of that release. It has to go somewhere," he said.

"I'm having a hard time with all this stuff," I said, "Energy. Harmonic buildup. My story. It kind of makes sense, but I keep trying to imagine how I'll ever explain this."

He shook his head. "This isn't set up so you can explain it. You need to forget everyone else and just be in the experience. Again, you're addicted to your story. You are addicted to how everyone sees you and whether or not you can maintain your stature with them."

"My story, my story…" I said, "What do you even mean by that?"

He sighed.

"You'll get to see what I mean soon. Your story is everything you think you are. In your case, it's also everything you imagine other people think you are. You have a number of stories mixing inside. That's the trouble. You don't know who you really are, so you're forced to keep dancing with the shadows of yourself. You don't have the perspective to understand this yet, but it will come."

A half-buried question raised itself, something he had said before we started our drive together. "You said earlier that some people are waiting for us. Who are they?"

"Oh, them." He paused and didn't say more. I expected him to continue but he just watched the road in silence.

We were navigating the tortured curves where Highway 21 summits at fifty-eight hundred feet and starts to descend into Lowman. The rain hitting the windshield had turned slushy and white flakes whipped past the window like tracer bullets when I peered into the night. I leaned back and rested. Fatigue settled like a black hood over me. I closed my eyes. *Just for a few minutes,* I thought.

Chapter Eleven

I emerged into consciousness the way that a mirror clears when fog fades from its surface. Sleep evaporated from my brain but I kept my eyes closed and reoriented myself. Perhaps it was the sound the tires made when we left the pavement that woke me. It took three seconds to connect the dots and remember that I was riding in a truck with Lucius. I moved my hands and felt the soft leather book under my palms. My fingertips recognized the embossed characters on *Emerson's Bible*. I had fallen asleep holding it on my lap. I opened my eyes and leaned forward. Lucius looked over at me.

"You're awake. Good. We're almost there."

I rolled my stiff shoulders and looked out the window. It was completely dark.

"How long did I sleep?"

"Not sure. Maybe a couple of hours."

Two hours on the road would put us close to the town of Stanley right at the base of the Sawtooth Mountains if we stayed on Highway 21 the whole time. That may not be the case, though. We could be anywhere in Idaho's interior wilderness for all I knew. Ahead of us, the headlights lit thick falling snow that covered the road and muffled the sound of our tires on the gravel.

"How are you feeling?" Lucius said, "Did your rest help? You did a lot of work."

I thought about this. He was right. My body was sore in places.

"I feel okay. I'm nervous, I guess. Not sure what I should expect next." I'd never been skydiving, but I imagined this must be like sitting strapped into a parachute for the first time. Anticipating that leap into roaring nothingness through the open hatch.

"I keep thinking about my business and my wife and kids. I've never done anything like this. I'm wondering what I got myself into."

He gave a little laugh.

"You want me to let you out? It's not too late."

It wasn't funny, but I laughed anyway and tried to settle my racing heart. It was warm in the truck, but I kept suppressing a shiver that ran up my spine and constricted my chest.

"It's all right to feel what you're feeling," he said. "In fact, that's all you need to do right now. Just be with the experience. Your anxiety is natural. You aren't comfortable with the unknown yet. Most humans, scratch that, all humans feel fear when they approach a threshold they've never crossed before. With practice, you will learn that fear isn't a solid object. You've built barricades against the unknown in your life. You've tried to create certainty. See this as a castle in your mind. You're well defended against fear and you do your best to keep it outside the walls. What you are getting ready to do is open the gate and follow me into territory you've never explored. Your mind tells you that this is crazy."

"But is it crazy?" I said, "I mean, will everything come out the way it should?"

"Ha! You really mean is it safe? You mean, will my life still be comfortable? don't you."

"Well," I thought about it, "Yes. I showed up today because I couldn't ignore the feeling you gave me. The entire week, I sat at my desk and looked at everything… It all felt different."

"Different how?"

"Different in the way I just knew that if I didn't meet you again, I wouldn't be able to face myself for the rest of my life. Pushing through hardship and doing what it took to grow my business always motivated me. After you and I met last time, my head was messed up, or something. Following my plan for the next twenty or thirty years seems, I don't know...bleak?"

He nodded. "I need to be clear about something. You have a lot of courage or you wouldn't be here. Nothing about what we're doing here is safe. Real? Yes. Safe and comfortable? Anything but."

At that moment, we hit a patch of ice. The truck fishtailed sideways. We skidded toward the huge gnarled trunk of a Ponderosa pine. It was right there on my side of the vehicle, coming fast. I wrenched away from the door but the seatbelt constrained me. In the instant before crashing, just before the black bark shattered my window, I looked at Lucius. He was chuckling. He spun the steering wheel in a couple of languid turns and the truck pivoted away from the tree. One slow-motion second later we were fifteen yards down the road—driving like nothing happened. My heart pounded hard. I blinked to get my eyeballs back in their sockets. The inside of my nose stung. I was still tense against the seatbelt. I righted myself and tried to breath. Eyes shut tight. *That was close.*

"Close to what?" Lucius said, reading my thoughts again.

"What?" I rubbed my palms on my pants.

"What was that close to?"

"I don't know," I said, feeling frustrated. Angry. We had almost crumpled the truck around a tree three seconds ago and now Lucius wanted to give me a pop quiz. *Damn it. Do we really have to examine everything that happens?*

"No, you do know," he said, "And, yes. We do have to examine everything."

"What do you mean I know? I don't know. It was just my automatic reaction to nearly crashing into a tree. I'm over it now, but why were you laughing?"

"When you say automatic, that's what I'm talking about. You have all these reactions to things that happen. They run beneath the surface and control your life. The guy who swerves in front of you on the freeway pushes your *'murder button'* for just a second. You never stop to think about why. You just yell and flip him off and pound on your horn. Maybe you feel a little ashamed later. Maybe not."

"But that's normal, isn't it?" I said, "A self-preservation thing."

"We're going way beyond normal here," he said, "What I'm talking about is how to start unraveling your unconscious. You have to become like a hunter. Actually, track down your random thoughts and reactions. Follow them back to their source. See where they really come from. It'll surprise you."

"Who does that?" I said, "It sounds like a whole lifetime of work. Where would I find time to live if I'm always analyzing my life?"

"We'll help with that. There are some ways to bypass the mind. In fact, what you humans call 'the mind' must be transcended. It's too slow. It always wants to organize and analyze. It's a function of the ego and although it's a powerful tool, you've allowed it to take control. You'll learn to control your mind. See? I said, *you*. Will learn. To control. *Your* mind."

"Yes, I heard you say that. I like the idea but it sounds like you mean something more. What?"

"You didn't hear the big clue, did you? I said you, as in the real you, will learn to control your mind. You don't recognize any distinction between mind and body and the authentic *you*. You're just one sloppy overlapping reaction machine. You'll learn Who You Really Are is the owner of your body and your personality and your mind. Eventually, you will be able to direct the actions of your mind and body consciously. This is mastery. By rising above and taking control of these tools, you can get on with your life experience. Right now, your tools are using you. Oh, and most people do spend a whole lifetime learning this. Many never even get a peek and those who do are usually near death."

I didn't like the idea that I had so much to learn. There was a whole ocean of knowledge previously unknown to me. I was dipping my toes into one tiny tributary.

At that moment, we turned a corner and I saw a spot of light ahead. It was distant and above us. On the side of a mountain, perhaps.

"That's where we're going," Lucius said, pointing with his chin. He must have known that my heart was racing. Whatever was in store was almost upon me. I felt as if I was huddled beneath the gaze of a giant invisible tiger who was crouched, ready to spring.

Lucius reached across and rested his hand on my shoulder. "You don't need to be afraid."

"I am, though." My hands were clenched, pressing down hard on the book in my lap.

His hand disappeared and materialized a moment later before my face holding a pen. I took it.

"Here, this will help. Open your book and turn to the second page."

My fingers were shaky as I loosened the knotted ties. I found the second page. It was filled with blank lines except for one sentence at the top.

"Read it," he said, "Out loud."

"Generally speaking, a howling wilderness does not howl: it is the imagination of the traveler that does the howling," I read, "That's written by Thoreau."

"Read it again. Slowly."

I did. He looked at me. "Now. Breathe very deeply, let it out and then read it one more time."

The intake of breath filled me with warmth. I held it for a couple of heartbeats and the air rushed out as I read aloud for the third time. This steadied me somewhat.

"Take the pen and write," he said, "Go back to your feeling of fear. Write that. Don't think about it. Just write the words as they enter your mind. They don't have to make sense. Name your fears. Quickly now. We don't have much time."

Thoughts filled my brain and I scribbled them on the empty page. Later I would see that my pen was so erratic that the words were barely legible.

At the edge of something, I can't be sure. Black and heavy. Much bigger than me. Why did I come here? I want out. Stop the train. Please don't make me do this. No that's not true. I can't go back, but I'm afraid. My toes are hanging over a cliff and it's not safe. No guard rail here. He says trust and all is well. I don't feel that way.

I can't breathe. My heart is pounding. This weird story is moving too fast. It can't be happening to me. Only crazy people believe this stuff. It's like an alien abduction. If I ever get home again, no one will believe me and then what will happen? What will become of my life? I'm afraid that soon nothing will be the same as before. I will be alone and no one will know who I am. Not even me.

My hand stopped moving. I closed my eyes. Beneath us, the truck downshifted and began to climb. I floated alone in my thoughts. The pit of my stomach was still hollow but my body stopped shaking. The angle of our ascent grew steeper and I heard Lucius adjust something on the gearshift that caused a lower growl from the engine.

"Good," he said. I opened my eyes and looked at him.

"That's all for now. Hold that feeling. Just be with it," he said.

"Which feeling? The sick-to-my-stomach-afraid one?"

"Yes, that one. Just feel what you're feeling. Don't think it. Feel it. Then, when you're sure you feel it all the way, breathe and let it go. That's the key."

I worked at this. *"Just be with it,"* he said. It was a struggle at first. I had never tried to isolate a feeling before.

"Where do you feel it in your body?" he asked.

I thought for a minute. "At first all over, but it's the strongest in my gut."

"Good. Observe that now. Can you move it somewhere else?"

I concentrated on the feeling but it had already begun to evaporate. It was floating away like steam from a cup of hot tea.

"See?" he said. I looked at him blankly so he elaborated.

"When you allow yourself to move into the experience and actually feel it rather than resist, it's manageable. You locate it in your body and then hold it. This way, you can be fully present to whatever happens. You'll find this cuts fear short and allows you to grow your times of joy. You aren't always living ahead of yourself."

"I'd love that," I said, "I'm always in a hurry. If life sucks then I want to get busy and make it better. If things are good, I always think ahead, plot the next step. Kind of like going on vacation. As soon as I get to the resort, I can't relax and enjoy it because I'm already thinking about having to going back and face the normal stress again."

"There it is!" he said, "One of the basic causes of human suffering, always wishing you were somewhere other than where you are. You wish you had more money, a bigger house, a different partner, a nicer body, on and on. It never stops."

"What can we do about that?" I said, "It's just part of the human condition, isn't it?"

"Later. We'll talk more about this. Look." He pointed. We topped a steep uphill grade in the road. Ahead of us in a large clearing, stood a house set tight against a dark mountain. The windows glowed with yellow light that spilled out across the expanse of snow. My impression was all about the light and the shape. The warmth that radiated outward filled the space around it. The house was round. The top was covered with a glowing dome of glass. I looked at Lucius. He was smiling.

"We're here," he said.

Our tires crunched and made soft squeaking sounds in the snow as we plowed through the last few yards to the house. Lucius braked and we sat for a moment in the stillness. The engine ticked and steamed as it cooled.

"Do I need to know anything before we go in?" I said, looking for reassurance.

He snuffed a short laugh through his nose. "No, just go with the flow." This gave me no comfort.

"Get your bag," he said, "And don't forget your book." The moment his door opened, bitter night cold rushed in and stung my face. The smell of wood smoke blew in with the wind. I got out and grabbed my suit jacket, shivering and wishing it was a real coat. I looked up to see the snow had stopped. The moon was bright and distant in the black sky it shared with millions of stars. The hairs in my nostrils prickled with each sharp breath.

"Let's go," Lucius said. I followed him up the drift-lined path to the front door. The powder clung to my pant cuffs like confectioner's sugar. Lucius stopped before the door. On either side, frozen bushes sat mounded high with snow. Some had the shape of bonsai trees, only big. Each well-trimmed clump of needles seemed a fairy's cake frosted in white.

The huge door could have been stolen from a medieval castle. It was made of thick oak planks held together with riveted iron bands. The top was rounded and a yellow glow came through a small barred window. I noticed carvings in the wood and felt a jolt. I recognized many of them from the cover of *Emerson's Bible,* symbols and ancient characters with meanings lost in time. Lucius raised his hand to knock but the door suddenly swung inward, music and warm food smells inundated us. Light flooded the night's darkness—illuminating a woman standing on the threshold with open arms.

"Lucius! You've come," she said and hugged him around the neck. I felt awkward standing there holding my bag while the wind turned one side of my face into a frozen mask. Looking over his shoulder, she caught my eyes and smiled. She released Lucius and pushed him aside to better look at me. She had dark hair pulled back in a thick braid and an indefinable exotic cast to her skin and eyes. It's a cliché to say that her smile was radiant, but it was. She opened her arms to welcome me with a hug, too. I hugged her briefly, feeling shy. She was delicate, almost gauzy, but not fragile. She placed her hands together as one would to pray. Holding eye contact, she offered a little bow.

"Hello, Jacob. We've been waiting for you. Namaskar!" I just nodded.

"Come," she said catching my arm, "Get inside. You're shivering. Oh, I'm Kaitlyn, by the way." Lucius proded my back with his fingertips and I shuffled through the doorway. Kaitlyn herded us to a mat in the entryway and we stomped loose snow from our feet. She shut the heavy door and pushed an iron latch into place. She turned to us, ready to take our coats.—Neither of us were wearing one.

"You boys," she said, "What are you thinking, no winter gear? Okay, come this way." She led us to the right and started up a twisting staircase its banisters were made of peeled fir limbs. They were hand-rubbed and gleamed like honey in the light. From down a hallway I heard conversation and cooking sounds. Someone played guitar. Incense drifted back in Kaitlyn's wake. We followed her up the stairs, Lucius ahead of me. On the landing of the second floor, she stopped and turned to a high window that looked out on the clearing. She held up her finger.

"Shh," we stopped climbing, "Did you hear that?" Lucius nodded and smiled. I hadn't heard anything and shook my head.

"What?" I said, "What is it?"

She peered out the window, shading her eyes to see better through the frosty glass. She motioned for me to join her. She pointed to the edge of the clearing where the trees formed a black wall that blended with the darkness.

"There," she whispered, "Do you see it?" I saw only the wide blanket of luminous snow stretching out to the trees in the distance. I leaned in closer but my breath fogged the glass. I stopped breathing for a few seconds and focused in the direction she pointed. My breath-mist evaporated from the window and my vision grew painfully clear. Suddenly, in such detail that it caused me to recoil from the glass—I saw an enormous white wolf. Seated on his haunches some yards from the edge of the woods, he shook himself and seemed to look straight at me. He pointed his snout at the moon and let out a mighty howl that rose high, changed pitch, then faded among its own echoes.

The alarm racing inside me wasn't due to the howl itself, one expects a wolf to howl in the distance. What shocked me was my sensation that the window had vanished and that I was soaring on a current of energy the wolf's strange, ancient song created. It was loud and hoarse and primitive. I was terrified and exhilarated to be alone in the presence of this primordial lupine entity. The howl came again and I felt as though I were ascending above the landscape and able to navigate on my own through the crystal air. My whole body vibrated with the power of the sound.

"Hey!"

A hand on my shoulder pulled my face back from the window. It was Lucius. He and Kaitlyn regarded me with sober expressions. Kaitlyn turned to him.

"It's already happening," she said, "He's more ready than you told us."

Lucius nodded. "The drive up was intense, too. I expected to prod our boy here along a little more. It's moving quickly."

Their voices were distant. I wanted to keep flying on the invisible energy reverberating under the bright moon outside. Lucius still had his hand on my shoulder, weighing me down. Kaitlyn leaned close.

"Wolf medicine," she said near my ear, "It's not time for that yet. You have other things to see first."

Yeah, well I wanted to lose myself in—whatever it was that just happened. Even though my feet were on the ground again, the big animal presence was still very real in my mind. The pure, joyful ferocity was tingling in my veins.

Lucius turned me around. "Listen now," he said, "You're not in your world up here. You must follow instructions very carefully. There will be tests and many opportunities to become disoriented. I'll say it again. This isn't your *normal* world anymore. Be sure to take direction only those I introduce to you. Kaitlyn is one such helper. You can trust her, but under no circumstance assume your usual tools and defenses will keep you safe.

"If you wander alone and follow the advice of strangers you meet at this stage, you could easily lose your way. If for some reason, you find yourself alone and someone approaches you, it's critical that you determine whether or not they are a friend. If they appeal to your vanity or try to use your fear to manipulate you, run. Get away. Listen to your own inner voice, you'll know if they are a messenger of love and wisdom—or just an impostor who could lead you astray."

I nodded without words. Lucius and Kaitlyn guided me down a long hall and into a snug, warm bedroom. The bed stood in the middle of the room, covered with quilts and a goose-down comforter. The blue flannel sheets were turned back inviting. A small lamp glowed on a bedside table made from a large pine stump. A candle burned on a bookcase beside a comfortable chair. There was a small attached bathroom, too. Lucius place my duffel bag on a low dresser at the foot of the bed. I sat on the bed overcome with weariness, I wanted nothing more than to collapse under the heavy covers.

Lucius tugged at my shoes. Kaitlyn rolled me out of my suit jacket and pulled off my tie. I swung my legs under the blankets and pulled a pillow under my head. Sleep came to me like an old friend. Before I surrendered to unconsciousness, I wondered what was cooking for supper and who else was downstairs waiting to be met. My last thought was, *I sure am sleeping a lot lately.*

Chapter Twelve

Pain in my cheek and pressure from a full bladder awakened me. I opened my eyes. Sleeping with one wrist under my head, the pain was caused by the corner of my cuff link. The room was dim. I propped myself on an elbow and leaned over to switch on the lamp beside my bed. The sudden light made me wince and I looked around, my head in a fog. There was no alarm clock with glowing red numbers, unlike my room at home. I looked at my watch, 6:33 A.M. The house was quiet.

After using the toilet, I was about to wash my face, then thought better of it and decided on a shower instead. I was smelly and disheveled from sleeping in my clothes. A thought nagged me. *Something about the clothes.* I took them off, draped them on the end of the bed and got into the shower. I stood under the jets of hot water and washed with soap that scented with lavender and sage. I took stock of my body, I didn't like the slippery handfuls of fat. Must do something about that—fatness. Finished, I was toweling off in the steamy little bathroom wondering what to wear. I spotted a thick robe hanging on the back of the door. Plush black terrycloth with gold piping and a crest embroidered on the pocket. Nice. I put it on and stepped out.

The clothes. There was that thought again. They were still on the end of the bed. *Why did Lucius make me wear my best clothes and then let me trash them like this?* They were wrinkled and stained beyond repair from the ordeals of my journey.

Someone tapped on the door. I opened it to see Lucius there. He smiled. He held a tray with a steaming cup of tea and a plate with fruit and toast.

"Good morning," he said, "May I come in?"

I stood aside and he brushed past me. He was wearing curious garments. They resembled a karate *gi* but were made from soft unbleached linen, or maybe woven hemp. His tunic was tied around the waist with a long silk sash dyed the teal color of a mallard's head. He was not wearing a hat and I realized this was the first time I had seen him bareheaded. His hair was thick and almost black with a few silver streaks. It curled a little in back where it touched his neck.

The smell of the food reminded me that I was terribly hungry. He handed me the tray, crossed to sit in the chair. I perched the tray on the rustic table and sat on the bed to eat.

"How are you feeling?"

"Rested," I said, "I can't believe that I was able to sleep at all. After conking out for two hours on the drive up, I should have been up all night." I held the cup between my hands and warm vapor drifted around my chin. It smelled of honey, mint, flowers and some exotic spice.

Lucius crossed his legs and leaned forward. "I came up early to talk with you before the day gets started. We haven't spoken much about what will happen. I can't tell you all of it because most of it is beyond words and can only be experienced."

I nodded and sipped tea. It was like liquid springtime in my mouth, sweet and pungent with a flavor that can only be described as green. Green like new pine needles and still-curled fiddlehead fern shoots are green. My Starbucks-jaded palate was electrified. I must have made a happy face because Lucius chuckled.

"What is this stuff?" I asked.

"None one really knows," he said, "Kaitlyn gathers her secret herbs in the forest and dries them all summer long. It's her own magical blend. Do you like it?"

"It's not about liking! It wouldn't matter how it tastes, there's something about this. It feels...alive."

"Many things will surprise you here and they should. We've arranged the surroundings to feel familiar, things like mountains and bathrobes and food. You'll soon see that we aren't very concerned with your comfort. However, we can't move you from your world directly into ours without some transition. It's just too foreign. You'd be so distracted by the unfamiliar that you'd miss the point, or maybe even die of fright. So drink up and eat while I explain things."

The gong had been silent awhile, it crashed again, vibrating in my belly. *Boomsheee... Here we go,* I thought, *peeking over the edge of the skyscraper. How long until I jump?*

"Mmmhmm, that's pretty close isn't it?" he said, answering my unspoken question. "That's decent picture. You're at the edge and think you'll have to jump, maybe to your death. That's the fear, yes?"

I just nodded, chewing a bite of toast. His mind reading didn't alarm me as much as it first did.

"If you remember the first time we met by your campfire, I said time is short. Great changes are coming to humanity and most of your so-called civilized people are completely unprepared. They're fast asleep, so to speak. Preoccupied with the game. Messengers have been sent. Long ago, measured by your time, beings incarnated to help the people of Earth. Masters and ancient ones have appeared to bring the light. In earlier days men were more simple, natural. They lived with the Earth and were guided by the Great Mother's voice. In those days, miracles and prophecy were part of the fabric of everyday life. Why do you suppose this doesn't happen much now, or if it does, you're quick to dismiss the people who dare to see as crazy?"

I swallowed and thought about it. "I don't know. Maybe we've moved past some of those things? Maybe that's not the way God talks to people anymore? I was taught the scriptures were written long ago and that was that. Period. We're supposed to learn everything we need to know from what happened back then. What are you saying? We're going to start seeing supernatural things again?"

"Well, perhaps that depends on your definition of super and natural. Looks to me like you're in the middle of a 'supernatural thing' now, as you'd call it. One of the Old Testament prophets said, 'It will come about after this that I will pour out My Spirit on all mankind; And your sons and daughters will prophesy, Your old men will dream dreams, Your young men will see visions.'"

"Wasn't that Daniel?" I said, trying to remember.

"Joel," he said, "The point is, you're actually living near the end of an age in human history. It's big. So, yes, you are going see things that appear supernatural. In fact, these things are always happening. They always have been. If you go to the Australian outback right now and sit with the old aborigines, you'd notice that miracles and magic are often part of the conversation. Same thing in Africa and South America. Anywhere on Earth where people live close to nature, Great Mother talks to them."

"Why not in places like Europe and America?" I said.

"Great Mother is speaking everywhere, always—you just don't listen. Your modern ways traded ritual and meaning for science. In the many centuries since the man you call Jesus incarnated, you've abandoned anything that can't be measured by your science. Your lives have grown easier but you've bartered away the ability to see and hear beyond your concrete reality, your stuff. The symbolism and mystery has vanished and taken with it much of what makes your life meaningful."

"Yes, but isn't that the way it's supposed to work?" I said, "People gradually learn and technology improves. We become more rational. Things change. Are you saying that's wrong?"

"It's not about right and wrong. You're going to have a hard time with that, aren't you? Anyway, the point is mankind has become quite clever with creating their massive illusions. People once had to cooperate to produce food and shelter. It was hard work and people knew that when they actually had to do it. Now, almost no one living what you call a normal life, ever sees the source of their clothes, shelter or what they eat. When was the last time you butchered a cow?"

"Me? I've never butchered a cow myself."

"Yes, but you've fed one and smelled the hay. You looked in her eyes and scratched the hair between her ears, right?"

"Yeah. My family kept a cow for a while when I was a kid. I guess I did see it butchered. I stood a long way off, I was horrified at the time."

"I know," he said, "And you are one of the few children of your generation ever to interact personally with the creature that would one day be your food. If you asked your own children right now where milk comes from, what do you suppose they'd say?"

I chuckled. "Oh, they'd say it comes from the store. They've never seen a cow udder up close."

"Right," he said, "That's it! In your society, people live so far away from the sources of life that it's no wonder you're isolated, stressed out and sick. You sit in sterile little cubicles, fooling with plastic machines under artificial lights, trying to earn money to buy more stuff you don't even need. You wonder why people go psychotic and lead broken lives? And we're still talking about the tangible plane here."

This made me uncomfortable. Lucius had just described my own lifestyle.

"But I grew up splitting wood to heat the house and working in our garden," I said. *Maybe my poverty-stricken childhood would earn me extra credit in this conversation.*

Lucius nodded. "I know. That's part of the reason you're here."

"What?"

He sighed. "As I said on the ride up here, you were given a gift in your life. You didn't have what most people call a normal childhood. You didn't watch TV, you didn't go to movies, you didn't have video games, you didn't mix normally with society, you moved around a lot. You were ruled by an overbearing church. Your family grew a lot of its own food. You helped to cut and split the wood that kept you warm. You even hauled water up the hill to your cabin when you lived in the mountains that one winter. Remember?"

I shook my head at the memories. I remembered all right. I remembered fiercely resenting my father's lack of ambition that forced us to live like peasants. I remembered wondering why I couldn't just be normal. I remembered...

Lucius held up his hand to slow my torrential thoughts. "Yes," he said, "We'll deal with all of that soon. I wanted you to recall those feelings. I said this before, you were given a gift of not fitting in. That very fact is the reason you are here now. There is just enough of an anomaly in your world view, that we can use it as leverage to crack your shell and let in some other truth. Most people have a shell so thick and dense it's impossible for them to open up and see outside of what they call reality. Does that make sense?"

"A little, I guess."

"Good. That's all I need. A little crack. You'll begin to see the rest of it soon."

"A crack sounds..." I struggled for the right word. It finally emerged, "Unsettling."

He laughed his knowing little almost-giggle and shook his head. "Oh, the unsettling-ness of it all! You've entered a world where nothing is very settling. That's partly why I wanted to talk with you this morning. You've been brought here to see things. If I could wave a wand and allow you to perceive Who You Really Are at once, I would. It would save time. The trouble is, you would either shatter completely, never be a functioning human again, or you would just disappear. You would die—as you might call it."

A hard knot formed in my chest and rose up, squeezing my throat to trap my breath. The room grew dim.

Lucius waved his hand to capture my attention. "Don't go into fear right now. There's plenty of time for that later."

I breathed again and the lamp glowed bright on its pine stump table.

"See," he said, "Even the merest mention of death makes you go all wobbly. That will change, but it is this very propensity of humans to cling to the known that makes it difficult for them to break free. To dance to their inner music. While you're here, we are going to help you loosen your grip on what you call reality. Here, close your eyes for a minute so I can illustrate."

I sat with my eyes shut and heard him moving. A drawer opened and closed in the small dresser at the foot of the bed. He crossed near me and stood beside the table. The orange light glowing through my eyelids diminished.

"Look," he said finally. I opened my eyes. He was standing by the lamp now covered in layers of colorful silk scarves. I saw only a dim glow beneath the mass.

"This represents the state you're in now," he said, "You can see a little light through all the filters, but only a little. Watch." He plucked the edge of the topmost cloth and flicked his wrist. It floated to the floor.

"See? The light grows a little brighter," he said and tossed the next layer aside. "And brighter." *Toss.* "And brighter still." One by one, the translucent scarves drifted away. Faster and faster. The lamp became more radiant after each discarded covering fell. I was caught in the movement and the play of color and shadow and light. My feelings grew buoyant and I found myself weaving back and forth in a sinewy motion along with the fluttering silk. Lucius stopped after he dropped the lamp shade on the floor and splayed his hands on either side of the naked bulb. Light burst out from the space he created and filled me with an indefinable joy. I was part of the radiance itself. My eyes were wide and I took the golden light into my body with each breath. I felt that I could rise and soar on any small puff of air.

Lucius tapped me on the shoulder and nodded. "There. That's the feeling. The light of Who You Really Are is hidden beneath all these layers. By coming here, you have chosen to explore and delve beneath the surface. The coverings represent old programs and inherited traits and the junk that stifles the light."

I rocked in place among the rumpled sheets and squeezed my hands together. My body was glowing with gentle electricity. I looked at him. He gazed at me with a little smile wrinkling the corners of his eyes.

"What is...this?" I moved my hands out in a slow circle, half expecting traces of light to follow their path with tiny crackles like a burning sparkler. He raised an eyebrow.

"This?"

"You know, this...feeling." I said, trying to express it by moving my hands around some more.

"Ah, well," he said, "That's just a taste of what I'm trying to tell you. It's like licking a drop of honey, no?"

"Only more," I said.

"Yes, only more," he echoed.

"How does that happen? One minute everything's normal, the next instant, I'm floating around. Like last night, too...the deal with the wolf. Is there something in the air up here?"

"Something in the air, something in the water, something in the light. Certainly," he said, "What is different here, is not the place. When you took action to meet me yesterday and journey into the unknown, against many obstacles and your own fears—you consciously and unconsciously entered a different space of awareness. It is this altered awareness that allows these new experiences. You are assisted by my presence and energies. Many other helpers have gathered to help create a portal to a sort of 'classroom' where you'll learn what you must. So far, you have only poked your nose in the door and caught a whiff."

"So that's what you were trying to explain yesterday on the drive up? When I got sick?"

"Trying to explain?" he said.

"You told me these strong feelings that come over me aren't normal. It's a relief actually, because they are out of proportion compared to what triggers them. I mean, one minute I'm telling you about my childhood. The next, I'm puking in a ditch beside the road. That's excessive...not normal."

"Well, yes," he said. "If you'd ever read Carlos Castaneda's books, you would've already noticed that your shifting is similar to his 'second attention.' It's like you're walking at the boundary where two bubbles of different awarenesses press together. You're open to moving back and forth between them a little. This isn't easy for you and it wouldn't happen at all without help. You don't have enough clarity of intention yet. By being here with me and the other helpers, the boundary between the bubbles is weakened. We lend you some of our power at times. We have to be very careful with this, though. The human part of you can't handle much voltage. Just a touch of it gives you strong physical sensations which transcend anything you've felt before. Is this true?"

It was true and this new understanding helped me connect a few dots. It also raised other questions.

"But, what is the purpose of this? I assume I'll return to my life somehow. Is this way of seeing things going to make a difference back there?"

He waved his hands, dismissing my questions. "Don't worry about that. We're just talking and words are only entertainment. It's like your incessant book reading. Up to a point, useful. Beyond that, procrastination."

"Procrastination? I thought..."

"I know what you thought. Read the wisdom of other great people. Model their behavior and presto! you're a great person, right? You can check the box and give yourself a high score for reading all the correct books, the important stuff. Some exposure is good because it helps you develop your mind. After a certain point, too much reading is just one more way to escape from embarking on your own mission. That's what I mean by procrastination."

"But it was you who gave me *Emerson's Bible*. It's you who makes me keep reading it." I was happy to catch him in an inconsistency.

He chuckled, not concerned in the least. "Listen now, I have to deal with you as you are. If you believe a thought is very deep and important, you'll pay attention. The quotes in *Emerson's Bible* are just hooks. They snag your busy mind and stop it in its tracks. They jolt you out of your story-chatter for a second. Why do you suppose most of the book is blank?"

I was feeling irritable. "Because I'm supposed to write in it."

"*Bravo! Bravo! Molto bene!*" he clapped his hands, mocking me. My face flushed.

He held up a hand. His voice was gentle when he said, "Easy now. I'm just tweaking you. You're such an important person...such a smart person. Everyone is impressed by you. You're impressed by you. That self-importance makes you an easy target. Anyone can toss out a red herring and you'll follow the bait every time. You're rarely in balance because you're too worried about always being right."

This was getting uncomfortable. I looked down at my hands.

He continued speaking. His voice was quiet. "I'm here to introduce you to Who You Really Are. Who is wise and powerful. Who isn't constantly playing politician and protecting a reputation. But come now, we've talked enough. More than enough. Finish your breakfast while I check some things."

I picked at what was left of the fruit on my plate. Lucius gathered the scarves from the floor and replaced the lampshade. He crossed the room and out of the corner of my eye, I noticed him fiddling with my duffel bag. *Zzziipp!* I turned my head and watched as he ransacked through my things. He held up a couple of the books I had packed and examined the titles. Then he picked up my wrinkled suit, made a ball of it and shoved it in the bag with everything else. My shirt, shoes and tie were next. He must have sensed my bewilderment because he looked up and grinned.

"What are you doing?" I said.

"Oh," he said, still jamming my expensive clothes in the bag. They didn't fit and the pack gaped open like a loaded baked potato with its innards bursting out. "I'm taking these. You can wear the robe for now." He started toward the door. I didn't argue or try to stop him. He turned just before closing the door. "Kaitlyn will come for you in a little while. You might spend some time writing."

The room felt very small and quiet after he was gone. I got up and paced between the bed and the door a few times. *Emerson's Bible* was there on the low dresser where my duffel bag had been. I picked it up and saw a pen tucked in the pages. I untied the bow and it opened. Lucius, with his quiet voice, left me stinging. *"You're such an important person. Such a smart person...self-importance makes you an easy target...you're too worried about always being right."* I flipped through the first couple of pages, past what I had already written. At the top of the next empty page was a quote in cardinal red calligraphy.

> "Do you wish to rise? Begin by descending. You plan a tower that will pierce the clouds? Lay first the foundation of humility."
> — St. Augustine

Is this damn book writing itself to match the lessons I'm learning at the time? I half-wondered. It wouldn't have surprised me at all to see an invisible pen trace a bright red *"Yes!"* right there as I watched. That didn't happen, though. I was left staring at blank lines and thinking about everything Lucius had said. My hand twitched and I started writing without forethought.

I've been living unplugged from some big reality. As confused as I am right now, and I am confused by everything here, my gut says go ahead. I can finally see the door that I've been knocking on my whole life. Who will answer the door and what will happen when I walk through it?

These questions terrify me. Yes. But I can't walk away now. I can see the door and hear footsteps approaching from the other side.

My pen stopped moving. I was lost in thought. The faces of my wife and children appeared in my mind. I felt love for them, then deep loneliness as their images grew distant and faded.

Chapter Thirteen

Dark clumps of hair fell down over my forehead, then softly rolled off my nose to pile in my lap and on the floor. I had my head bent forward and felt the clippers vibrate on the back of my neck and then buzz over the crown of my skull. With each sure stroke, my head felt lighter and more naked. *Exposed*, I thought, *I'm exposed*. Even though I usually kept my hair short, I'd never been completely bald.

The monk-like man moved around to my right side and shaved the hair around my ear. He kept rising up on his tiptoes to reach the high spots. Transfixed sitting on the low round stool, I wondered, *Is this really happening?*

A few seconds later, my left side was likewise shorn. The little man stood back holding the buzzing clippers in one hand while resting the fingertips of his right hand on my shoulder. He cocked his own bald head from side to side, surveying his handiwork. His features crumpled into a mask of tan, wrinkled leather. He nodded and grinned, revealing his toothless gums. He turned without speaking and started working the bristles of a brush inside a stout brown mug.

A mushroom-cap of white lather rose over the rim of the cup and he placed it on the nearby butcher-block table. He flipped open a bone-handled straight razor and began to strop it on an ancient looking strip of leather. *Schwipp, schwipp, schwipp.* He was engaged in his task and I watched him in silence. After a dozen strokes, he tested the blade with his thumb and was satisfied. He picked up the mug and advanced on me with the foam-covered brush. He worked the lather all over my prickling scalp, cheeks and throat. It was warm and smelled of an herb I couldn't identify but it had a pleasant cool burn similar to peppermint oil.

I wanted to recoil when the razor touched the skin on my forehead right at the hairline, but I concentrated on breathing and forced myself to remain still. He was gentle but as efficient as a surgeon with the blade.

The short, friendly man was dressed in the same singular attire as Lucius. Except the sash around his waist was the orange of a monarch butterfly's wings. For some reason, he made me think of a butterfly, serene and silent, but happily present in his work. He moved quickly but with floating grace.

I tried not to swallow as he drew the razor's edge over my Adam's apple. My mind could not resist picturing him as the demon barber — slashing my carotid artery and cackling while blood gushed in fountains spurting on the floor. He didn't of course and was soon working away on the safer parts of my cheeks.

Then he touched his thumbs to my eyelids and drew them down. My eyes popped open in alarm, but the Monk put a finger to his lips and closed my eyes again. I breathed and clenched my jaws. I felt his fingers on the left side of my face and then the cool blade began to scrape away my eyebrows. For some reason, this terrified me and I had to squeeze both hands together and tighten the muscles of my legs to keep my balance on the stool.

About ten minutes earlier, Kaitlyn had tapped on my bedroom door and led me down the stairs. In the morning light, the house seemed much larger than it had the night before. She didn't let me spend any time checking out the amenities. Instead, she hustled me down a long hall past several closed doors. Behind one of them, I could hear muted music playing. Although we didn't see any other people, I could sense the presence of several others somewhere in the house. As we walked, I got the impression that the house was built to resemble the sun. The hallways radiated out from a center point. It was bright and open with light blazing in from the winter sun shining through tall windows. Kaitlyn was subdued and meditative today. Her sparkling eyes would meet mine briefly and then slip away into private musing.

I was now sitting in what appeared to be a mudroom that also served as a laundry area and pantry. One wall was devoted to all manner of winter gear hanging on hooks, on the other side, large open cupboards held food preserved in shiny jars and mesh sacks full of root vegetables. Kaitlyn had parked me by myself but quickly returned with the old man. She hadn't told me what he was going to do. Just mentioned in an offhand way that he would "prepare me for the ceremony." She never introduced him by name. Just said that he was a helper and I should follow his instructions.

His instructions took the form of a few simple gestures and an occasional nudge with his fingertips. Without urgency, he had guided me to a seat, wrapped a sheet around my neck and showed me the clippers. I had shrugged, looked into his wise old Asian eyes and nodded my head. I was along for the ride now. No holds barred.

In a matter of minutes, The Monk, that was the name I imagined for him, finished shaving me. He untied the saffron cloth around my neck and laid it neatly on the floor. Then he squatted and swept all of my hair into a heap. He scooped this onto the cloth and spent time picking every strand from the tiles. At last, he dusted his hands over the cloth and gathered the corners together in the middle and tying them into a bundle. This he placed on the table and stepped back to face me. He placed his palms together and smiling, bowed. This seemed to be the custom of the house, so I returned the bow.

The Monk nodded at me and did a sweeping upward gesture with both hands like a concert master. I raised my eyebrows and pointed at myself. He nodded and made the gesture again. I stood up. He then moved toward the door that led outside. He opened it and sunlight burst in along with a blast of frigid air. My freshly shaved head burned and I hugged the robe across my chest, hairs prickled on my bare legs.

He stepped through the doorway and for an instant became translucent in the sunlight. He turned and beckoned. I was barefoot and had nothing on beneath the robe but I followed him out to a wide terrace. The snow under my feet was like a bed of hot coals. I drew in a breath of air so sharp and pure that it shocked my lungs. The Monk seemed untouched by the cold. He stood there with a beatific grin and watched as I danced from one foot to the other and beat my arms for warmth. He pointed to the side of the house where a large copper shower head was fixed to the end of an iron pipe. I looked at him, alarmed. *He doesn't really want me to take a shower out here*, I silently hoped. But he did.

The Monk came close and pulled at one end of the plush tie around my waist. He motioned that I should give him the robe. I shivered and shook my head. He threw his hands in the air and laughed. It was the first sound he had made since Kaitlyn left me alone with him. It swirled around me and created a momentary envelope of warmth. I looked around for observers. The windows on this side of the house were all shuttered and vacant. Reluctantly, I shrugged off the robe and handed it to the Monk. He nodded pointing to the shower. I was freezing again and naked. I took a couple of quick steps on the balls of my feet through the snow and stood under the shower head. A rope pull hung from a lever. I tugged and was instantly surrounded by steam as the hot water sluiced down my body and melted the snow around my feet.

The Monk disappeared behind clouds of vapor and I reveled in the warmth. I rubbed my head with both hands and was amazed by its crystal-globe smoothness. I stood there and let the water run down my back. Through the steam, I saw the tops of jagged mountains piercing the bright blue sky. They appeared to be part of the Sawtooth range, I wasn't sure. At the moment, nothing mattered. I was blissful, shiny, clean. My skin tingled where the air touched. The hot water everywhere else made a delightful contrast. I did a full turn under the shower and was surprised to hear a loud *Caw! Caw!* near my head. I shook water from my face and saw a large raven swoop down toward the deck. It disappeared behind the steam cloud. I looked for the Monk but he was gone.

A light breeze swept around the house and momentarily cleared the air. I cringed as the curtain of vapor vanished and I stood naked in the daylight. There was no one in sight but the raven and I. He hopped twice toward me and cocked his head a few times, looking at the absurd human trying in vain to cover himself. My skin began to goosepimple just as the gust mercifully died and the steam surrounded me again. I let the water warm me and peered through the mist. The Monk was there as if he'd never left. He clapped his hands and motioned me toward him. I pulled the shower cord and stopped the water. The Monk pointed to the unbroken snow covering the granite terrace, then rolled his hands over and over then pointed at me. *Roll in the snow now?* I thought, *Seriously?* He nodded emphatically and made the rolling gesture again.

I took a few exaggerated steps on tiptoe. The snow came more than halfway up my calves. I clenched my teeth, took a breath and looked at the Monk. He grinned. *Okay, here goes...* I bent at the knees and shallow-dived headfirst into the snow. Thousands of ice-hot needles stabbed my skin, but I was in full motion. I rolled over and over. Twice, three times, then stood up trying to catch my breath. The Monk was already there wrapping the robe around me and patting my back. I looked at him. He was laughing with his eyes squeezed shut. I laughed, too. My whole body flushed with life. Every capillary was awake and the blood sang in my veins.

The Monk led me into the house and turned me toward a mirror on the wall. I was shocked by my reflection. My denuded skull was bright pink with steam rising from it. I had never imagined myself without any hair at all. I looked like a cancer patient in late-stage chemotherapy, but I was grinning like a mad man. A small chunk of melting snow slid down my nose. I stuck my tongue out to catch it as it fell.

Lucius appeared over my shoulder and shook his head at my appearance. We stared at each other in the mirror and burst out laughing at the same time.

He turned me around and put his fingertips on my gleaming head.

"Bless you, my chubby son," he said with overdone pomp, "I have brought thee more fitting garments."

"Speaking of the chub," I said and bunched flab in each hand, "I'd love to lose some weight."

"In time," he said.

"Look over there," he pointed to where the Monk was holding up a set of garments.

"Those for me?" I said.

"They are. Try them on."

He took my robe and I hurried to get the loose pants up over my hairy nakedness. The Monk helped me into the tunic and I looked down at myself. The clothes were plain and functional. All made of very soft cloth, lighter in weight than it appeared. Lucius handed me a sash made of the same material.

"Put this around your middle. Comfortable?"

I nodded. The Monk left the room for a moment and returned with a small white pot and two cups. With elaborate care he arranged the cups near me and filled them with the tea Kaitlyn made. The Monk looked at Lucius who nodded. He moved in front of me and placed his hands on either side of my face. He held my gaze for a long moment. Then he stood on his toes to kiss the top of my head, blessing me. He bowed to Lucius and I, each in turn. We honored him with a bow and he left us.

"So, how're you doing?" he said.

We were sipping tea. I had a mouthful of it and used this as an excuse to think before answering.

"Mmm. I feel good. Great, actually." I smoothed a palm over my head. It made a little squeak, like when you rub a moist paper towel on a mirror. "What can you tell me about this?" I pointed to my scalp.

"Nothing just yet."

"Uh, okay. I liked the Monk. Does he have a name?"

"Not really. He may, but it's never been important. He's a shapeshifter." He said this casually. Just part of the conversation. Like mentioning that the new neighbor down the street is a stamp collector.

"Shapeshifter?"

"Yes. He can change forms and appear in different ways. Sometimes he'll show up as an animal. You didn't notice anything like that?"

I remembered the raven on the deck. "I might have, actually." I told him about it, then added that "I didn't think much about it."

Lucius was silent and sipped slowly from his cup. He glanced at me and said, "You're going to learn that everything in this place has a meaning. Nothing is wasted. The Great Mother is always speaking. You don't know how to listen yet, but you will. It is significant that the raven appeared. That's no accident. I don't suppose you have read much about the raven legends, have you?"

"No," I said. None of my books on business were useful in this world.

"You'll understand this better later on, but the Indians believed the Raven had great magic. They associated ravens with powerful medicine that can give humans the courage to enter the Void. The wise ones taught that when a raven appears, there will be a change in consciousness for the better. The stories go back all the way to the creation of the world. They say that Raven brought light into the darkness and created part of *Maka*, Mother Earth. He named plants and taught animals. Raven could see all and find things that are hidden. In fact, this being you call the Monk was probably making a little joke showing up in that form. Raven is the hallmark of shapeshifting. See, he's being playful while sending a message with many layers."

I wasn't sure I wanted to ask the next question, but it popped out anyway, "So, what's the message?"

Lucius narrowed his eyes, "I can't give you words for this. You'll know soon enough."

That sounded ominous. I swallowed the lump of hard dread that kept rising in my throat at odd moments.

Lucius stood. "Come with me. I have something for you to do."

He led me down the hall and we turned into another room, one I had not seen. At one end was a fireplace with a hearth made of sandstone and river rocks. Quiet music was playing. Lucius pointed me to a seat on the large leather couch. It sat near the wall and a hand-loomed rug spread over the floor planks. I walked over to sit and noticed *Emerson's Bible* on the cushions. I looked at Lucius. He nodded for me to pick it up.

"Find a blank page," he said. I did so and waited with my pen at the ready, he continued. "What I want you to do now is close your eyes." I looked at him.

"Go ahead," he said, "Do it now. Allow the dark to come and let yourself drift. Here, breathe with me." With my eyes closed, his hands covered mine. I drew in a long breath that continued for eight beats and held it. "Release," he said. We did this three times and with each outgoing rush of breath, I felt lighter and my mind became more quiet.

"Now, I want you to imagine yourself as a creature with many faces, many masks. This is the you that you've always known, only seen in a different way. These faces are how you interact with the world. Do you understand?"

"You mean the way other people see me?"

"This isn't about them, it's about how *you* see yourself. I want you to look through the eyeholes of your many masks. Recognize the faces you wear as your masks. Then, you'll to be able to take them off your true face — and see each mask for what it really is."

"When you say my masks, it sounds like you're suggesting falseness."

"Let's not get tangled in philosophy, he said. I'm not sure you feel what I'm talking about yet. Tell me, what's your sense of the meaning? It's simpler than you think."

"Is it the way I go through my days, always putting on the face I believe others want to see?"

"Yes!" he said. It felt good to have the right answer for once. Then he continued, "But it goes beyond that. You're conscious of that at times, you almost know when it's happening. I'm also talking about the masks glued so tightly to the face of Who You Really Are — that you don't even know they're masks anymore. Okay, open your eyes."

I did. He was straightening from finding my pen on the floor. Strange, I hadn't even noticed its fall. He handed it to me.

"Write now. Keep your pen moving. Come up with as many different roles as you can think of in your life. Your jobs, the hats you wear. Go. Say these words and then write what follows. I am a..."

Ah! This was starting to make sense. I heard the voices of many thoughts and started writing as fast as possible.

> *I'm an Entrepreneur*
> *I'm a Father*
> *I'm a Husband*

"Think about all the roles, all the different ways you move through the world," he said. I kept writing.

I'm a Son
I'm a Brother
I'm Salesperson
...CEO
...Friend
...Leader

"Imagine old roles you thought were gone but still seem to affect the way you think. Maybe even some you're trying to forget," he said quietly. I thought about this one for awhile.

Church member
Student
Fundamentalist
Poor kid

"You're doing well," he whispered, "That's good. Keep going. How about loyalties? Say it to yourself 'to whom am I loyal?' and then write that."

America
God, some kind of God
My family
My business partners
My customers

"How about things you own or that own you?" he said. This took a minute.

Business Owner
Home owner
Tax payer

Lots of business debts. Debt Payer
Debtor

"Rest now," he said, "I want you to close your eyes and feel your attachment to all of these labels. Hold each one in your mind. It goes very deep doesn't it? We merely touched the most obvious things. There is much more. This is about your identity, who you've always believed yourself to be."

The image of myself as Jonathan Swift's Gulliver floated up again. I was tied down with hundreds of ropes and couldn't move. Everything had its hold on me. I opened my eyes, Lucius was looking at me.

"It's my whole life," I said, "All of it. My whole life. It's everything, Lucius."

He touched my knee. "It isn't everything, but it's everything you've been paying attention to." He turned the book on my lap so he could read what I had written. "Jacob, what's interesting here is that none of these big important masks truly define you."

"I didn't even think of them as masks," I said, "This is just my life. Am I going to come unglued now that I see this way?"

"Some people have," he said, "You could. You are here to discover the nature of your true being. Tell me, when you say 'unglued' what does that mean?"

"You know, go crazy, lose it. Crack up. My whole world would fall apart." My hands made little frantic gestures. "If none of what I *thought* I was sticks to me after this, that will mean the end of life as I've known it."

He didn't say anything.

"I mean, wouldn't it?"

"How is life 'as you've known it' treating you so far?" he said.

"It was actually going pretty well until you showed up," I shot back. "I'm sorry, that came out badly."

He shook his head. "Don't apologize. You spoke the truth, or at least what feels true. Get in the habit of that. If you feel it, say it—gently. Tell me more."

"I really didn't think I was on the wrong track until I met you. I was stressed out with my business most of the time, but I kind of liked it. I felt important...like people needed me. Then I met you and it was as if someone pulled back a curtain. Everything looks different and now I'm not sure how to deal with this big stacked-up life I've built. Before you came along I was motivated to keep going. Then you showed up and I just feel tired of it. Is that what's supposed to happen?"

"What's supposed to happen is that you wake up and embrace who you really are. Here, look at the top of your page."

I hadn't noticed the quote before he pointed it out.

> "A nice definition of an awakened person: a person who no longer marches to the drums of society, a person who dances to the tune of the music that springs up from within."
> — Anthony de Mello

"Yes," he said, "How does that sound? Are you dancing to your own music yet?"

I sighed. "Not really. I can hear it sometimes, but I haven't had the courage to actually dance. I thought that I was really going for it by starting a business. I suspect I've been ignoring my real music."

"Well, that's why you're here," he said, "You're going to wake up and dance."

"But will I have to fall apart in the process?"

"Only what isn't real will be lost," he said, "People looking on aren't going to understand everything that happens. The you who's attached to what they think isn't going to understand either."

"That part scares me," I said.

"It always does," he said.

"But what about my duties? The promises I've made. My wife and kids. I can't just stop being everything all at once, can I?"

He held up his hand. "One step at a time. First you have to see the masks. You have to go on a journey to discover who you really are. Then you can become more intentional with the roles you choose to play. You're carrying burdens without discrimination. You've always done this, haven't you? Taken on whatever was handed to you? People know they can load you up, so they do. Why not?"

"Am I so different from everyone else?"

"Jacob, we aren't talking about everyone else. Most people are sleepwalking through life. You have agreed to wake up. Part of your mission is to help others wake up to Who They Really Are. However, you're not ready for that yet. First we have to help you crack the shell."

He touched my knee again.

"I'm going to leave you for awhile. Sit here in the quiet. I recommend you close your eyes and concentrate on your breathing. See where that takes you."

I nodded and closed my eyes. He made no sound as he left. *Breathe in...Breathe out...Breathe in...Breathe out...*

Ten minutes must have passed, then twenty. I desperately wanted to get up and move around, talk or watch television.

Breathe in...Breathe out... Slowly, the stillness flowered inside me.

Breathe in...Breathe out...Breathe in...Breathe out...

Without effort, my jagged rushing thoughts faded. I was floating, a lillypad on the surface of a pond with only a single stem rooted in the darkness below. I breathed and followed the stem down. Deeper into the cool black water. Deeper still into silence.

Chapter Fourteen

Dancing. I was dancing in the center of an enormous bonfire. The round patch of earth in the middle was bare and had been raked clean of debris. The rake's iron teeth had left markings on the ground that held deep secrets. I knew this without understanding why or how. The heat was intense and sweat ran down my face in great shining rivulets. I had already torn off my shirt and tossed it into the fire. I was conscious of my slippery torso whenever I crossed my arms or touched my sides. I danced harder. My bare feet pounded on the scorching dirt. Animal groans and cries burst from my throat.

Beyond the flames, with orange light flickering on their faces, my family and friends were crowded, watching my strange contortions. Afraid, they beckoned to me with frantic gestures. "Come out...come out of the fire! Are you mad?" they seemed to say. My wife and children were there, hands pressed over their mouths in horrified confusion. I wept in sorrow for them but I could not stop. The flames climbed closer. My skin was searing. I shrieked and danced. Terror and wild joy struggled inside me. I could not say whether the crackling sounds came from the burning wood or from my bones.

The fire roared along with my breath and I became a human bellows. I sucked a great draft of blazing air to make a long howl of pain and bliss, but as I did the flame rushed into my lungs. I fell down then and was wrapped in a blanket of molten light. I heard, from far away, a many-tongued wail of sorrow from the gathering of my loved ones but I had already merged with the pyre. The vortex was converting my body into a different kind of energy. Sparks and glowing ashes from my incinerating form blew away with the smoke and were lost among the stars in the black night sky.

From a great distance, I could hear a voice calling. The stillness was so deep that I had no desire to answer. Instead, I examined the words as they entered my ears. It was like watching a fly walk on a window without caring where it went. I had no feeling for them, they didn't attach to me or require anything. They were simply sounds, waveforms crawling around the beautiful emptiness inside my head. I focused on them and they became personal. There were two voices talking with each other. I surfaced, returning to consciousness, but I didn't move—just listened.

"It was the fire vision," he said.

"Oh," her voice was hushed and compassionate.

"Yes, the most intense so far," he said.

"It would be, up here," she said.

"Yes, it would."

"He's ready now, isn't he?" she said, "I sense he's shedding density quickly."

I felt them on either side of me, each resting a hand on my shoulder. I opened my eyes and looked straight ahead. The room rushed at my face and then retreated until I could focus again. I moved my eyes from side to side but not my head. My whole body locked in stillness. Like I was an iron bar gripped by a powerful magnet. It was comforting to be held. My whole life felt like one long mad dash. In this moment, I was quiet in a way I'd never been before. I couldn't move and didn't want to. There was nowhere else for me to be. Nothing that needed doing.

I found movement in my thumbs first. By staring down past the tip of my nose, I could see my hands clasped in my lap. I looked at my thumbs and smiled inside. They were inexplicably funny. I moved the left one just a little and the right one went along. I tapped them together a few times and looked out of the corner of my eye. Lucius was there, leaning close.

"You're doing so well," he whispered near my ear.

"Don't hurry," Kaitlyn said softly on the other side. I turned to look at her. She smiled. "Sit with this for a little while. Are you comfortable?"

I nodded. I was sitting with my feet underneath my legs, but I couldn't feel them. The magnetic grasp was fading, but I still had no desire to get up or move around. Both helpers patted me on the back, I squeezed my hands together and moved my fingers. This broke the spell and I began to topple into Kaitlyn's lap. They steadied me on each side and we all laughed.

I leaned back on the couch cushions. My new friends looked at me, their faces bright and open.

"You haven't meditated much, have you?" Kaitlyn asked.

I shook my head.

"Well, you went deeper than many people do, even though they've meditated for years." I felt a tingle of pride over this but Kaitlyn held up a finger. "You should be grateful and just know that you are assisted. Don't give yourself a gold star. It's a gift and has a purpose."

"Not a lot happened, though," I said, "I sort of sank into a quiet place and then I had the dream about burning."

"That's all you remember now," Kaitlyn said.

Lucius nodded, "Any time you go below the surface, lots of invisible things start to happen. It's common to not recall much when you're in normal awareness later."

Kaitlyn moved her hands in slow circles and said, "You enter Silence and these energy wheels go into motion. Things are happening, you just can't see them."

Lucius jumped up and stretched. He motioned for me to join him.

"We need to get some wood in. We can talk more about these things at lunch."

Kaitlyn patted me and gave a little push. "Wear a coat out there, you hear? Lucius never does but you need one. Oh, and a hat, too, for obvious reasons." She tapped my shiny scalp and smiled.

We spent the rest of the day eating lunch, splitting firewood in the shed behind the house and snowshoeing through the timber. Exercise was a welcome break from my emotional heavy lifting of the past week. Lucius showed me the wolf tracks out by the edge of the forest. We followed them through the trees until they disappeared into a ravine too treacherous to navigate by snowshoe.

Kaitlyn joined us after a while. She and Lucius were playful in the snow. They challenged me to snowshoe races, then rolled on the ground laughing when I tangled my feet and stood up with a faceful of frozen powder. Kaitlyn possessed amazing powers of mimicry. She would whistle a bird call and then, after a moment of silence, we would hear an identical answer from one of her friends in the trees. Once, I heard a raven *caw-cawing* in the distance. I looked at Lucius. *Was that the Monk?* He raised his eyebrows, grinned and shrugged.

The rays of the sun angled over the fir tree tops, Kaitlyn produced a picnic from her pack. We sat on fallen logs in a round meadow sipping hot chocolate and eating peanut butter sandwiches. I tried to imitate the slow enjoyment with which my helpers ate their food. Kaitlyn was wearing a hat like I'd seen in pictures of Laplanders. It was made of woolen yarn in many bright colors. A few strands of black hair escaped and fell down to frame her glowing cheeks. Lucius looked as he always did: strong, capable, comfortable. He wasn't wearing a coat but had on a pair of ski pants.

We sat there, chewing and enjoying the food. Sun touched one of the mountaintops and the light turned golden. At that moment, through the trees from the direction of the house, the sound of a gong crashed in the stillness. *BoomSHEEE!* The sound echoed and faded. It was strange; I was actually hearing a real, live gong just like the one that had thundered in my gut for more than a week. I looked at Lucius. He was already helping Kaitlyn pack up the food. They moved fast. He looked at me and said, "Come on. Let's get back. It's time."

I hung back as we started through the trees toward the house. We came to the clearing and Lucius pointed at the sky. A pair of turkey vultures were circling high above us. The undersides of their wings glowed as the late sunlight caught them when they turned. Kaitlyn and Lucius waved at them, then looked at each other and nodded.

We went inside and Kaitlyn disappeared. Lucius hustled me up to the little bedroom. As soon as we entered the house, his manner changed. His easy cheerfulness of the afternoon was replaced by intense concentration. We climbed the stairs and I glanced out the window where I had seen the wolf. The field of snow was empty of everything but the long blue shadows the fir trees cast as the sun descended behind the mountains.

The outfit Lucius gave me that morning was folded, lying on the bed. Lucius pointed.

"Why don't you shower and put that on. I'll be back for you in a few minutes."

I nodded and he left the room.

My lighthearted spirits were morphing to somber expectancy. No one had given me details about what was coming, but intuition said I was nearing the edge of the precipice.

I showered and dried myself with more care than usual. In the mirror, I noticed a mild sunburn, my shaved scalp was bright red. It wasn't painful, but I found some strong smelling lotion in the cabinet and rubbed it on my head and neck. I put on the clothes and glowed. I felt restored, fresh and warm. I hadn't experienced this kind of vitality in years. Thinking back over the day, I realized that I had eaten enough, but much less than usual. I didn't feel hungry now, instead my body was saying "yes!"

Underneath the clothes I found a pair of strange looking brown socks with separated toes. I wiggled my feet into them and smiled. *My kids would love these. They'd probably call them monkey socks.* I stretched my sore muscles and sat to wait for Lucius.

The room was quiet and the silence grew palpable. I didn't move, I simply sat there—feeling.

Tap. Tap. Tap... Someone knocked. Outside the door Lucius said, "You ready?"

"Come in," I said. The door opened and Lucius poked his head in.

"Are you ready?" he repeated.

I nodded and pushed up from the chair. My legs screamed and I put a hand out to steady myself against the wall. Lucius smiled and the corners of his eyes crinkled. He shook his head.

"You in pain?"

"*Ooh, ow!* Yeah. I'll be all right. I need to get back in shape."

"Where are you sore?"

"All over." We had split wood and snowshoed for hours. My shoulders and chest were sore. I could feel muscles along my rib cage that hadn't been used for years. It was a good kind of hurt.

"Remind me later. I have some tea that will help. Oh, and I'll show you the hot springs, too. That'll put you right."

He turned and I followed him to the left. We were walking down the angled hall away from the stairs. I had not gone this way before. We were moving toward the center. I became aware of an ambient sound. It was music, but just one note. It grew in volume as we walked, but my impression was less one of decibels and more of increased vibration. It was the voice of a single note that flourished within itself. It came in waves. It gently ebbed and flowed. It sounded like the swelling tone of a pipe organ which was a voice at the same time. I imagined a radiant giantess lying on her back in the sun, exhaling with a gentle humming *aaaaaaauuuuummmm...* Not quite a song and not quite a sigh. The sound was both hypnotic and magnetic. I wanted to sit right there on the floor and merge with it. Lucius put his hand on my back.

The wide passageway was dim. Gas lamps set in sconces on the walls provided the only light. Almost obscured by shadows at the end of the hall, I could make out a closed door. We stopped walking fifteen feet from it. Lucius turned and placed his hands on my shoulders. The door had captured my attention and I broke eye contact and looked at it. Like a portal, it was completely round, set into the wall and held with heavy carved beams. Similar to the front door of the house, it was also very old and covered in markings. Behind the door came new sounds. *PUM pum pum pum...* A rhythmic drumming joined the vibrant tone that filled the space around us.

Lucius caught my attention with his eyes again. He held me with his gaze and we stood, just a few inches apart, while the seconds ticked by. Finally he said, "Here we are. You've been waiting and searching your whole life for this, long before you had the first inkling of what *it* might be. I must warn you, though. When you step through that door, there's no going back to the way you were before." I must have flinched because he paused and raised his eyebrows. I shook my head, there was nothing to say.

He continued, "We are going to join a group of helpers. They come in different forms. You will see how they use ritual and ceremonies from other times and places. Don't get fixated on the form or the story. They are only here as teachers. Just be in the experience and learn."

He was quiet for a moment, thinking. Then he said, "This council was gathered for you in particular. We are all here at this moment to assist you. I say this only so that you will fully invest yourself. Your ego will desire to either invalidate the experience, or co-opt it. You must only surrender. Remember that word?

"Turn down the volume on your rational voice. Know in advance that it will try to say it's all too weird, or it will try to inflate your self-importance. Both of these are distractions. Remember, everything here is real, realer than real. By using the illusions of this house and the ceremonies we are now entering, you will step across the threshold and experience the nature of Being with your eyes wide open. This is a gift which comes to you in a way most humans are never offered. Treasure it."

I nodded. The sounds around us, the light, the words Lucius spoke, all combined to move me into a different state of awareness. Lucius seemed to know this. He let go of my shoulders and moved to the door. I followed. He had his hand on the latch but paused and pointed above the door. Carved deep in the wooden beam was the inscription "*Rumi's Gate.*" He shook his head and smiled at me. I saw him then as one radiant glow.

"Remember the round door?" he said. I nodded again. Fragments of the quote in *Emerson's Bible* danced through my mind, "*People are going back and forth across the doorsill where the two worlds touch...the door is round and open...don't go back to sleep.*" Based on how I felt at that moment, I didn't care if I ever slept again.

Lucius pulled the latch and the heavy round door swung open. The rhythmic drumming faded as the music of a single note surged through the round entryway.

Chapter Fifteen

I stepped up behind Lucius as he swung the door on its oiled hinges. If you can imagine a wind of energy, one that doesn't blow your hair or rustle the leaves on the ground, that's what I felt as the round gate opened. I was drawn across the threshold, both pushed from behind by the mysterious wind and pulled by the magnetic center of the chamber. Lucius moved aside and I put one foot through the door, then the other. I knew, without any doubt, I had entered a different domain. Behind us, the portal thumped shut with a deep thundering echo. The pervasive note I had first heard in the passageway was much stronger here, but grew in power on the subaudible plane. My whole body vibrated.

I thought we were alone. I stood still and looked around at the remarkable space. The room was round and perhaps sixty feet across. *Temple*, I thought. That was my first impression but as I looked closer, I couldn't understand why. There were none of the usual religious symbols one would expect in a temple. Nevertheless, the feeling persisted. The floor was made of wood and stone. It had a curious pattern. I blinked and tried to focus on the whole design.

Skilled craftsmen had used wood from many different trees and slabs of quartz, granite, limestone, marble and other stones to create a huge inlayed mosaic on the floor. My eyes adjusted to the soft light and the image of Earth appeared beneath my feet. The spaces between the carved floor were filled with translucent glass that was lit from below. The whole surface gleamed with thick varnish. I stood on the ocean off the coast of the western United States. Across from my familiar continent to the east, Europe and the Far East spanned the floor covering the other side of the room.

Looking up, I saw a great glass-paneled dome in a copper frame radiating from a central point shaped like the sun. Above us was the sky, darker in the east as the last orange light of day faded in the west. The moon and first large evening star were of evening shining where deep blue turned to black. I took a breath. Lucius put out his hand to steady me. He tapped my shoulder as before when he told the story of the scarves and lamp. Lightness filled my body. Like a helium balloon floating on the end of a cotton string, a puff of wind could have lifted me into the sky.

Blinking, squinting, I tried to clear my vision. The combined effects of expanded sound and light invaded my senses. I floated a few feet above my body, suspended between Earth and Heaven in the vibrant, glowing atmosphere of the temple-chamber.

Lucius pressed my shoulder again. I reassociated with my wobbling feet as he walked me clockwise around the circumference of the room. We approached the large compass-direction letter "E" on floor, set with gilt edges on the shape of India. Lucius turned me toward the center and whispered in my ear.

"Take this and follow the line to the middle, where the light comes up from the floor. Spread it out, then sit and wait." He took a rolled rug from a large basket near the wall and put it in my arms. "Go now," he said.

I obeyed him, taking each step deliberately as if balancing on a shining railroad track, sure I'd be swept off my feet by the oscillating waves of sound and light. A brilliant shaft of radiance like a spotlight was shining from a point in the center of the floor. I came near but was reluctant to place the rug over it. Finally, I knelt and unrolled the rug. The light below was so strong that it glowed through the rug. I fidgeted, making tiny adjustments to be certain that it was exactly centered. I crawled to the middle to sit directly on top of the luminous orange patch, legs crossed, facing roughly north. Warm stillness folded around me. Lucius moved through my field of vision around the room.

I noticed a large circular frame. Hanging from it—an enormous bronze gong.

Lucius stopped and took the long teakwood beater from its hook. He raised it high over his right shoulder with both hands and paused. His body coiled like a golfer poised to swing. Then he whipped the mallet into the shining disc.

BOOOMSHHEEEeeeeeeEEEEEeeee...

Powerful reverberations of the sound rocked me. He raised his arms and brought them down again.

BOOOMSHHEEEeeeeeeEEEEEeeee...

I was sure I could see the waves of energy burst from the massive impact and ripple back and forth across the room. He raised his arms for a third blow, just as the crashing roar exploded from the gong, he cried out in a loud voice,

"Now...!"

Like steam rising in reverse, figures began to emerge and coalesce from the thin air. The sound from the gong faded, again I heard the gentle drums beating in the circle. I moved my head slowly and watched as a group of people materialized around me. They seemed to have been there all along, sitting crosslegged on rugs. They used short leather-topped strikers to thump on round drums made of animal hide stretched over wooden hoops. *PUM-pumpumpum. PUM-pumpumpum. PUM-pumpumpum.*

I looked at them. The shapeshifting Monk was seated in the direction of the east. His eyes were closed and he was swaying lightly as he tapped his drum. I turned toward the west and recognized

Kaitlyn sitting with the sealed portal door at her back. She was shaking an egg-shaped rattle along with the drums and looking at me. My face must have registered the joy I felt in seeing her because she smiled and nodded slowly, her eyes full of care. She glanced to her left and I followed her gaze. Lucius was taking his place. As he sat, the circle felt complete.

Lucius began to drum with the others and I looked at them. I recognized no one else, but they didn't feel like strangers. I turned my head and counted. Sitting surrounded by twelve people, I was the thirteenth. I saw a man from India and a woman who looked to be of an Aborigine tribe, perhaps Australian. A tall African sat straight like a prince. The Monk was Asian and Kaitlyn seemed to be of Middle Eastern descent. The music of the drums went on and on. Lucius was gazing at me and I nodded at him. He smiled and then looked behind me.

A presence drew near from the south. I straightened and sat still as a drum grew loud above my head. Its tones throbbed in my solar plexus, filling up the spaces in my lungs. The drummer suddenly increased the tempo. Everyone in the circle kept pace. *Faster. Faster. Louder. Stop.* Then silence.

The drums disappeared. Everyone sat in magnificent silence. They all looked at the person standing behind me. I wanted to turn my head. To look, but dared not break the reigning stillness. I closed my eyes and took a breath. I was suddenly feeling solid again. Not just solid. Nervous. I swallowed hard to suppress the tension rising in my throat. I opened my eyes and alarm bells jangled my body.

Directly in front of me, seated crosslegged with his knees almost touching mine, was an old Native American man. I had not seen him before. He was the archetypical Red Man in some ways, long black braids, beaded headband, sun-weathered skin. In other ways, he was clearly one of the group. He wore the same simple garments as everyone else and bore no obvious symbols of leadership.

Something about his gaze pierced me. I was sure he could flip me over or pin me to the glass-domed ceiling with nothing more than a glance of his eyes. He sat looking at me silently. After a few seconds of nervous looking around, I met his direct stare and held it. I don't know how long we sat like that. The stillness around us formed a bubble and I was rooted to my rug. Then he blinked. He nodded and uncrossed his legs to stand. I followed his example.

When we were both standing, I saw he wore a leather pouch decorated with beads and fringes. He reached inside the flap and produced a gray-white dried sprig. Then, he struck a match and lit it. A small flame burned for a moment then died, leaving glowing ash. The smoke was sweet and pungent. He motioned for me to hold out my arms. I did and became a human cross. He waved the smoking leaves slowly in front of my body and followed the lines of my arms and legs. He circled behind me and repeated this motion. Facing me again, he smudged above my head and making circles with the smoke. Earth-spice filled my nostrils.

Kaitlyn appeared holding a large abalone shell. He stubbed the smoldering twigs on the mother-of-pearl lining and dropped them in the bowl. He nodded at Kaitlyn. She knelt and set the dish on the floor near our feet, then returned to her place.

When the circle was complete again, he raised his arms and spoke. "Brothers and Sisters, let us welcome this man into the circle of Light." He placed his palms on either side of my bald head. "Ah ho, Jacob," he said. "Ah ho!" the gathered helpers echoed and the room filled with their voices. They clapped their hands and laughter rippled around the circle.

His hands dropped to my shoulders and he pushed me down. After I was settled, he addressed the council. "We will open the ceremony with a pipe." Everyone placed their palms together and made a small bow of assent.

The man opened the pouch and drew out a leather-wrapped package. He seated himself then and opened the bundle on the floor between us. With great care he arranged the parts of a peace pipe and a smaller pouch I assumed contained tobacco. He smoothed the wrappings, then relit the sage and smudged himself and the items on the floor before him. Smoke lingered in the air and I breathed in its sharp aroma.

He lifted the pipe pieces and held them over his head. He closed his eyes and his lips moved silently. After a moment, he fitted the two pieces together and pressed them tight. He lowered the pipe, reached into the pouch and took a pinch of shredded brown mixture. He raised this above his head and began to speak.

"We thank you, Great Spirit, Father of All That Is, for the life that we hold in these bodies. Thank you for this day, for this moment of light. We ask for the light to guide the journeys of the seeker and to bless this doorway between the worlds." He paused and moved the pinch down and touched it to the floor. "Mother Earth, thank you for the abundance and goodness that springs forth from your womb. We ask you to aid us in our prayers and meditations today as you have always done. Allow us safe passage and guide us back to you in perfect time." He silently offered the tobacco to the directions of the four winds, each in their turn.

He loaded the bowl of the pipe with care. When he had completed this task, he sat back and looked at me. He held up the pipe and said, "The sacred pipe is at the heart of my people's culture as we travel the road of balance within creation. The smoke that comes from my mouth is a symbol of truth that is spoken. The smoke that drifts up from the pipe offers a path for prayers to reach the Great Spirit, also a way for the Great Spirit to travel down to Mother Earth. You are here today to learn of the connection between the world of form" he touched my knee, "and the world of Spirit." He swept an arc through the air with his hand. "You see?"

I nodded. He regarded me intently for a moment, then nodded.

He held the pipe to his lips and lit it with a match   He drew on the mouthpiece and flame sucked down into the bowl. An orange coal appeared and he drew twice more to be sure it was lit. Then, he took a mouthful of smoke and turned to the south. He blew out a long breath letting the fragrant smoke stream. I smelled tobacco and willow bark as it drifted around my head.

"We offer smoke to the Spirit of the South, for fire and passion, for summer and sunshine. For medicine and growth."

He drew again on the pipe, turned and blew smoke toward the west. Kaitlyn was seated there with her head bowed.

"We offer smoke to the Spirit of the West, to the thunder and rain that waters our plains, to rivers that run down into the sea. For the spirit world that lives in the night and always surrounds us."

He shifted toward the north and faced Lucius across the shining expanse of the floor. Smoke drifted in the air between them as he exhaled.

"We offer smoke to the Spirit of the North, *Waziya ahtah*, the white giant from the north. We are thankful for your strength and endurance, for purity like snow."

He turned at last toward the old Monk, seated in shadows before the eastern wall.

"We offer smoke to the East, where the daybreak star of knowledge appears. Like the rising sun, bringing us new visions and new experiences, causing the night of ignorance to fade away."

Then he pivoted to face me again and drew several times on the pipe to revive the coal at the bottom of the bowl. It glowed brightly as it burned. He tilted his chin and let a long blue-gray steam of smoke drift toward the clear dome above us.

"We offer smoke to the Above, to all the gods and goddesses, to all the invisible helpers and other unseen ones. We thank *Wakan Tanka*, the great creator of All That Is."

He puffed on the pipe for the last time. I heard the ember crackle and die.

"We offer smoke to the Below, to the mysteries and that which is yet to be known. We thank all that walk upon the Earth, the four-leggeds and the two-leggeds, the people of the rocks and trees. And for the spirits of the great mountains."

He held the pipe at arm's length again and said, "For All That Is, we are very grateful." He took a breath and looked around the circle and said, "Ah ho." We all responded together with reverence, "Ah ho."

He placed the pipe carefully on its leather wrappings after tapping the remaining ashes from the bowl and into the abalone shell.

He stood and spread his arms. "The circle is now open!"

For a moment, I surfaced and experienced a lull in the energy that had been so strong. It was a let-down, to sit there with my ankles cramping. My back itched and I scratched it surreptitiously. The pipe ritual had moved me, but I wondered what people from the real world would think if they could peek through a window and watch the proceedings. These thoughts seemed unworthy of my surroundings but they persisted. I began to feel annoyed with myself and anxious. Perhaps I wouldn't be able to come up to whatever standard of enlightenment was expected of me in this place.

There was motion in the group. They were moving closer to me and to each other. The circle grew tighter. I was seated in the center like the hub of a wheel with twelve spokes. The Medicine Man, a title I gave him mentally for his mysterious mantle of authority, sat down across from me and crossed his legs. He reached into his pouch and brought out a small handkerchief tied at the top to form a bundle about the size of a child's fist. He loosened the knotted leather thongs and opened it. I caught the scent of incense from the little pile of what looked like dried bark and crumbled leaves. He pinched a clump of it and dropped it in the abalone shell. He looked at me, then lit it.

A thin stream of smoke appeared. My nostrils stung as I inhaling the heady bouquet. I immediately felt myself sliding back into the luminous state of being. The Medicine Man sat with his hands on his knees. His eyes closed. My lids had drooped and watching him through my lashes, he seemed to join the floating incense haze and hover in the air. I saw him pick up his drum again and tap it softly.

PUM-pumpumpum...

I closed my eyes, too. The sound grew, one by one, the voices of the other drums joined in.

PUM-pumpumpum... PUM-pumpumpum...

The music thrummed faster and its many separate streams intermingled until they formed a sinuous, glowing river. That in turn merged with the scented smoke and carried me with it, up, up . . . swirling and floating high above the ground. I don't know how long this lasted—I just hoped it wouldn't stop. Images and thoughts wandered through my field of vision. Unlike the rushing torrent of normal consciousness, in this temple space I saw them as a dispassionate observer. They carried their normal payload of emotion and urgency, but I was seated beyond their range. I was like a preoccupied child playing a few feet outside the reach of a pitbull who snarled and raged at the end of his chain, but could not touch me. I saw my office and all the people in it. They were busy, frantic it seemed from where I watched now. The picture was heavy with fear.

I reached out to put my hand in, to help, to take action. That was my job. The face of Lucius came into focus. He didn't say anything, just slowly shook his head and smiled compassion with his eyes. He moved his finger so that I'd turn away from that scene and look at something else. He faded as I saw my own living room at home. My wife and children were together. My mind's voice whispered, "Get attached! You should be home, being a Dad right now." Before I could act on this obligation, the image moved away from me, receding into the distance, it disappeared. Bliss and detachment filled me. I wanted to stay on that rug forever.

The Medicine Man was talking. I hadn't opened my eyes, but I could see him in front of me. He was still drumming, but very slowly now. The round leather pad on the end of his striker barely touched the drum's surface. *Tum... Tum... Tum...*

"This is good but it's time to see beyond," he said, "Many have journeyed to where you are now. They dip their feet in the water of joy and never wish to go any farther. This is not the purpose for which we are gathered. Do you know what is to come?"

I shook my head. Something in the question filled me with dread. I felt transported to the camp chair in the mountains on the night of my first meeting with Lucius, that same sense of creeping to the edge and fearing that I must leap returned.

He placed his drum on the floor and clapped his hands twice. A command. I opened my eyes. He was looking at me, then his gaze moved past my shoulder. I sensed motion behind me, coming from the south. Lucius and the African prince appeared, their backs bent as they carried a heavy stone slab by handholds chiseled into its sides. They positioned it at the east side of where the Medicine Man and I sat facing each other and left us.

Lucius returned a moment later carrying my near bursting duffel bag. He set it down beside the stone. The Monk appeared bearing the bundled saffron cloth that held the hair shaved from my head earlier in the day. He laid this next to my bag, bowed and returned to his place.

Events shifted into inexorable motion now. Nothing I could do would stop what was to come. The Medicine Man leaned forward and turned me clockwise on my rug toward the strange collection of my belongings. I could not imagine what was about to happen, but I was clearly going to be the center of attention. The circle of helpers moved closer. They were now sitting with their knees almost touching one another. At a motion from the Medicine Man, Lucius rose and walked inside the circle clockwise until he was standing beside the stone slab. I looked at him. His face a mask of unyielding concentration. He knelt and began pulling things out of my bag.

First, my shirt with the cufflinks still fastened. He folded this loosely and laid it on the stone. My shoes and tie followed. I heard my car keys rattling around inside one of the shoes. He placed my pants on top of them. He held up my suit coat and shook it a couple of times. He reached into the inside pockets and began sorting through what he found, my business cards in a platinum case, my Mont Blanc pen, my wallet. Without speaking, he held my business card up so that I could see it. It had my picture on it—a flattering one. It was taken when I was probably forty-pounds lighter. Below my name was my title, Founder & CEO. I remembered having these cards designed. I had felt such warm pride at finally seeing a printed confirmation of my success. Lucius glanced at me, then put the cards and pen on the growing pile.

He opened my wallet and began pulling things out of their clear plastic covers. My driver's license, pictures of my family, business cards from friends and associates. He held them up for me to view and then put them on the slab. I had no idea what he was doing. The group was in deep concentration. They had their hands together in a prayer-like attitude and were rocking in place with their eyes closed. I had difficulty catching my breath. I kept sucking in big gulps of air, but it didn't relieve my growing anxiety.

Lucius found my credit cards and slips of paper with my bank account codes. He opened the hidden compartment inside and pulled out a stack of cash. It wasn't all that much, maybe two or three hundred dollars—but I felt the pleasure that always blossomed when I looked at money. He put all of these on the heap. I had often thought about my wallet, how it represented a passkey to hundreds of thousands of dollars in buying power. Even though it really wasn't all my money, it felt great to know that I had this armor against poverty close. I could always put out my hand and touch it if I needed to.

He reached out and grasped my wrist—the one with my Rolex. I watched him fiddle with the clasp and pop it open. He slid it over my hand and tossed it on the pile. He did the same with my wedding ring. *Where is this going?* I thought. I had the sudden desire to jump up and push my way out of the room, to do whatever it took to fight my way clear of this place. Lucius and the Medicine Man must have sensed this. They each put a hand on me. I took a deep breath and the feeling passed.

Lucius fished inside my bag and brought out my "power books." He turned them so I could see the titles. I looked them over and nodded, still confused. He found my copy of *The Secret* movie and placed it with all the others. He had to turn and arrange the books on top so they wouldn't slide off. He pulled the bag open and looked inside. It was nearly empty now. He pulled out my old King James Version Bible and put it in my hands. I held it, felt the worn spots on the black cover and thought of how far it had traveled with me in life. Lucius held out his hand for it and placed it carefully on top of the pile. He reached for the wrapped sheet that contained my hair. He untied the knotted corners and dumped the loose clumps over everything in the pile. Then he folded the sheet and tucked it under one side of the heap. When this was done, he nodded at the Medicine Man and returned to his place with the others.

The leader pursed his lips and frowned gravely. Finally, he spoke. "You see this *stuff*?" he waved his hand over the pile. I nodded.

"Well that's *all* it is, but it means a lot of things to you. Does it not?"

I nodded again. Emotion made my Adam's apple swell and clench, it was a fist in my throat. I tried to swallow and tears stung my eyes. The man from India approached. He squatted and handed the Medicine Man a small round pot full of liquid. The two of them nodded their heads toward each other and the Indian moved away.

The Medicine Man looked at me again and then held the pot above my things and poured the contents out in a shining stream. I could smell it now, honey-colored oil suffused with potent herbs and spices. It soaked into the cloth of my suit and ran down through the loose hair clippings in tiny streams that dripped from the edges of the books. I sat there stunned as the oil pooled on the porous surface of the slab. *Ruined. My things are ruined. Why?*

Then the Medicine Man flicked his thumbnail on a match and tossed it, flaring, on the saturated pile. Flames caught the oil first and began to consume it, racing around like a burning serpent among my belongings. Time stopped and I was caught in an airless vacuum. I opened my mouth to scream, but no sound would come. There was something so terrible, so final, so gapingly death-like in the fiery mass. I clawed the air and gasped. The drums were beating again. The Medicine Man knelt beside me with the abalone shell full of smoldering incense in his hands. He passed it close to my face three times and I found a way to catch a ragged gasp of air. With it, I drew in a lungful of fumes from the blazing altar and the incense haze.

I felt myself falling backwards. Hands beneath my shoulders lowered me, but I was gone. Falling and flailing. This was it. I had finally taken that last stumbling step off the edge into the terrible unknown. I thought I heard a raven's harsh *caw-caw* and an owl answer *who?* amidst the confusion and clamor of my disintegrating world.

Chapter Sixteen

Like being ejected from a burning fighter jet, I blasted into the sky with unimaginable speed. I tried to scream but I was tumbling... falling upward too rapidly to catch my breath. *My breath!* Somehow I knew that breathing was the least of my worries. I had exploded out of my body and was expanding without form. I moved much faster than the velocity of thought, so these realizations were just instant imprints of knowledge...shining watermarks of wisdom. I knew them but didn't know how or why. My dominant impression was of the most intense terror I'd ever experienced. It was as if the sum of all my adult fears and childhood nightmares had been visited upon me in a single instant. *Death. Falling. Darkness. Looming apparitions.*

I rolled face up and felt myself bursting away from the gravitational pull of Earth. It was as if I was trapped inside a membrane of living liquid newspaper. It was a web of panic. Faces, information, headlines, emotions, they blurred together and stretched to the horizon in every direction around the globe. I bounced and struggled to get free from the dense layer of frozen fear. I heard a loud shrieking voice cry out to me and recognized it as my own. *"Come back!"* it said. For a split second, I struggled to open my eyes and did. I saw the faces of Lucius and the Medicine Man above me.

Together, they each raised a single finger and pointed to the sky. I looked toward where they were pointing and instantly resumed my flight.

The presence of my helpers seemed to give me extra power and I crashed against the inside surface of the matrix which wrapped itself around the planet. I bounced back and the realization hit me that I was weighted down. With every cell, I was clinging to my earthbound self. A word appeared and grew into a solid three dimensional object, SURRENDER. It was the answer I had been seeking. *Surrender.* The idea swept through me bringing another wave of fear, but now I knew what must be done.

Nothing.

Nothing must be done. I must simply let go. Then I did it. My fingers broke away from their death grip on what I had always accepted as reality. In that instant, the universe as I knew it, exploded like a shattering kaleidoscope. Color and lights splintered in every direction. I billowed out into the pitch blackness of forevermore with crazy delight. I was boundless...without limits. The powerful knowledge that there was no longer any "me" downloaded into my being. I roared with relieved laughter. It was as if I had finally been pried loose from hanging on and when I fell, the rules of gravity were broken. I had fallen up, into the arms of a divine embrace so comforting that it embodied everything that could ever be meant by the word "home." If there were no more me, then I was fully absorbed into the ultimate Reality. This came as a blinding flash of infinite release.

In this state, there was no judgment, no obligation, no weary searching, no struggle. There was only One. I was it and It was me. I was blossoming outward through the vastness of the universe and simultaneously hovering at the edge of the Void.—Reclining in an ultimate expression of blissful peace. My attention was drawn by this and I swam through a field of unconditional love to explore the Great All-Nothing. Without effort, I was there, face to face with what could only be the Mystery of Mysteries, Yahweh, Bahá, Wakan Tankah, Allah, Krishna, God the Father-Mother, Rah, All That Is. I could look into the depths of this without any sense of separation from It. I was Its breath. The very fabric of Existence was, as it turned out, love.

I hovered and merged, an amorphous blissful expression of the pervasive intelligent Love. If there were a consciousness of a heaven other than this, I had no need to learn of it. Laughter like thunder boomed from the vast depths. Another imprint of wisdom appeared: *Nothing is personal*. At first glance, this seems trite, perhaps, but the astounding truth of it rolled around and through me like joyful, wrestling nimbus clouds. *Nothing personal!* If this were true and it clearly, unquestionably was, then I was released from a lifetime of anxious, obsessive maintenance of a facade that never meant anything in the first place. Could it be that I was free? Yes. The whole universe answered, "Yes!"

Images appeared, welling up from some womb-like Mind that I was experiencing now for the first time without any filters. Impressions more than mental images, I noticed sexual energy and it transformed itself from glowing pink-wrapped fluid ecstasy into a gateway of pure power. Like a mysterious, delicious opening in the protective covering of the Universe through which humans could momentarily reach their ravenous arms and touch All That Is. A lifetime of judgment and guilt melted away. I saw a spiraling trace of humanity that swirled like campfire smoke, twisting in the breeze flowing beyond the eons before time.

All of human history, infused with knowledge and emotion, birth, growth, learning, achievement, tragedy, death, floating in the timeless, spaceless realm. I laughed again, rather, Everything laughed through me. I had the knowledge that nothing, NO-THING is real in the way I had always believed it. This circulated and I realized that Nothing *is* Real as well. In very fact, there is no thing as real as Nothing. This struck me as the grandest joke of all. Somehow All That Is could play a trick on Itself like this.

My entire Being experienced itself as a formless transparent eyeball. I had only to shift my attention and I would immediately surround and suffuse whatever interested me. A tiny blue rock, shining in the distant blackness drew my gaze. Instantly, like a powerful telescope, I zoomed in on it and was manifest. It was the Earth. I watched it spin silently. For the first time, I was free of its gravitational pull. I was unaffected by its drama and power struggles and endless trivial convulsions. Deep compassion for the inhabitants of the planet swelled inside me. I wanted to surround every human who walked the dusty streets with the same all powerful embrace that absorbed me. This yearning created a pull that drew me closer. I passed through light years in a flash and entered the atmosphere of Earth. The vapor of clouds parted and I was looking through the dome of the strange circular house. It rested in a field of snow and trees.

Music, prayers and scented smoke drifted up through an opening in the copper sun at the top of the glass canopy like an ephemeral umbilical cord. I saw warm light and beings kneeling with hands outstretched toward the figure of a man lying in the center. He had fallen with his arms spread out as if he were nailed to an invisible cross. I felt such love for this creature. At his feet, the smoking ashes of something burnt on a stone altar still glowed. One of the kneeling figures picked up a drum and began to beat it softly.

Pum...pum...pum...pum...

It created a magnetic pathway of sound that I followed down into the bright circle. Then I somersaulted backwards into the inert body of the man.

I opened my eyes. My body felt very still. I dared not move. Didn't want to move. Lucius knelt nearby holding his hands a few inches over my chest. He opened his eyes and smiled. "Shh..." he whispered, "There's a lot happening here. Just be still with it." I closed my eyes in bliss again and this sent me soaring back into the ice clouds high above the Earth. I floated and settled. The face of each helper in the circle appeared. I loved them and wept with gratitude.

"Thank you thank you thank you thank you," my lips kept saying. I heard happy laughter from the group. I laughed loud and long with them. The sound of my own voice both buoyed me higher into the air and also returned feeling to my body lying there on the rug. I moved my fingers first but then relaxed back into glorious repose. I felt shiny and scrubbed clean. *Newborn. I just died and have been born again,* I thought. This made me giggle. The expanded sensation of infinity began closing as if silk veils were piling up, obscuring my transcendent vision. Still, I had many new knowings engraved into my soul. I hoped I could excavate them later. It seemed that I had accessed the answers to life, the universe and everything.

The small voice of fear approached. I recognized it as myself, the Earth-self. With compassion even for this ever-present saboteur, I simply smiled and turned away. The words of Saint John comforted my mind, "*There is no fear in Love; but perfect love casteth out fear...*"

I moved my hands up, fingers splayed and looked at them. I had no desire to move, but I could feel myself filling out my own limbs with life and vigor. I closed my eyes again and heard humming, haunting music very near my ears. Hands touched the sides of my face and I realized my head was resting on something. I opened my eyes and looked up into the shining black face of the Aborigine woman helper. She was singing a kind of wordless song, my head in her lap. It had a deep, ancient quality to it. Like the sweep of wind across the desert after a thunderstorm carrying the smells of rain soaked dust. Like the cries of wild dogs calling to a bright full moon.

She looked down at me with tremendous compassion and kept crooning, moving her face from side to side. I turned my head and looked around the circle. The rest of the helpers were also gazing at me, saying with their looks, "Yes. We understand." And I knew they did. Whatever they had observed, whatever humiliating contortions I had exhibited, they had seen it all and held me with reverent care.

The song ended and the woman gently rested my head on the rug again before she moved back to her place. The Medicine Man knelt beside me and sat silent, his silver-streaked braids swaying. Then he reached his hands for mine and nodded. He pulled me to a sitting position and looked at me.

"And, how are you?"

"I..." my mouth moved, searching for the words. None approached. He smiled and touched my knee.

"Never mind. Words aren't necessary. Did you see? Do you know?"

I looked at him. My eyes glowed and I could only nod.

"Yes. I can see you did. Now, take care with what you have been given. Already your little mind is weaving a basket, trying to tell you a story that will make sense from an Earth perspective. Do not try to stop this. Just observe it and remember. Just remember. You now know what's real."

Fresh tears sprang into my eyes for no reason. I shook my head and they slid down my cheeks. My body buzzed with high voltage energy. The Medicine Man motioned and the whole group came near and reached out to touch me. I sat bent over with tears dripping from the end of my nose and the skin of my whole body radiating reverent gratitude for what I had experienced.

"Ah ho, Jacob," he said. "Aho," they echoed in unison. Then they moved away and the drums began again, very softly.

Coolness like a gentle wind came up and touched the back of my neck. I looked around. The sounds and the images of the helpers were slowly fading. Only Lucius was still there, kneeling beside me before a broad stone slab. There, the ashes of all that I had ever thought important were growing cold and gray. He took me by the hand and helped me to stand. Together we stepped across the altar and made our way around the room to the round door, open once more toward the west.

Chapter Seventeen

What if you slept, and what if in your sleep you dreamed,
and what if in your dream you went to Heaven and there
you picked a strange and beautiful flower, and what if when
you awoke you had the flower in your hand? Ah, what then?
— Samuel Coleridge

I was propped on an elbow in the bed. The lamp made a warm circle of light on the blankets. *Emerson's Bible* was open and I stared at it, lost in thoughts with my pen in hand. Coleridge's words written across the top of the page captured my state of mind perfectly. Here I was, covered with heavy blankets and feeling rested. Feeling normal. I scratched the tip of my nose with the pen. Every time I inhaled, I thought I could smell the incense from the ceremony the night before. Had it not been for this reminder, I might have convinced myself that the entire thing was imagined. After all, I'd dreamed plenty of strange dreams lately.

As if I held Coleridge's strange and beautiful flower in my hand, each time I breathed, the scent triggered memories of the experience. I kept being transported back to the round temple room, back into the vibrating music, back into the great comforting infinity. I had indeed "gone to Heaven" and wasn't sure how to deal with what I'd seen. Something fundamental seemed to have shifted in my consciousness. My eyes drifted further down the page. This one had a second quote near the bottom.

> *We are not human beings having a spiritual experience. We*
> *are spirit beings having a human experience.*
> — *Pierre Teilhard de Chardin*

I had seen this quote before. Something from a Wayne Dyer book, maybe? This thought sent me backward in time. The public library shelves were full of books. I had frequented the self-help and success sections for years. The titles were familiar and inspiring. During that visit on a rainy day in October of 1998, I was scanning the covers looking for something different. *How To Be A No-Limit Person* seemed to slide itself off the shelf and into my hand. I turned it over and a mustached, balding guy smiled up from the face of the book. The title tickled my fancy, wasn't that what I had set out to be, after all? A no-limit person? I checked it out and drove to a nearby Starbucks to immerse myself in a *venti* latté and the book.

So opened the gate into a new thought-path for me. Reading that book uncovered a fascinating labyrinth of decisions and exploration. Prior to it, I was locked in a rigid religious environment where nothing was left to chance. What we thought about God, how we dressed, how we entertained ourselves, how we spent our time—all of it was predetermined for us. After pulling an intriguing little string on the sweater of my belief systems, the whole thing began to unravel. By the time Lucius visited me, I had a big pile of snarled yarn instead of the usual comfy dogma I wore. I had no idea what to do with any of it. I went on with life as best I could—glancing at the messy heap only when it was unavoidable.

I read almost everything Wayne Dyer wrote. His clear, down-to-earth explanations seduced me to walk trails that led to uncharted territory. He talked of deep honesty, quoted the Bible and the Bhagavad Gita, Ram Dass and Saint John. It was confusing and disturbing to suddenly see patterns that connected all the great teachings on Earth like a radiant web. Naturally, I could share my discoveries with no one in my life as it was. I became a secret agent hiding under the religious radar in my search for truth. If I admitted my doubts or growing certainties, I would face excommunication. Eventually, the new ideas springing up could no longer be hidden and I confessed my heresy.

The pain of those days was horrendous. I was terrified by the implacable progress of truth in my life. Admitting that I could not adhere to the doctrines that had always governed me was almost unbearable. My wife continued taking our children to her father's church. I, lonely and confused, wandered through the religious landscape. Each Sunday I visited a different church. I sat in the mega-churches with thousands of people cheering the evangelists of easy, prosperous religion. I visited Catholic and Lutheran masses. I sat in synagogues on Saturday. None of it pierced the cloud bank of questions that remained after my sky fell.

People raised in less intense religions would have a hard time understanding this, perhaps. When I was growing up, God was everything. He was often angry with "the world," so they told us, therefore we had to work hard to avoid His wrath. We needed to do a lot of things—and not do a lot of other things to escape hell fire.

When I let that fade, I was left with no solid answers. I decided to shift my focus to business success. A hole remained in the place where my beliefs about God had been, but I did my best to fill it with new pleasures. I started drinking and watching movies for the first time in my life. I dived into making money. If people couldn't understand me as a religious person, I could at least force them to approve of me for material success.

Now, here I was. The door I had been knocking on my whole life was flung open. Not just opened, shattered. Destroyed. Up in smoke.

My view of what waited on the other side was both beautiful and terrifying.

I began to write.

This place I find myself. It's too big for me. Not for me I felt last night when I was part of Everything. But too big for the self I've always been before. I feel the truth of what I've seen but have no idea how to translate it into my life. There's no way to tell anyone about this so they'll understand, but I'm sure that nothing will ever be the same again, either. This all might vanish like a dream, but I don't think so. Something big happened. This could change everything.

Like what?

Like, how I live my life. If there really isn't anything to fear, if nothing's personal, if it's all a big made-up game...then what have I been doing all this time? I've been running around worried about what everybody thinks. Everybody! I worry about how I look, whether people think I'm successful, whether people like me. Seems I'm wasting my time with that, but...

But, if I really start living the way I want to, start really walking my own path, it's going to piss off a lot of people. If I'm really not afraid of death, then I'll probably quit trying to stack up stuff around myself to prove how important I am, to try to leave a legacy. But everybody thinks that's who I am. They think I'm a smart guy. A successful guy. A responsible guy. If I stop being that person, they probably aren't going to like the new me—or the real me, whatever. And who is that anyway?

I don't know how to be anybody else, I guess. After what just happened, I know there's more going on than I ever imagined.

I also just realized that I never knew what surrender meant before last night. That was out of control. I hated it. It felt like death. Hell, it WAS death, but then it turned into LIFE like I never believed possible before. I can't ever see life or death the same way again. Now I know for sure I'm a nonmaterial energy somehow here having a physical experience, but...why? What's next? The rules have all changed and I don't know anything about the new ones yet.

The pen stopped moving, I leaned back and closed my eyes. For the moment, I was too confused to think, too overwhelmed by the volumes of instant knowledge I had experienced the night before. The big answers were in there somewhere. I knew this but couldn't wrap my brain around them. I didn't even know which questions to ask.

I was content lying there, remembering the experience. Flying, merging, being, loving. With my eyes closed, the feelings returned. Surrender, billowing up and into the Unknown. I realized that for the first time in my life, all my doubts about God were erased. Along with the doubts, my preconceptions had also shattered. My hands moved in slow circles as if I were sifting layers of energy.

I probably would have spent the entire day like that, but my reveries were interrupted by a knock on the door.

"May I come in?"

I opened my eyes and tried to orient myself. "Okay."

Lucius came in with a tray of food and placed in on the bedside table. He sat in the chair. I propped myself up and looked over at him. He smiled. "So?"

I smiled back and shook my head. "So...what?"

"How are you doing today?"

"Assimilating."

"Ah. Assimilate is a good word. We call it integrating, too. What's going on?"

I handed him *Emerson's Bible*. "Here. Hope you can read it."

While he read my recent entries, I sat up and ate. I could really get used to this whole room-service, breakfast-in-bed thing. My usual habit was to drive through some fast food place and eat in the car on my way to work. Lucius finished reading and looked up at me. He was quiet. Deciding.

"Interesting, isn't it?" he said, "How you can journey to the far edges of the universe and then wake up and wonder how your amazing adventure makes sense in the real world."

"That's exactly how I feel."

"I can see that in what you've written."

"How do I grab hold of all these new realizations and pull them into my life? They're so...big...I'm not sure how they possibly fit."

"Now perhaps you can see why most prophets and mystics were called lunatics. How do you suppose your golfing buddies would react if you tried to tell them about your journey?"

I snorted. "That's not going to happen. I wish I could, though. I wish everyone could see. Could know."

Lucius leaned forward. "What would you like them to know?"

I closed my eyes and drifted back into memories of the leap into the Unknown. I said, "I'd like them to know that there is nothing to fear. That it's safe to let go. I'd like to show them how everything, *everything*, is Love and that what we call life is just a game. None of it really matters. All the stuff I thought was so important turns out to be just stuff. That's it."

"What did you have to pass through before you realized that?" Lucius quietly asked.

Sudden tears wet my lashes. "My whole world shattered. Everything in my life disintegrated and blew away. All my worst fears combined."

"And what was left?"

"Only reality. Only what I've always really wanted. It's as if everything I've searched for my entire life revealed itself, but it wasn't anything like I thought it would be."

"Better? Worse?"

I laughed. "Now you're trying to trick me. There wasn't any better or worse out there."

A seed of knowledge planted itself even as I spoke the words. I didn't know where it came from, but there it was. Lucius nodded. "Yes, let that one grow. How would your realization change things if you could bring it into your life here?"

"Well, I could stop judging everything. Everything out there just *is* and that's enough. It's perfect. Everything is perfect."

"And how do you feel about this idea?"

"It's not possible. Not in this fucked up world." The profanity slipped out before I could catch it. It floated out there in front of me like a turd in a swimming pool. My face flushed. Lucius was unfazed. Maybe he didn't know that word.

"That's how you feel?"

"That's how I feel and that's how it is."

"Is it?"

"Circles," I said, drawing the shape with my finger, "You're making circles again. I feel dizzy. Yes, I think that's how it is."

"You *think* that's how it is? Do you see anything in this statement? A clue?"

"Not really. Not yet."

"That's all right. It may come to you in time. Let's go back. You said you experienced what you've been searching for your entire life. What else can you tell me? Oh, and by the way, I don't care what language you use. Whatever you feel is what I want you to say. Maybe you can't help judging yourself for saying words you call bad, but it's not important to me. What is important is that you feel and speak honestly. Okay?"

"Okay. But, I don't know how to deal with this judgment-free zone, Lucius. It's like walking on the moon or something. Zero gravity. I don't know how to behave and I'm afraid I might do something inappropriate."

"Inappropriate for what?"

I sighed, "It's hard to say. I'm used to filters. Limits. With no boundaries, I might cross some lines that shouldn't be crossed."

"Were there any lines 'out there' as you call it?"

"No, there was only Everything. Only love."

"Were you afraid you would cross some lines, do something inappropriate out there?"

"No, it just isn't possible out there. That's different. There wasn't any separation. There wasn't any point where I ended and Everything began. I couldn't cross lines because everything was one thing." The light began to glow from my soul, I wasn't ready for it. This realization was too bright. I forced my mind's eye to look away before it was scorched.

"If I understand what you're saying, out there you could do no wrong, but back here you can?"

"Yes." Safe again. Some rules.

"What does that tell you about the nature of being, about the true order of things?"

I sat for a couple of breaths. "Um, I don't know."

"You actually do know, Who You Really Are does, I mean. It's perfect to think you don't, though. It's all part of the process. See, you had a taste of Who You Really Are last night. Just a taste. Don't mistake that for the whole thing. There's much more. You've awakened to the fact that you are more than you ever imagined, is that true?"

My mind raced back to that distant point in time a couple of weeks ago, before I met Lucius by my campfire. Today the entire world looked different. I knew I'd never see things the same way again. "Yes, it's true. The whole game has changed. Everything."

"And it will always and forever continue to change. How do you feel about that?"

"Like...I don't know where I'm going anymore."

"Did you ever know? Really?"

"I thought I did. I had plans, goals, dreams. They were written down. I had pictures of them on my vision boards."

"And now?"

"Now I don't know what to think."

"That's perfect. Don't think about it. Just experience. Feel... Act... Breathe... Be... Back to last night for a minute, if you had to describe your experience in just one word, one word that would help you remember the entire journey, what would it be? Don't overthink this. Just say what you feel."

The word was there in my mouth instantly: "Surrender." The memory erupted inside me. I was caught up into All That Is again, the billowing stillness, the vibrating love.

Lucius was quiet and allowed me to soar. After more slow seconds, I shook my head and grinned.

"That's it, isn't it?" he said, "Surrender. Hold that. Let it grow in you. It's all you are asked to do. Answer me this: if you actually lived that way, how would you describe your life?"

"Honest. Brave. Afraid of nothing. At peace. I would be *with* everything that happens in life. I would love everything and everyone for exactly what and who they are."

"And how does that compare to the way you've been living?"

"I've been running. My whole life. I've been trying to outrace time, poverty, my own weakness. Fear. I've been running away from fear."

"How's that working for you? Are you staying ahead? What would happen if you stopped running?"

"Last night happened and I'm not running right any more. But I'm terrified to sit still, because whatever I've been running from is this close to catching me now." I snapped my fingers.

"And if you let it catch you?"

A momentary video clip of hungry flames devouring my possessions flashed up. My stomach knotted. Lucius nodded.

"Right. Everything will burn down to ashes, won't it?" he said.

"That's what I'm afraid of," I said.

"Why do you suppose we created that scene for you? Do you think it was actually necessary to torch your clothes and books?"

"I think you wanted me to experience myself without the props and crutches." *Wow, where did that nugget come from?* I wondered. It rang true, though. I could feel it.

"And how was that for you?"

"It was terrifying. Liberating. I've writing about it all morning, I just don't know how to bring the lessons back to my real life."

Lucius smirked. "How do you know you're going back? Maybe you've died and gone to Heaven."

I gave him my best deadpan look.

He chuckled. "Well, how would you know for sure?"

I thought about this. *Disturbing, but he's right.* I had discovered up-close, first-person the night before, that the universe contains many versions of Reality. Moreover, they all appeared to be only a single blink apart. Close your eyes in one, open them in another. Just like that. Heaven, hell . . . they weren't places. They were simultaneous dreams existing in parallel states of Mind. I had crossed the bridge between them faster than the speed of thought. One reality shattered and as soon as I let go and a new one took its place.

"Remember," he said, "Surrender means walking through doorways marked 'I don't know.' You wouldn't want to explore a couple of ideas with me, would you?"

"What? Of course I do." There was the damn red herring again. He knew exactly how to pull my strings.

"Okay. Buckle your seatbelt. This is your pilot speaking; we will be talking at high altitudes of consciousness. There may be turbulence at times, please remain calm and in your seat for the duration of the flight." We both started laughing.

We spent the next few hours together. I wrote notes in *Emerson's Bible* as fast as I could, but even so, the fabric of wisdom Lucius wove as we talked spread itself beyond the limits of my comprehension. I only captured a bit of the essence. I read my notes later, they were breadcrumbs dropped along the path of memory to lead me back.

> *...when we surrender fully, we can access wisdom of the Super-Mind. That's what I experienced with the instant imprints of knowledge "out there." Some people call this the Akashic Records. Like a vast Library of Consciousness.*
>
> *...the Earth is a palette for creation together, a learning space, a place where Life (All That IS) has the experience of Itself and evolves.*
>
> *...we have carelessly cut off our mystical connections to the Divine Source even as our technology and knowledge has exploded.*
>
> *...the people of Earth are unconsciously moving closer together and striving to give birth to a different kind of collective story.*
>
> *...this birthing is accompanied by terrible pains which will increase as the momentum toward the Great Shift grows.*
>
> *...many individuals are becoming awake to this reality and their combined consciousness serves as a catalyst.*
>
> *...the powerful nations of the Earth would experience the most painful humiliations because they were so invested in their pride and their story.*
>
> *...the stories were breaking up but those most attached to them would have terrible difficulty moving into the new way of living.*
>
> *...I am supposed to experience the passing away of my own story, then hold space in this world for others to do the same.*

I wrote and listened with intense focus. At one point, Lucius touched me on the shoulder and said I should not be so worried. He said it was impossible to grasp it all in one sitting. That he was plowing the ground and planting seeds. He said I would be taught and retaught these lessons in different ways until they became self-evident. This was a comfort. I relaxed and allowed his words to flow through me.

There was a lull in our talking. Lucius stood and stretched, then he clapped his hands together, "Come! It's time we were off. I have someone you need to meet."

"Who's that?" I said.

"He's called by different names. Some people say he's the Hermit. A few call him the Wizard. I think he'd prefer you just call him Jack. Hang on, I have something for you."

He left the room and returned in seconds carrying a bulky knapsack.

"You'll find some clothes in there. Dress yourself and we'll get going. I'll come back in a few minutes." He picked up the breakfast tray and walked out.

Chapter Eighteen

It was almost noon. The sun was high and bright in the sky. We were climbing a trail cut into the round-topped mountain behind the house. During the night and through the morning, a warm wind had blown in and melted some of the snow. Stepping carefully using the chunks of granite that jutted from the path as stairs, I looked out from the top of the world. I now recognized the Sawtooth Mountains' jagged peaks gleaming in the distance with a pure white intensity.

"Indian summer. It's too early for real winter yet, even way up here," Lucius had explained when I stepped out the door and was surprised by the warm air.

My pack was heavy with clothes and food. I was already sweating and my lungs burned trying to keep pace with Lucius. He was carrying a pack even larger than mine, but his steps were light and easy on the trail.

"How far is it?" I asked when he signaled a short rest near the top.

He pointed to a place two ridges over. "See that?"

"What? I see mountains and trees."

"Can't you see the smoke? Over there." He traced his finger in a snaky pattern.

I strained to see. There it was, a faint gray line drifting along the top of a ridge and fading into the sky. It was almost invisible. "What is it?" I asked.

"That's were Jack lives."

"There aren't any roads to his place are there? What does he do way up here?"

"Do? Nobody knows much about what Jack does. He's not a big *doer*. Jack is kind of a mountain monk. Don't tell him I said that, though. He doesn't care for titles."

"But, how does he live? Eat?"

"He's very self-sufficient. He lives on the land and sometimes people visit him. He has no use for money, so in return for the work he does with people, sometimes they bring him food. Why do you think we're carrying all this stuff on our backs?"

The mention of food reminded me that I was hungry. Lucius was one thought ahead of me, as usual and pulled an orange from one of the side pouches of his pack. He handed it to me and I dug into the peel with my fingernails. The sun was warm on my face and a trickle of sweet juice ran down my chin after biting a plump segment. At that moment, I could not imagine wanting to be anywhere else. There was no story, no ringing telephone, no deadlines, no expectations. I looked at Lucius. He was gazing off into the distance and chewing a bite from his own orange.

The sweat on my shaved head felt cooling in the breeze blowing up the side of the mountain. Lucius finished eating, scrubbed his fingers in the snow beside the trail and started walking again.

I had no watch now, but the sun moved with us. I judged it to be about two o'clock by the time we hiked the ridgeline path and started down into the forest. We must have been close to Jack's dwelling because I could smell wood smoke in the air, but there was no visible sign of a house. The trail led into the shadows with deeper snow out of the sun's reach. Small birds chased each other through the dense patches of huckleberry and mountain laurel. A wiry dark squirrel ran to the end of a branch in an aspen tree to scold us as we passed.

We came to a place where the path crossed a creek. Lucius squatted and plunged his cupped hands in to drink. I did likewise and saw raccoon tracks in the wet earth at the water's edge. After more than two hours of hiking with the heavy pack on my back, I was sweating freely. The clothes Lucius gave me wicked the moisture from my skin but I still shivered in the shady forest.

"Up," Lucius said, "Let's keep going."

He crossed the creek in three quick steps on granite boulders just below the surface of the water. I tried the same method but slipped and staggered like a drunken water buffalo in the rocky shallows. Lucius turned back at the sound of my splashing and caught my wrist before I toppled in completely. He hauled me to the bank and helped me sit on a large fallen log while he pulled off my drenched boots. He wrung out the wool socks and handed them back.

"Go ahead, put them on. You won't be comfortable but we aren't far now."

The socks were damp and became resaturated the instant I forced my feet into the wet boots. I lamely tried to squeeze some of the water out of my soaked pant legs.

"Here," Lucius said. He packed handfuls of snow around the sopping wet jeans. When he brushed it away, the denim was damp but not dripping. I would live. I tied the boots and we resumed our descent through the trees. Several minutes passed. I heard wind in the tree tops, a few birds talking amongst themselves and my boots squishing with every step. We came to a round open patch where the light flooded down on a huge flat rock. Lucius pointed to it and I sat, grateful for the warmth.

Lucius also turned his face up to the light and smiled with his eyes closed. "I should warn you a little about Jack," he said.

"Yeah? How so?"

"Well, he's…different. Most of it can't be explained, so I won't try. Just keep your expectations loose. He has a lot to teach you, but you'll really have to go with the flow. He's not much for hand-holding."

"Go with the flow. That seems to be the motto here."

"Yes, but until now I've been spoon-feeding you explanations and spending a lot of time talking. I don't know for sure what Jack will do. You'll need to keep your eyes open. He doesn't always make the lesson obvious. Write in your journal regularly. Keep a record of your impressions."

"Where will you be? Aren't you going to stay with us?" I felt anxiety at the thought that Lucius might be leaving me.

"No, I have some things to attend to elsewhere. You'll be fine." He chuckled to himself.

I started to reply, but that very moment we heard a sudden splintering crash in the woods behind us. I almost levitated from my seat on the rock. My heart pounded loud in my ears. Lucius had his hand on my shoulder.

"Shh," he whispered and nodded toward the direction of the noise. I heard harsh panting and more thumps and loud thrashing in the brush, but still couldn't see anything. Lucius crouched and began to creep, half bent over, into a stand of aspens. He turned and motioned to me. "Come on," he mouthed. It seemed like such a bad idea.

Whatever was out there sounded huge, powerful and probably angry. Lucius was already disappearing into the thicket and I didn't want to be left alone. I followed him, doing my best to avoid stepping on dry branches that might snap and draw the attention the creature crashing about. We moved through the tangle of brush and trees. I saw a flash of motion up ahead. Something about the size of a small horse was rearing and struggling. I glimpsed patches of tan and dark brown fur between the thin trunks of the aspens.

Lucius, still hunched over, ran and took cover behind a huge tree. He turned and jerked his head, telling me to hurry up. I joined him on hands and knees and looked around the massive trunk that hid us. Now I could see it was an elk, maybe a yearling. His antlers were short spikes with a few shreds of velvet hanging from their base. He was performing a crazy dance around a bending aspen sapling. He rolled his eyes and let out a harsh bellow that rang loud in the forest. His breath came in short huffs. Then I saw the rope around its neck. It was made of braided leather and tied to the top of the small tree. We were only ten feet away. The colors of the scene were made vibrant with drama and adrenaline.

"Snare," Lucius said close to my ear, "Watch now." He pointed to the right of the young elk. Low to the ground, I saw a lump of something purple moving toward the animal. I shook my head and looked again. Now the lump was standing up. It was a man. He sprang on the elk's back with his arms around its neck. The terrified animal suddenly stopped thrashing and surrendered. Like a program on the Discovery Channel I'd seen showing a gazelle give up the fight in its last moments—when the cheetah's jaws clamp down on the back of its neck.

A fountain of steaming blood spurted out and stained the bent sapling. The big creature bucked and tore at the air with its front legs, then went still. The man held the elk with a kind of tenderness and spoke a few words to the sky before easing the animal down on the trampled snow. He turned, hands covered in bloody hair and I almost laughed.

The moment was intense with primal fierceness, but this bearded man was draped in what must have once been a very fat woman's purple velvet bathrobe. He thrust his arms out to push the sleeves back and I saw he held a dripping knife.

Lucius stood up. His motion caught the man's attention. He turned and glared in our direction. Lucius raised his hand.

"Jack!"

The man's face softened as his eyes focused on us and he grinned wide, revealing his missing upper teeth. "Hey, brother! Who's this with you?" He pointed at me with his knife.

Lucius started to answer but Jack turned back to the fallen elk and yelled over his shoulder, "Help me with this, will you? You fellas came along at a good time."

By the time we leaned our packs against a log, Jack had untied the rawhide rope from the sapling and started cutting a long slit in the young bull's abdomen from anus to throat. "Each a you grab a leg," he said, grunting with his effort. Lucius and I pulled the elk to its back and held the legs apart to make Jack's work easier. He field-dressed the animal, leaving its entrails in a steaming heap. He showed us how to pack snow into the body cavity to dissipate the heat. Jack carefully wrapped the heart and liver in a large bandana and set them aside to cool in a snow bank. Done.

We all took a break. Jack sat on a stump and found a mostly clean patch on the back of his hand to rub his nose. I got a good look at him.

Jack's hair hung down on his shoulders in gray strands. He wore a rusty black beret with a single eagle feather stuck into the front at a fascinating angle. He had parted his beard into two braids that dangled nearly to his waist in front of an ancient Grateful Dead T-shirt. He reached down and washed his hands in the snow, then wiped them on his often-repaired jeans.

Then Jack pushed the purple robe aside and fiddled with a beaded leather pouch that hung from a cord around his neck. I noticed two tiny brass bells hanging from a belt loop. He produced a small rectangle of paper and a pinch of shredded tobacco. Lucius and I watched him lick one edge of the paper, sprinkle the tobacco in a line down the middle and then roll it up. He stuck it in the corner of his mouth and fished in the sagging pocket of his bathrobe for a box of matches.

Jack struck a flame, drew on the cigarette and leaned back with the sun on his weather-stained face. He released twin streams of smoke through his nostrils. I was amazed by the sense of raw, blissful beingness radiating from this strange man. He was fully immersed in his moment and didn't appear to remember that he had two visitors seated nearby watching him. The smell of burning tobacco infused the air and immediately brought back the memory of the old Medicine Man with his ceremonial pipe the night before.

"Jack, I brought Jacob here to stay with you for awhile," Lucius said. "He has some things to learn that only you can teach."

This brought him out of his reverie. He popped one fierce blue eye open to look at me while squeezing the other eye shut against the smoke in his face. He cocked a frosty eyebrow, frowned and looked at Lucius. A few beats passed. He drew on the crooked cigarette again then shifted his gaze to me.

"I ain't sure that I want him here," he said.

This bald statement felt like an invisible hand had just smacked me on the back of my head. I was usually welcomed and appreciated. I was somewhat famous for having friends everywhere. I was a friendly guy. *No one gets to not like me at first glance,* I thought. *Who is this old buzzard, anyway? He must not know that I've been chosen by Lucius to wake up and be a messenger.*

"That is e'zactly the shit I'm talking about," Jack said and tried to spit a speck of tobacco off the end of his tongue. *Pthh! Pthh!*

My eyes widened in alarm. *Oh, great. He can read my mind, too.*

"Yep," Jack said and squinted down at the tip of his tongue as he picked off the offending shred with his thumb and forefinger.

Lucius held up his hand. "Jack, please. I know I didn't ask you first, but we're moving him along. He needs a dose of what you can give him."

The ridiculous old guy closed his eyes and took a long drag on his cigarette. It had grown so short that I was sure he'd singe his wispy mustache. *I hope he does. It'd serve him right,* I thought but then caught myself. *Sorry about that. I didn't really mean it.*

Jack roared with sudden laughter. The stumpy end of his cigarette flew out and sizzled in the snow. He flapped his arms wide, making me think of a giant purple bat trying to take flight.

"Damn! I gotcha," he said. Lucius was laughing, too. They cackled and hooted. I joined in after a few seconds. I was relieved. Jack gasped for air and wiped tears from his cheeks.

He stood up. "Come on you two bag-a-bones. Let's drag this elk back to my place before it gets any later." *Guess that means I'm in,* I thought.

"We'll see about that," Jack yelled back over his shoulder. He was already striding back to where the young bull was stiffening in the bloody snow. I hoisted my pack and followed him.

In minutes, Lucius and the old mountain man crafted a rough travois from two aspen saplings and trussed the elk on it. I imagined the animal must weigh at least a couple of hundred pounds, maybe more, even with all the innards removed. I hoped Jack didn't live far away.

It may have taken only half an hour, but I was scratched, sweaty and exhausted by the time we reached the clearing. Jack had handed me the rope and said, "Here. You're young and strong. You pull the sled. I'll carry your pack." When I first put the rope over my shoulder and leaned into the load, I thought it was impossible. I bent my back and dug in with my toes. The ends of the poles that bore the weight of the elk scraped forward in the snow a few inches. Sweat collected between my shaved eyebrows and ran down the ridge of my nose.

Lucius and Jack had already started walking ahead. I pulled with all my might and the load moved some more. I found if I concentrated my attention on my legs, they became like pistons in an engine. *Push. Push. Push.* A foot at a time, I was making progress. I couldn't see the other men, but I could hear their voices ahead of me. After twenty yards, I stopped to catch my breath and looked back over my shoulder. I saw an enormous black bird with an ugly red-skinned head descending through the trees to the scene of the fresh kill. *Vulture*, I thought. *That was fast.*

Each step was impossible but I kept going somehow. My lungs burned and I felt resentful every time I heard Jack cackle up ahead on the trail as he talked with Lucius. *I shouldn't be the only one to haul this thing. This isn't fair.*

I smelled the smoke from Jack's chimney before I noticed that I had caught up with my companions. I had pulled the dead weight on the travois with my head down and teeth gritted for the last ten minutes. Several times, lost in effort, sharp branches that reached across the trail scratched my face. The pain almost brought tears to my eyes. *Story of my life*, I thought. *Always getting myself in situations where I do all the work and end up hurting.* I entertained several cycles of angry thoughts before I realized that Jack and Lucius were right in front of me. They stood in a small clearing that had the marks of human habitation. I noticed the house first. *Surely, surely he doesn't live in there.*

Jack and Lucius stopped talking. "I surely do live in there," Jack called over his shoulder. We all turned to look. Like Jack himself, the house was a bizarre caricature. It was, in fact, a school bus backed into the side of a hill. On the sides of the bus was a vivid psychedelic mural. A covered porch was built over the spot where the door had been. It extended down half the length of the vehicle and I saw a hammock hanging between two of the supporting posts. The door itself now appeared to be made from two-by-fours and a sheet of rusty corrugated metal roofing.

The back of the bus was concealed inside the earth. At one point, someone must have dug it in and mounded dirt over it. Bushes and wild grass covered the scar, giving the impression the weird dwelling had sprouted directly out of the hill. A chimney stuck out of a hole in a sheet of tin over what had been a window. Smoke drifted up from it in a lazy stream and disappeared into the blue mountain sky.

On the other side of the clearing were traces of a long-abandoned road. The surrounding forest had nearly reclaimed it. I imagined that it was once a logging track. I was glad to see the remnants of this road because it gave me a logical solution for how the school bus had ever made it here. Otherwise, I might be forced to conclude that it had actually popped up on its own like a rainbow-colored mushroom. In the clearing was a large timber-frame tripod with a block-and-tackle assembly.

Jack turned to me and said, "Well? Let's get that meat hung up. Haul it over there." He pointed to a hook that dangled from the end of the rope on the hoist. Standing there, my muscles had relaxed, when I tried to move my load again, they rebelled. My legs cramped and I would have collapsed had I not been leaning against the rope. Jack and Lucius were already climbing onto the low porch. *Damn them*, I thought, *I'm struggling here.* I immediately tried to unthink these words, but knew it was too late when I saw my two guides shaking their heads laughing at me.

I breathed deep, closed my eyes and summoned every last shred of willpower. *PUSH!* That burst of energy propelled me forward faster than I had anticipated and I nearly fell on my face. The snow in the clearing was slushy but my toes found enough grip so I could cover the last few feet to my goal. I rested against one of the slanting poles and allowed the rope to slide down my back. *Ahhhh...*

Lucius and Jack came down from the porch and unstrapped the elk from the travois while I wandered into the trees to find a place to pee. By the time I returned to the clearing, they had hauled the big animal into the air, suspended from the hook by its hind legs. Jack patted the swinging carcass on the rib cage.

"That worked out nice," he said, "I been eating rabbits and ground squirrels for weeks. Looks like them hunters down below finally forced the elk back up here into the high country. I'm grateful to have this guy." He looked at me, "You'll be happy, too. I have a hunch you wouldn't like my rodent stew much."

My face twitched involuntarily.

Lucius dusted off his hands and looked at us. "Well, I better be on my way. I have other people to visit for a few days. You two have fun."

Jack sniffed and spat on the ground. I opened my mouth to beg Lucius to take me with him, then thought better of it. He patted me on the back, grinned at us both and clapped his hands. He vanished right before our eyes leaving me open-mouthed. I knew that sort of thing must be possible for him, but it was the first time he had displayed his abilities.

Jack grunted and shook his head. "Damned parlor tricks," he said.

Chapter Nineteen

"You smoke?" he asked as he assembled another of his little cigarettes. We were seated in ragged old camp chairs in the sun. The late afternoon air was mild and smelled of autumn leaves and melting snow.

"Just cigars. Never did try cigarettes," I said.

"Huh," he said, "Gimme a minute." He pushed out of his chair and disappeared inside the house. A couple of minutes passed and he reappeared. He was grinning and chuckling, pleased with himself. "Here, give this a puff." He held out a cigar. I was surprised. It looked well preserved. I took it and bit the end cap off with my teeth. A cutter would have been nice, but that seemed like a lot to ask. He handed me his box of matches and I lit up, turning the cigar in the flame until the end glowed.

"Thank you," I said.

He nodded. "Sure. It's Cuban. I got some off a guy who visited me a while back. Any good?"

I drew on it and released a cloud of smoke into the sunshine. It smelled wonderful.

"Perfect," I said.

We sat back and enjoyed the warmth on our skin. I stole a glance at him and couldn't help but smile. He was sprawled in his chair, the purple bathrobe draped open. His pants were hiked up to reveal he was wearing cowboy boots without any socks. His eyes were closed and he held his crumpled cigarette to his lips. He puffed with more pleasure than I had ever seen on the face of any partier in the most lavish Las Vegas nightclubs. After a while, he dropped the smoldering butt on the ground and seemed to fall asleep. I sat and observed the surroundings in silence.

Despite the overall eccentricity of the man and his dwelling, I saw that he had created a simple, functional order in the wilderness. Between two trees on the edge of the clearing, he had built a lean-to and under it were several cords of stacked firewood. The remains of a summer garden poked up through the snow. A large, weathered copper pipe stuck out of the hillside. A stream of water poured from the end of it into a rock basin that, in turn, drained into an irrigation ditch. *A real-live Robinson Crusoe, this guy.*

Wonder why I'm really here now, I thought.

"Ain't that the question most people try to figure out their entire lives?"

I looked at him. His eyes were still closed but he was scratching at the thin hair under the front edge of his beret. The eagle feather waggled up and down.

"What? Oh...no. What I mean is, what am I doing here with you? Everything else has been so otherworldly. No offense, but you seem pretty normal, down-to-earth."

He huffed and frowned. "Well, I been reading your mind haven't I? That ain't completely normal."

This made me laugh. "Far be it from me to suggest you're normal. It's just that..."

He interrupted me, "It's just that spiritual stuff is supposed to come out of people who look a certain way, ain't it?" He had me there. "I suggest you just pay attention. Quit thinking so much. Out here, you can learn a lot by being quiet with your eyes open. Hell, even with your eyes closed. Try it. Close your eyes and keep your mouth shut awhile."

I took a big pull on the cigar, closed my eyes and blew out a cloud of smoke.

Seconds passed. Nothing. Not a single sound. It was eerie. I discovered that I was holding my breath, that all creation was holding its breath around me. Then, far away to my left I heard a crow. Caw, Caw, Caw! With that, it seemed a great symphony director waved his baton to start the concert. Wind blew through the tops of the fir trees. My heart beat audibly in my ears. Drops of water splashed like liquid notes of music from the copper pipe. I felt my body swaying in time with the natural rhythm of everything. Warmth grew in my belly and spread throughout my chest. I kept my eyes closed.

A pair of birds fluttered past and chased each other into the bushes behind me. I heard them chattering as they played. Jack must have stood up. The little bells on his belt loops jingled. I heard footsteps in the soft snow, the door squeaked open and banged shut. Then, clanging pots and pans. I kept my eyes closed and breathed.

I found myself in a strange borderland. I was between the sensory banquet—the sounds, scents and tactile richness of a sunny afternoon—and the universe of Silence barely concealed behind the veil. The sheer energy of the encroaching All-Nothingness was both magnetic and terrifying. I thought that I heard Kaitlyn whisper from the cosmic wilderness. *"Breathe,"* she said. *"Bre-e-e-a-a-the... Surrender."*

I did. *Breathe in...relax. Breathe out...relax.* Rather than push me back into my chair and normal awareness, however, this exercise cleared my confusion. The prickling fear evaporated from my spine and I allowed Silence to possess me. It flowed in and filled my body. All the external sensations remained, but they grew distant and muted. I felt myself bathing in mysterious ecstasy, the undercurrent of All That Is in a realm beyond thought.

I could still hear my mind chattering to itself, but its voice was not my own. It seemed to be merely tuning in to a ceaseless frequency. It was like a tiny internal newscaster reading from an endless teleprompter of thoughts. I sat and watched this knowledge emerge. A question formed: *If I didn't originate the thoughts, where do they come from?* The newscaster began reading louder, trying to drown out this consideration: "And in other news, your-nose-is-itching...wonder-what-Jack's-doing... you-should-probably-get-up-and-see-if-you-can-help-with-something...isn't-that-a-bird-out-there?...hey-what's-that-coming-up-behind-you?"

"*Shh...*" Kaitlyn's whisper came again. I turned away from the incessant voice and allowed Silence to blossom. The cigar dropped from my fingers and extinguished itself with a sizzle in the snow. I paid no attention.

"You wanna come back and have something to eat now?"

My eyes popped open and zigzagged. It was like someone turned the volume knob on my head to full-blast normal awareness. The jolt was abrupt. I squinted and my eyes focused on Jack, who was staring at me with his face just a few inches from mine. I smelled tobacco, woodsmoke and food odors coming from his clothes. He grinned and shook one of my knees.

"What'd I tell you? Lot happens when you do nothing and listen. You ready to eat?"

I nodded and squeezed my hands. I felt like I was slowly materializing back into my camp chair, growing dense and solid again. And I was hungry. Jack disappeared into the house. He came back carrying two pie tins. He handed one to me and sat down with his. The makeshift plate was warm in my hands. I looked at its contents. Some kind of dark meat was accompanied by roasted potatoes and carrots. Whatever it was smelled good. I was ready to eat but didn't have a fork.

"Just eat it," Jack said, "I got no silverware. Go find a sharp twig to spear stuff if you can't stand eating with your fingers."

I gave it a try. It was different. My mother's family had enjoyed the last generation of old money. She had drilled proper etiquette into me so thoroughly that this felt like a violation of the Ten Commandments. I pinched a dripping chunk of meat and stuck it in my mouth. Trickles of broth ran down my fingers so I licked them. I glanced at Jack to see if he had noticed my *faux pas*. He was busy chewing.

After a while, he looked at me. "You got nobody to impress up here."

"But I..."

"You're always thinking about how you look to other people. There ain't nobody here but you and me. You think I'm worried about your table manners?" He grinned and some potatoes showed through the spaces where his top teeth should have been.

"No, but..."

"But nothing, son. Ain't nothing wrong with manners except when they become a prison. You been running your whole life by rules, rules, rules. Other people's rules. You think you got no choice in the matter. Time you broke a few rules just to see how it feels. You gotta live your own life. Quit worrying about what other people think all the time."

"That's easier said than done."

"Yep."

We ate for a while. The food was good.

"Jack, this is delicious. What is it?"

"Elk heart. I roasted it while you were being quiet. Didn't know I'd have that much time. You were gone for awhile."

"Well, thanks. It's great. May I ask a question?"

He sniffed, "You already did. You want to ask another one?"

"Uh, yes. Is that okay?"

"Spit it out. We're wasting time. Say something. What do we got to lose?"

Crotchety old bastard, I thought, then cringed. No private thought was safe from him.

"Okay. How did you get up here? I mean, can you tell me your story?" I looked around the clearing, "It looks like it might be interesting."

"Interesting, how?"

Frustrated, I gestured with my hands. "I don't know. You live like a hermit in a school bus that could have come straight out of Bob Marley's marijuana dreams. You have a...unusual style of dressing. Lucius said that you have a lot to teach me and I believe him, but the pieces are hard to put together. I want to know..."

"You want to know if I took a certain path to get here. You want some facts that would help you believe what I say, don't you? You want to be sure my papers are all in order."

I thought it over, then nodded. "I can't argue with that. I'm going to be blunt and tell you that you seem too weird to teach me much. We speak totally different languages." That sounded harsh, I hoped he wouldn't take offense.

He carefully set his pie-tin plate on the ground and took off his beret. He scratched his head and squinted up at the sun. It was nearly touching the mountain tops and the air had grown crisp. He nodded to himself and looked back at me.

"Okay. Looks like we gotta do this. I was hoping there'd be another way. Get up."

"What?"

"Get up. Give me your plate." I handed it over. "Now, take your clothes off."

No way! I thought, *No way, no way, no way!* I started shaking my head.

"Do it. Now."

"I can't, Jack. I mean. Really?"

"Yes, really. You think I ain't seen a penis before. Nobody else up here to worry about. Do you trust me?"

"No. Not very much."

"Fair enough. You trust Lucius?"

"Yes."

"Okay, well then, he wouldn't have left you with me for no good reason. You got a choice to make. Follow my instructions or leave."

"What are we going to do when my clothes are off?"

He sighed. "I know this is tough, but you just got to do what I say."

The moment of truth. If I obeyed his orders, I had no idea what would happen. If I refused, I was pretty sure it would mean failing an important test. Still...

My fingers found the zipper of the jacket Lucius gave me earlier that day. *Am I really doing this?* Piece by piece, my clothes came off.

"Boots, too," he said.

No point arguing. I untied the boots and pulled them off, my damp socks still inside. I stood there hugging my chest and shivering. The tender skin of my privates shriveled in the cold. *What happens now?*

Jack held my bundled clothes in his arms and pointed to the woods with his chin. The two braids of his beard swung along with his movements. "Go out there. I'll come find you in the morning."

"But, I can't...Jack, I'll die out there! You want me to spend the night in the woods—naked?"

"It's the only way," he said.

Goosebumps prickled the hairs on my legs and back. The snow burned under my feet. I looked out toward the edge of the woods, beyond the dead elk swinging from the engine hoist. Ominous. *This is madness!* "Seriously, Jack, I could die."

"You could," he said.

"What about animals? There are wolves up here."

"That there are," he nodded.

We stood there looking at each other. The time for arguing had come to an end, I could see it in his eyes. I shrugged in disbelief and turned to go. *Might as well get this nightmare started.* I felt Jack's hand on my shoulder so looked back at him.

"You know the way," he said. His fierce furry eyebrows drew together. "Breathe and surrender. Go within. You'll find what you need." He gave me a push and a wink. "You'll probably be okay." He was chuckling to himself as he trudged through the snow toward his warm house — carrying my clothes.

The situation was ridiculous and terrifying. If it's possible to be naked-er than naked, I was. I was humiliated, confused and breathless with rising panic. *Breathe, he had said.* I gulped some air. The sun was a dim glow at the tree tops. I was standing in the long-blue shadows cast by the forest. A gust moved across the open snow and wrapped itself around my body. I took one step toward the woods and then another. The snow crystals were hardening as the warmth of the sun disappeared. They crunched underfoot and scraped the sensitive skin on the sides of my feet. *Maybe I'll survive somehow if I just keep moving all night long.*

Chapter Twenty

The next couple of hours were painful and terrifying. The cold as it turned out, was the least of my problems. Demons of panic swirled around my head and I found myself running through the trees in the gathering darkness. I couldn't catch my breath and my heart pounded in my chest as terrible thoughts overwhelmed me. I knew better than to lose my head, but knowing and doing are different things—especially when the poison of fear has entered your bloodstream. In blind confusion I ran, seeking shelter, seeking sanity.

I tried to recall old survival lore. Stories I had read about trappers and Indians who used their wits to endure impossible situations. All memory of their techniques fled before me, just beyond the fingertips of my mind. The shadows of the forest were very dark when I tripped over a fallen fir tree and crashed through its branches. Sharp twigs and icy crust tore at my skin as I fell and rolled on to my back. I was exhausted and lay still, panting and surprised to find sweat running down my chest. Snow on my body stung, but under my back I felt softer matted fir needles and dry grasses. I looked up to see the trunk of the tree above my face angling like a tent ridge. I wriggled to my side and rested on an elbow to peer through the sheltering branches.

It was a natural lean-to. I couldn't sit up, but I could rest for here, protected from the night winds that sighed through the trees.

I pulled a few sticks from beneath my hip bones and worked my body deeper under the low canopy. Some dry needles showered down and caught in the hair on my legs. I rested my head on my arms. *Surrender and breathe, the old coot said. At least I can breathe for now.* I drew a deep, shaky breath and held it. A few more breaths steadied me. I closed my eyes and took stock. I wasn't comfortable. Still freezing. I was also certain my skin was lacerated from falling through the sharp branches. I was totally exhausted. It had been quite a day, the long hike, hauling the dead elk and now—this naked venture into the night. *What can I possibly learn from this?*

I considered for awhile and lay very quiet. My exertion still warmed me but the sweat turned cold as it dried on my skin. Night had grown dark around me. Without warning, thoughts of my wife entered my mind, no doubt she was at home in our warm bed. For some reason, this rattled my sense of safety in the cocoon of branches and snow. I didn't move, but my body shuddered and thoughts raced.

Seriously? What the hell am I doing? I pictured my children, with their sweet faces. How many days had it been since I had given them a hug? I had lost track of time. *If I die out here and never get to see them again...* A wave of self pity crested inside me and my eyes stung.

What the...? I must be nuts. My life was going great. Well, at least it was better than lying naked under a dead tree out in the snow. Where's this going anyway?

My heart was pounding again. My breath came fast. *Pointless. This is all pointless.*

On my left leg, down by the ankle, something started creeping on my skin. I conjured a spider in my imagination immediately. *A black widow.* My whole body was rigid with terror. I wanted to leap out of my shallow cave, brush the horrible creature into the snow and stomp it to death. I felt it moving up my leg and tried to be completely still. I imagined myself twitching and the alarmed spider burying her fangs in my flesh. Fatally poisoned, I would die out here under this fallen tree in the snow. Coyotes and buzzards would eat my body. My bones would be scattered through the forest. *What a sad, meaningless way to die.*

The spider crept up my calf. I was sure I could feel its tiny arachnid feet moving through the hairs on my leg. I couldn't catch my breath, cold sweat sprang out on my back. I was shivering but trying not to move. It was a waking nightmare of the finest order. I shook my head and sharp pain stabbed the skin behind my left ear. I had forgotten that I was in a cave of sharp, broken twigs.

"Ouch!" I yelled. My voice and the pain shattered the terror-reveries. The spider disappeared. I lay very still and held my breath. Nothing. Sweat prickled my skin but I dared not move. Seconds passed. No spider. It was almost worse. Before, I knew for sure that I had a poisonous creature crawling on me. Now, I wasn't certain if it had ever been there or if I was hallucinating. Maybe it was climbing through the twigs and I'd feel its feet tickle my neck soon.

I was angry. Angry with myself and at Jack. On one hand, I was not receiving the lesson he had intended, but why the hell did he need to be so tricky about teaching it? He was both rough and subtle at the same time. One thing was clear, I needed to pass some sort of test out here alone. Jack's ultimatum was still fresh in my mind, "Follow my instructions, or leave." *Yes, but what exactly were his instructions? He was vague about everything except the fact that I had to walk around naked all night.* I really needed to figure this out. I knew that I was on the threshold of something critical, but the door I was knocking on refused to open.

Breathe and go within… I remembered that part and tried to obey. I was shivering in the aftermath of my encounter with the spider—real or imagined. With every breath, I tried to visualize warmth saturating my body, but I couldn't stop shaking. *Go within.* I closed my eyes and used all my will power to focus on memories of the fire in the middle of the sacred circle the night before. *If I could only return to that feeling!*

Just recreating those sensations in my imagination brought some peace. I followed the shining trails of thought back to the instant when I stepped off the edge of rationality and plunged upward into the arms of All That Is.

Light glowed brighter within me and breathing came more easily. *There is no fear in Love. Perfect Love casteth out fear...* Over and over, these words circulated through my mind. *No fear...perfect love...casteth out fear...* I was barely aware of my circumstances now. My body felt radiant and every breath filled me with greater buoyancy. Currents of Source energy swirled though me. As the light filled my body, fear vanished. A round orb of warmth formed near my solar plexus and began to grow.

I can't remember how I came to be standing outside my shelter. All I know is that I walked upright through the forest and was not afraid. Perhaps I shined with physical light so bright that it illuminated my path. Maybe the inner glow superseded my need for normal vision. The woods were transformed and became a charmed garden. In this state of awareness, the flow of all Life was tangible to my senses. I leaned against the trunk of an unusually large tree. With no surprise, I noticed that it was a giant oak. This should have given me pause because oaks are not indigenous to the high altitudes of that area. Instead, it seemed quite natural that it should be there. I pressed my back against its bark and felt myself merge with the energy of the tree.

Not only was I one with the fiber and sinew of the ancient trunk, I was absorbed by the essential tree-ness of its consciousness. I raised my arms and found them reaching for the sky in much the same pattern as the limbs of the great oak above me. My fingers splayed in the moonlight and I breathed along with the tree itself. A breeze moved through the branches and I also swayed. A fresh taste filled my mouth and I imagined it must be the sap seeping through me. Then the tree began to speak, not with words but with deep, eloquent silence. On some non-verbal level, I was communing with the tree.

Telling the story now, I know this sounds weird and hard to believe. At the time, it was the most natural thing to do, like chatting with a friend on a sunny park bench in late spring. I followed the tree's story as it wound backward in time, back to the first green sprig of leaves that had sprung up from the mountain soil. Back to the acorn dropped from the beak of a mischievous raven. I felt nourishment flowing upward from the roots that dug deep beneath the soil and wrapped themselves around enormous granite boulders. I saw the changing seasons, years upon years layered on top of each other. Birds built their nests in our branches, deer and elk rested in the shade beneath our leaves.

Without hearing any sounds, I felt my mouth forming slow words in a language I couldn't understand. It was strange, though. Something about being captured by this ancient giant silenced my racing thoughts. Standing there, enveloped by the living flesh of the old tree, I watched thought forms passing before me but my mind was immune to their energy. I could observe them moving, but was not required to participate or attach myself to them. One peculiarly dazzling bundle of thought-energy floated close. I read it, "*You are not your thoughts. You are greater than what you know as your mind.*" It began to move away, but I summoned all my focus and held it there a few moments more. To my great surprise—that worked. In fact, I appeared to be exerting magnetic force on it.

The scintillating mini-nova of truth reversed its path on the breeze, it moved back and stopped just inches before my face. I had a sudden intuition that I must fully absorb this "knowing." I focused on it. It drew nearer, its light warming my forehead and eyelids. I read it again, "*You are not your thoughts. You are greater than what you know as your mind.*" This shining realization floated in place before me, held in place by my intent. It was both inviting and austere. I knew it must enter and become part of me and that it would change my life forever if I allowed it to do so.

Nevertheless, there was no doubt that this must be one of the lessons I was meant to receive. I grew even more still than before and from deep within, a command issued. "Come!" The ball of light moved in a slow circle for a moment and then I felt its magnetic force touch the center of my forehead. All at once, I exploded with light. The tree was rocked by what felt like a bolt of lightning and I stood there swaying along with it. Powerful currents of energy ran through me from top to bottom and back again. The stunning realization spread throughout my consciousness like a benevolent virus. It's one thing to read the words and accept them on a rational level, but quite another to experience their truth in a way that transcends human comprehension.

I rested in the power of this revelation for a long time. Thought patterns continued to float by. However, I sat back—a detached observer who simply watched. I somersaulted backward into blissful unconsciousness. Yet, even without thought, my powerful underlying Awareness was present and awake. It may have been hours, or perhaps only minutes, that I stood there embraced by the great oak tree.

After a time, something made me look down. What I saw gave me a tremendous shock. Seated at the base of the tree, legs crossed and arms resting lightly on his knees—was my body. The few threads of sanity that anchored me to my earthbound self drew tight and threatened to break. I almost wanted them to go ahead and break to let the Self I was discovering fly away...fly free into the night.

I don't remember sitting down. In fact, I had not. This was confusing. I was standing, but my body was sitting. *Wonder if I can move?* I waved one arm, my body stayed still. This was weird. My body exerted gravity on me and I had to concentrate to stay detached. I circled around in front of the seated form. His—my eyes were closed. *Perhaps I'm dead. No... Obviously, I'm not dead but is this how death works? Maybe I can't go back to this body...maybe I can't return to my wife and children?* I watched for several long moments. The figure of a man, of my body, was quiet. I leaned close and saw his chest moving in and out very lightly. *Still breathing.* Okay.

I smiled at the naked bald man sitting in the snow that covered the great tree's roots. He was overweight and showed signs of premature aging that come with the stress of modern life. I sat in front of him and loved him. Every cell, every forehead wrinkle, all of him. I saw now that my body was just a vehicle for this transcendent energy of my true Self. I hadn't been taking very good care of my vessel.

A few more minutes passed. A question presented itself. *If you are not your body, then who are you?* At the moment, I couldn't come up with an answer for that one. My experiences over the last two weeks had infused me with direct knowledge that human beings are much more powerful and mysterious than they imagine. This was no longer a self-help theory or a cool idea. It was a knowing that swelled within like a sea tide under the full moon.

Language weaves the fabric of our memories. I recalled the concept. It came rumbling through my being with thunderclap force in the words, "*You...are...more.*"

The Energy-of-Self I was experiencing at that moment blazed with radiant light. I turned away from the motionless bundle of my flesh and observed the dark forest around me. The huge oak tree grew alone in the center of a round clearing. Light gleamed on the trunks of the tall fir trees standing like sentries around the circle. I looked to find the source of this light, but there was no one else present. I moved toward the trees and the light moved with me.

I looked to the sky but could see no obvious source of the radiance. Transfixed by joy, I stood and allowed the light to pulsate through me. Difficult as it is to explain, I knew then...without any question...

"*I am a radiant beam of light from God in this world!*" The words burst within, liquid sunshine in the still mountain night.

Impossible!

Preposterous!

Blasphemous!

Like doubt-arrows, those thoughts tried to pierce me. Yet in that resplendent moment, I was impervious and filled with wonder. I was giddy with joy. Stars in the galaxy called my name and my irresistible light answered them in a language that perhaps only angels can translate.

In deep worshipful dance for this marvel, All That Is pulsated around and above and below and within me.

How long this continued, I don't know. I basked and reveled in the absolute one-ness of all things. The entire planet was transformed into a temple. Every sight, sound and texture was holy. Every human was a fellow priest or priestess in the grand ceremony of existence.

I awoke inside my body under the oak tree's spreading limbs. The new day's first light broke over the peaks of the mountains. I was still seated with my palms and face turned to greet the sun. My eyes opened and I moved them back and forth—signaling that I was in control of my nervous system again, at least a little. With great care, I pushed myself to all fours. Then, I rose slowly to my feet. I felt the snow under my toes and rubbed my palm against the rough bark of the tree that steadied me. A breeze sighed and with it came a freshness from the sparkling dawn.

Then I remembered glimmers from the night before and started to run. I had to find Jack. I didn't need directions now.

I ran, laughing out loud.

Chapter Twenty One

Jack looked around the corner of his school bus house and grinned at me.

What a spectacle I must have presented, running through the tall dry grass at the edge of his clearing. Waving my arms wildly with the glorious rising sun behind me. And of course, I was still naked. Jack's head disappeared and I heard his door squeak open. I stood and closed my eyes. The sun warmed my back and I found myself swaying to music that only I could hear.

"Moses...come on back now, Moses." I opened my eyes. Jack was right in front of me holding a large blanket. His eyes laughed and he shook his head.

"Here, let's get you covered up. Running around rowdy like that with no clothes on..." he unfolded the blanket and wrapped it around my shoulders, "Did you get into a fight with a cougar? You're scratched all-to-hell back here."

I accepted the blanket. It felt good to be covered again, but I honestly had not given the cold or exposure any thought. Not since I stood up in a trance at the fallen tree shelter the night before.

I followed Jack up his porch steps and realized that I hadn't been inside the unusual house yet. My arrival yesterday seemed like a long time ago already. Since I got in the truck with Lucius, the revelations of each passing day were dramatic. I could see why he had said it might be hard to return to my former life. My perspectives were shifting radically right before my eyes.

"Well, you going to come in here or what?" Jack's voice startled me. I shook myself and discovered I was standing at the threshold in a daze.

"Yeah, I just," my voice trailed off.

"You just, what?" Jack put his hand on my shoulder and guided me through the doorway.

The room spun and Jack must have felt me get wobbly. He put his arm around me and helped me into another canvas chair.

"Here, close your eyes and sit a minute. You been through a lot. I'll fix up some tea. We'll talk in a bit."

My eyes were already drifting shut by this time and I gave him a faint nod. He shuffled off and I slipped into a hazy slumber.

I don't remember dreaming anything in particular. Instead of a storyline, I swam through realms of billowing energy that tossed and cradled me like the waves of a living ocean.

I may have slept hours, but I suspect it was less than fifteen minutes. I woke under the startling gaze of the old man. He was seated in a chair across from me holding a cup of steaming tea to his lips and looking at me over its rim. I blinked a few times and wiped my mouth with the back of my hand. Jack didn't say anything but kept looking at me, holding eye contact. We sat like that for long moments. Finally, I swallowed and tried to speak. My voice came out in a loud croak. Jack stood, shook his head and waved his fingers to silence me. He ambled toward the back of his converted school bus where a flimsy wall hid what passed for a kitchen. He returned with a second cup of tea. I took it from him and nearly dropped it in my lap. The enameled metal cup was hot and I realised I was shivering under the blanket.

Jack stood across the room, fiddling with something on a ledge. I heard a match flare and soon the scent of incense filled the room. I sipped tea and looked around. The interior of his little home was small. A realtor might have advertised it as a "cozy nook tucked away in the pristine wilderness," but it was really just a gutted school bus backed into the side of a mountain. It was stripped down to the metal and I could see that whoever had converted it had not bothered with insulation or any kind of wall finish. It wasn't needed. The room was warm, too warm, from the heat of an ancient wood stove that was also Jack's only kitchen appliance.

The windows were mostly painted over from the outside and the sun glowed through bright colors. I looked toward the front of the vehicle and saw that Jack had left the steering wheel and driver's seat in place. It appeared to be his creative cockpit. He had stacks of books piled on the floor and a beat-up guitar hanging from a screw. The windshield was not painted, but Jack had strung an old shower curtain from side to side. It was pulled back and I saw the glittering morning light reflecting on the patchy snow in the clearing.

"Well, what do you know," the old man's voice was raspy in the quiet room. I looked at him. We grinned at each other.

"You didn't die out there. That means something," he said, "And you gotta glow about you now. Want to tell me about it?"

I nodded and sat working through my memories, trying to put the chain of events into linear form. They kept trying to merge into a single, glorious mandala of light and sensation that defied description. Finally, I closed my eyes and started talking. I found myself muttering at first, just telling myself the story. Then, my voice grew louder and I forgot myself as the words burst forth. I must have stood and waved my arms in my trance of feverish inspiration. When the rant stopped flowing from my mouth, I opened my eyes and looked around. I was standing near the door. The blanket was hanging where I left it, flung over the camp chair. I was quite naked — again.

Jack slapped his free hand on his knee and laughed. I started laughing with him. The whole thing was so beautifully ridiculous and insane. After a while I composed myself, got back to the chair and wrapped myself in the blanket.

"Why don't you get some clothes on. I'm gonna go find something you need to see." He was pointing to my clothes draped over my backpack against the wall. Jack got up and disappeared into the gloom at the back of the bus. The little bells on his beltloop jingled with each step.

I pulled on the jeans, buttoned up my shirt and looked back. Jack was digging around in a big duffel bag that he pulled out from under a cot. Beyond him, way at the back, the shadows were so dark that I couldn't be sure of what I saw. It looked as if the old school bus door had been replaced with a wooden one. It was made of planks that were painted over with symbols reminiscent of *Emerson's Bible*.

Emerson's Bible! Lucius had told me to write in it as much as possible, but I had been otherwise occupied. I rummaged in my pack until my fingers touched the now-familiar leather binding. I grabed it and got back to my seat just as Jack returned and sat. He was holding a book, too. With a shock that sent a tingle up my spine—I recognized it. The old man peered at me from under his frosty eyebrows and held up his copy. I stared at him with my mouth hanging open.

"You have one, too? I mean…"

He nodded slowly, "Yep, I do."

"But, how did you…what…?"

He held up his hand. "Whoa there, give me a chance. I'll tell you how it happened." He put the book in his lap and his eyes drifted up toward the ceiling. He pursed his lips and seemed to fade into memory. I sat silent and watched him as he decided where to begin.

Then, he started to talk.

Chapter Twenty Two

"I was a young buck," he said, "Full of piss and vinegar. Of course, this was a long, long time ago, back in the fifties. Nineteen hundred and fifty-seven. I was almost twenty."

He paused and fished in his beaded pouch for a moment and came up with the little bag of tobacco and rolling papers. He concentrated on making himself a cigarette. When it was lit, he squinted at me around the ribbon of smoke drifting toward the ceiling.

"Where was I? Oh, yeah. I was not quite twenty. Grew up in Ohio. Raised on a farm until my daddy decided to move us to the city after the war ended. He got a job at one of the big factories like most men did back then. Can't remember what he made now. Ain't important. We started living pretty easy. You know, a new car, refrigerator, TV, all of it. That was all well and good, but after I finished school, I tried my hand at the factory. Hated it. Every minute. Daddy was happy with his life but I wanted more. I wanted adventure. Daddy told me stories about the war, he was in Europe. Even though I didn't want to be in the military, I knew it was no good for me to settle down. I had to get out of there. Didn't even matter where.

"My mother wanted me to go to college. Get a degree. Make something outta my life. Well, I planned some great things for myself, but they didn't include more school. I decided to just get going. You know, Jack Kerouac was a big deal back then. I read his *On the Road* and couldn't wait to go have my own journey. Made my parents furious, 'course. They were solid, God-fearing people. I was their only son. I left under a cloud. Put a few clothes and some books in a duffel and hit the road. I had saved up some money, not much. I left a note on the kitchen table. Told my parents I'd call them from somewhere.

"I never did talk to them again. I tried. After I left, I hitched rides across the country. I'd work a little whenever I needed a few bucks for food. I got down to Texas. Austin, it was. Along the way I sent some postcards, just so my folks would know I was alive. Anyway, I got down there and stopped in to a hotel. I wanted to make a long distance call home. It was evening and I wandered in to the big old Driskill Hotel downtown. There was guy at the little desk inside the front door, what do they call him?"

"Concierge?" I said.

"Yeah, one of them. He wasn't happy to see me. It's a swanky kind of place and I was pretty grubby. I told him my story and showed him I had a little money to pay for the phone charges. He took me to a back office and let me use their telephone. My daddy picked up on the other end but when he heard it was me, he slammed the phone down in my ear. Right before he did, I heard my mother ask him who it was. That was the last time I ever heard her voice. I was a mess after that happened. I tried to give the concierge guy some money, but he saw that I had tears in my eyes and he wouldn't let me pay. He said he had a son on the road, too. Lot of us doing that back then. It was quite a time.

"He took me up to a vacant room and told me to shower up. He gave me a menu and said to order whatever I wanted. I didn't know 'til later this was the room usually only Presidents and other big fish stay in. He put me up in the fanciest suite they had. I sat there in a plush bathrobe and ate like a king, but I was very sad. I didn't want to hurt my folks. I just knew that I had to get out and do something, not settle down and pile up stuff around me.

"Well, anyway, Sam, that was the hotel guy's name, he let me stay for a couple of days since business was slow that spring. He walked me around downtown and we sat and talked while we ate barbeque brisket and drank beer. I think he missed his son so bad that he wanted to just talk to someone else who was traipsing around the country. Maybe convince himself his son would be okay, too. I tried to pay him for the room, at least wash dishes in the restaurant. He wouldn't hear none of it. Just said he was happy to help out a little. He also told me to keep trying to call my folks, but I was pretty sore about Daddy hanging up on me.

"On the last morning, Sam took a break after the breakfast rush. He bought me coffee and we sat outside. I already had my bag packed. He never said I had to leave, but I knew it was time. Sam saw my duffel there on the ground and nodded at me like he understood. When we were drinking coffee, he showed me a picture of his son. Told me to take it. Asked me to keep my eye out for him on the road. Said if I ever saw him that I was to please ask him to call his dad.

"He drove me out to the edge of town. He would've taken me farther, but I knew he needed to get back to work. I made him leave me. Well, he gave me a hug and stuffed a wad of bills in my shirt pocket. I tried to give them back but he shook his head and pushed me away. Said to get on with my journey an' he was happy he could help me a little bit.

"Well, the rest of it's a long story, as you can imagine. I stood there at a crossroads with the warm Texas wind blowin' around me. It was springtime and the bluebonnets and Indian paintbrush were growing everywhere. I almost stayed right there, but then a car pulled over that was headed north. The driver leaned out and said he was going a long way, all the way to Idaho, did I want a ride?

"What the hell? I thought, Why not? So I jumped in. The guy was an Asian fella and he had no hair. Made me think of pictures in the National Geographic magazines my parents used to get. Looked like pictures of monks over in China or Tibet or somewhere. He said he was going to check out Idaho for some investors who were interested in mining claims. He didn't talk much, but what he did say got me very interested. We drove and drove. It's a long trip, even longer back then before the roads were good."

Jack lapsed into silence for a few seconds. I could hear the wind outside singing over the edges of the roof like a low wind instrument.

"Yep, that was the start of everything. Of course, I didn't know that then. I was on a lark and it didn't matter much where I went. I'd never been west of the Mississippi before I left home. I was seeing the country, eating new food and feeling the blood like sap rising up inside me. We drove through west Texas into El Paso and then up through New Mexico and Utah. I kept marking places in my mind. I gotta come back here, I'd tell myself...all that beautiful country. We stopped in Salt Lake City for a day or so. The guy put us up in a hotel. Said I could do whatever I wanted. He had some people to meet. I walked all around that town. The big Mormon Temple was right there in the middle of everything, maybe you've seen it. I was dumbstruck.

"After my driver—never did get his name—after he got done with his meetings the next day, we took off again. Took us most of the day to get to Boise."

He stopped to take a sip of tea and look at me.

"This boring you?"

"Not at all, Jack. I always wished I could've traveled like that before I plowed into business as a young guy. I might be in a whole different place in life if I had."

He snorted, "Yeah, you would. No doubt about that. Don't worry though. You'll get your chance to change things up if you keep going like you are now."

The gong that was so disturbing when it started reverberating in my gut a couple of weeks before—sounded again. I found it much less frightening after my experiences of the last few days.

"As I was saying, we got to Boise and the man dropped me off by the Union Pacific train depot, you know the one. He handed me this book all wrapped up in canvas. He said I might find it useful on my journey and then he left. There I was, standing by the train station with no reason to be in that town. I didn't know no one and had no idea what to do next. I unwrapped the book and flipped through it. It didn't seem like much at the time, so I shoved it down inside my bag and started walking down the street that runs across the river and right into the big Capitol Building. Things were a lot different back then. Boise was just a little place but it was growing. I got downtown and found a cheap little hotel room that only cost me a few bucks a night."

He got up from his chair and went to the front door. "Hang on a minute, will you? Nature's calling."

The door banged shut behind him and I could hear him whistling as he relieved himself off the side of the porch. He came back in grinning.

"Shoo! It's a nice day out there. Keeps getting warmer. Looks like we're in for some good weather. Where was I? You ready for some food?"

At the suggestion, my stomach growled.

"I'll take that as a yes," he said, "Sit still and I'll get something for you to gnaw on."

He rustled around in his makeshift cupboards and came back holding one of the tin plates. It held more of the stew from the day before with a thick slice of yellow cornbread on top.

"Ain't e'zackly hot, but I kept the pot near the wood stove. Should be edible."

I was ravenous and would have eaten a dead rat. He made himself comfortable and took a long swallow of tea.

"Well anyway, I spent a couple of days doing pretty much nothing. Hung around down by the river. Sat on the grass by the Capitol Building. It was colder than it had been down Texas way, but spring was in the air. I started getting restless about the second day and ended up in a rough little dive bar down in Garden City. I got drunk and started a fight, can't remember what it was about. The cops showed up and I landed in jail with my shirt torn almost off my back and a black eye. My jaw hurt. When I sobered up in the morning, I sat and talked to another couple of guys in there who were working for Boise Cascade—it was a big deal that year because of a merger they did with a couple other lumber companies. We got outta the clink and went before the judge. He wasn't too hard on us but said we had to pay fines. I didn't have much money left and that pretty much wiped me out. The guys told me I should come up and work the timber with them.

"Well, that seemed like a good idea, so I went along. That little bend in the road took up the next couple years of my life. The work was hard but it paid pretty good. 'Course, I was stupid. Drank up most of the money. Prostitutes... Old story that any sailor or factory worker could tell—but me—I was on the adventure of my life. I was different, you know.

"Once I mailed a letter home to my mother. Didn't try to call but I did want her to know I was alive and doing all right. We was lumberin' all over back then and the nearest town of any size was Sun Valley. Even that wasn't big but it had a post office and the trains ran to it. Hemingway was around in those days. He wasn't in great shape by then, '59 I guess it was, but I actually ran into him around about Christmas that year. He was in a corner at a little bar in Ketchum. Drinkin' by himself. I didn't know who he was at first. We were the only two people in the place so I asked if I could join him. We got to talking and pretty soon the stories started rolling out of him.

"He just got back from Spain where he'd been writing about bullfights for Life magazine. On and on we talked. He asked about my story. I told him quite a bit. He kept buying me drinks. Said he wished he had another big book in him. Said he'd write me into it, but he didn't think he was gonna make it much longer. After that, he got kinda snarly. I left him there. He was drinking even more than me, which was saying something.—He had him a whole little stack of whiskey glasses piled up like a pyramid.

"Turned out, that particular Christmas holiday was an important one for me. I didn't know it at the time. We were taking a break from cutting trees for a week or so. I had nothing to do, no family or close friends. I camped out in a hotel there in Ketchum and pretty much partied my head off. On Christmas Eve, I was playing poker with a bunch of guys in the hotel bar.

"We were playing for real money, an' more than I had to lose. Along about midnight, it was down to just me and another guy. We had both cleaned out the other players and it was turning into a personal thing between us. I had about six thousand dollars stacked up and he had near four thousand. The cards came out and I watched him close. He was pretty good and didn't show much. I took a look at my hand and I had a queen and ten of spades. Not bad, but could be beat for sure. I won't bore you with all the back and forth, but we really took our time and watched each other. We both got into the hand quite a bit before it was time for the flop.

"The dealer put down the next three cards and I was pretty sure I saw his eyes light up. There was a king of spades, ace of hearts and a three. Well, there I was. I didn't have much, but it was gettin' late. I could hope for a straight to win or just bluff him. I looked across the table at him and made a decision. I'm all in, says I. He blinked when I said that. I don't think he expected it. He screwed up his face and peeked at his cards and looked back at me some more. Finally he says, 'Okay, I'm in with everything here and I'm gonna raise you.' He went rummaging around inside a pack he was carryin' and came out with a little wooden box. He opened it and pulled out a stack of papers.

"He told us 'this here's my deed to a mine claim.' 'It's worth a fortune, but if I were just sellin' the rights at a bargain, I'd put it at ten thousand bucks.' He handed the papers to the dealer who looked 'em over and gave 'em to me. I didn't really know what I was looking at, but I shuffled through real quick. They was official looking, with seals and maps and such. I says, okay. I don't have anything else on me to call you with, but I'll sign a note to pay you if I lose. He thought about this for awhile and then he says, 'You're on. Let's see your cards.'

"We all turned our hands face up. I felt like I got kicked in the belly. He had a pair of aces and with the ones on the table, he had a triple. I didn't really have nothing. My heart started pounding so hard I was sure it would explode. He grinned at me and shook his head. 'Looks like I'm gonna own your ass for awhile, kid,' said he.

"The dealer put down the turn card. It was the ace of spades. Well, now things got tense! It all came down to the next card. I must have been holding my breath because I nearly passed out by the time the dealer flipped the river card. My whole body was shaking. I had done a fool thing and we all knew it. I'll never forget seein' that card turn over. It felt like lightning struck the room and ran through my bones. It was a jack—of spades.

"That's right! I got my straight flush with the last card. The other guy damn near fainted. His face went pale and he gulped, but there was nothing he could do. I had won it, fair and square. He stood and I saw his fists ball up. He leaned across the table like he was going to come at me but the dealer grabbed him by the collar and shoved him down. He made him sign over the deed and that was that. I watched my back for the next few days but the other guy must have left town. I didn't see him again."

I felt my fingers loosen their grip on my knees in relief and I let my breath out. Jack had drawn me into his tale with such skill that my own heart was pounding. He glanced at me and I nodded for him to keep going. He rubbed his nose and cleared his throat.

"Well, that's how I got here."

"Here?" I said.

"Yes, this property. It was a silver mining claim. I won it in that hand of poker back in 1959. I had about ten thousand dollars in cash winnings and the deed to this land. As a young guy, that seemed like a huge stroke of luck. How could it not be, right? I decided to take care of the papers right after Christmas so the land would be mine and then quit my lumber job. I didn't know nothin' about silver mining, but I figured I had a bankroll and could learn. I'd been playing around long enough, it was time to get busy making a fortune."

He stood up then and motioned that I should, too. "We gotta get going. I'll tell you the rest of the story while we walk."

"Walk where?"

"Where I tell you," he grinned at me, showing his missing teeth and waggling his eyebrows.

I sniffed and shook my head. I had learned better than to argue or even think rebellious thoughts around him.

Jack pointed at my boots where they stood by the door. "Put 'em on. Let's go."

Chapter Twenty Three

The sun was so bright it hurt my eyes when Jack and I emerged from his house. He had packed a knapsack with food and told me to carry it. He led the way back toward the woods where I spent the night. I didn't bother to ask him again where he was taking me—I just fell in behind him. The big elk was no longer hanging from the tripod in the clearing. He must have butchered it sometime after he forced me into the forest the day before.

Probably because of the mild weather, he had left his bathrobe behind, but the beat-up beret with its eagle feather was shoved down over his hair again. Outside, his gait was transformed from a shuffle into the limber strides of a much younger man. He walked fast—so fast that I had to break into a jog just to keep up. The pack jostled and rubbed against the scratches on my back. I grasped the straps with both hands and ran panting to catch the old man.

"Jack, are we going to a fire? You're too fast for me."

He glanced over his shoulder. "Ha. We gotta toughen you up, don't we?" He stopped and let me catch my breath. Overhead, through the branches of the fir trees, he pointed at the sky. A pair of vultures soared high above the Earth.

"Lucius ever mention vultures?"

"No," I said, "He pointed at them but he didn't say anything."

"Hmm. Well, you ain't an Indian, but the ancient ones believed that everything is connected and that animals show up to remind us about important stuff. They gave meanings—omens they sometimes called them—to most of the critters. The Indians saw nothing as accidental."

"You're saying that the vultures mean something?" I said.

"No, not necessarily, but I've lived close to the Earth for many years, so it's hard to say the Old Ones had it all wrong. Vultures don't kill things themselves. They have weak talons. They clean up the dead, rotting carcasses." He added that "they'll pick the last shreds of meat from the bones after the wolves and bears and such have their fill."

I watched the vultures disappear and waited for him to continue. He remained silent, so I cocked my head at him, "But what did they say vultures mean?"

He glanced at me. "The vultures are kind of a symbol of turning dead, rotten stuff in our lives into useful fuel. Like the bugs and what-have-you's that break down dead leaves and branches. Reminds us that everything has a purpose—even the stinky, ugly messes. You don't have to believe that about the vultures, but it might be a good way to help you shift your thinking when you see one show up. Say 'thank you' to All That Is for everything going on in your life."

I thought about this and nodded. It felt good to have a new way to look at nature and it was in line with my magical dance of unity the night before.

He started walking again—but more slowly.

"You said you'd tell me more of your story while we walk," I said.

"Yep, I did. Where was I?"

"You decided to come up here and find your fortune."

"Yes, yes. That's it. Well, it's a pretty long story but I'll shorten it up some. As I said, I knew nothin' about mining for silver. I asked around and most people laughed at me. I found some books and talked to old guys who had worked the mines. Turned out, I really didn't have enough cash to do it right, but I decided to give it a whirl anyway. The papers that came with the deed showed drawings and plans. Whoever staked the claim in the first place seemed to think that there was a vein of silver not far inside the mountain. Somebody had started digging a little already, but the hole was pretty much overgrown by the time I got there.

"Here, turn this way." He pointed to the left fork in the path and started on it without pausing. I felt I'd been here before, but couldn't be sure. The events of the night before were lost in a glowing haze of visions bearing little resemblance to normal awareness.

"So, I spent more than five years bustin' my hump trying to find silver. I scratched up a little now and again—just enough to keep me excited. Kind of like gambling, I guess. You lose and lose, then hit a pot big enough to make you keep believing. I was obsessed after the first year. Got to be skin and bones because I wasn't eating right. Didn't matter. I just knew I'd hit it rich pretty soon and be able to go back home with a big stack of cash. Then my daddy would have to say I was right to go my own way like I did.

"Well, as I said, it was just over five years after I won the game of poker and got my land. I was busted. Almost no money left. My clothes were rags. I barely had any food. I was living in a little shack with a dirt floor. It was early spring, lots of snow still on the ground. I decided to hike back to Ketchum with the little bit of silver I had. All that time I barely mixed with other people. The world was changing like crazy out there, but not for me. I was stuck in my own dreams and chained to my own ideas about how things needed to turn out.

"Anyway, it took me a few days to get all the way to town. I was exhausted and filthy when I got there. I took my bag of silver to the assayer's office, got it looked at and weighed. They bought it from me for under a hundred bucks. I was just sick to my stomach. That was all I could show for more than six months of hard work. Looked like my dreams of going home a big hero were pretty much worthless.

"I got a hotel room and cleaned up as much as I could. Then I went out and got something to eat and started drinking.

"Along about four in the afternoon, one of my old lumberjack friends came in. We had a fine time slapping each other on the back and whatnot. Pretty soon he told me that he'd moved into town and settled down. He went and got married and was working for the railroad. He said someone at the Western Union office was asking about me. Said they had a telegram and did anyone know if I was still around. He said that was about six months ago.

"Well, I never got a telegram before. I figured it must be pretty important. My friend told me where to find the office and I headed on over there.

"I'll never forget. No one else in there. I got up to the counter and a young lady asked if she could help me. I told her my name and why I was there. She fiddled around in a couple of files and then said she needed to talk to her manager. She went in the back and then came out with a yellow paper in her hand. Her face had changed. It was all tightened up and pale. She shook her head and handed it to me. I recall she said, 'I'm so sorry to have to give you this.'

"My heart fell down in my gut as I took it from her. I couldn't imagine what it said, but my first thought was that something was wrong with my mother.

"It was even worse than that. The telegram was from one of my uncles in Ohio. It was short. It said: 'Jack so sorry. stop. Both your parents killed in car wreck. stop. Tried to find you earlier. stop.'

"That was it. I almost fainted. The girl asked if I needed a glass of water. I said no and stumbled out to the street and sat on the wooden sidewalk.

"I don't remember much after that. I must have spent the night. I remember drinking a lot and crying 'til my stomach hurt. The next day, I got up and started back here. I don't remember a thing about the trip except it only took me a couple of days instead of three. I must have pushed harder, I don't even know why. There was nothing left for me.

"At my little clearing things got even darker. It was twilight when I came through the trees, I smelled smoke. That didn't make no sense. I was gone for almost a week and nobody ever came up this way, no reason to.

"I got to the edge of the woods and looked over where my shack was. Or where it used to be. I got no way of knowing what happened, but there was nothing left but a heap of charred wood. I must've left a lantern too close to the wall, or the wood stove chimney caught fire. Whatever, I was homeless. I had no prospects, no money. My mother and daddy had been dead for months. I was at the end."

He stopped for a minute and fished around in his back pocket. He pulled out a red handkerchief and wiped his face. I didn't think he was actually crying but it was hard to be sure. We were standing deep in the forest. The path we followed was little more than a narrow deer trail.

Jack looked intently at me, his eyes moist, he pointed off through the thicket of fir trees surrounding us.

"That's where it happened," he said.

"That's where what happened?" I looked but couldn't see much.

"Look again," he said.

I shaded my eyes and strained to see. Through the filigree patterns of the fir branches, about thirty yards away, an out-of-place tree trunk came into focus. A huge oak. I must have jumped in surprise because Jack put out his hand to steady me.

"Is that...?" I looked at him.

"The very one," he said.

"The tree from last night?"

"That's it."

"What happened to you there?" I said, "You said that's where 'it' happened." My breath got faster.

"And it did. Let's go there now and I'll tell you the rest. When you came back this morning, you didn't have to say nothing. I knew you found the tree."

"This tree is…"

"Something special, yeah. Come on. Let's get over to it and I'll tell you the rest." He turned and strode through the thicket, following the faint game path. I hurried along after him.

Three minutes later, I caught up to Jack. He was leaning against the tree, his arms wrapped around it in a hug. His eyes were closed. I stepped on a twig that snapped loudly, but he didn't look.

"This is where my life began," he said, "Right here. Right where it almost ended."

"How did it almost end?"

He opened his eyes and drew his brows together. "Here, sit down," he said and pointed to a couple of boulders nestled in the roots of the giant tree. We settled ourselves and he looked at me for a long time before resuming his tale.

"After I came upon my burnt-down shack, everything fell in on top of me. That's how it felt, anyway. I suppose I hadn't really let myself feel the shock of losing my parents and my own bein' pissed-off with myself. Right then, it all hit me like a freight train. I thought my head would split apart.

"I was angry and sad—sadder than I ever had been before. I felt trapped in a corner and life was standing there laughing at me. I don't remember all the details, but I just started running into the woods. I stumbled and fell down in the snow, tore my shirt on branches. I was crying until I thought my chest would bust open. Finally, I tripped over one of these roots right here and slammed against this tree. It was a little smaller then, but not by much.

"I still had my pack on my back so I ripped it open to get the rope. The one I always had just in case—you always need a rope in the woods. Anyway, I tossed it over that branch right there and made a noose. I put it over my head, standing on this very same boulder, ready to jump off and end it all."

He stopped to wipe his face with the handkerchief again—I suspected that the pause was also for dramatic effect. He looked at the ground and scuffed his feet a little.

"Jack, then what happened?"

"Oh. He showed up."

"He?"

"Yeah, Lucius."

It shouldn't have stunned me. By now, nothing should. For some reason, I kept forgetting that Lucius was more than a human being with interesting superpowers. He is, whatever he is, but not an ordinary man on high-grade steroids.

"I was balancing up on the rock," Jack said, "I could feel the rope around my neck and I was ready to jump. My mind was past thinking, I wasn't even afraid, as I should've been. It was all fight-or-flight and I was out of fight. Seemed like pulling down the shades was my only option at the moment. I was already leaning out for my big jump when I looked straight across this little patch and saw Lucius standing right over there. You know that thing he can do with his eyes?"

"Oh, you mean when you get frozen in one spot?" I said.

"Yeah, that. Well, that's what he was doing to me. I was surprised to see him there. Of course, you got to factor in that it was Lucius, too. You know what I mean. I almost fell over backwards off the rock and hanged myself anyway."

I shook my head, imagining the scene.

"He didn't say anything at first, just motioned for me to get down. I didn't want to. The end was so close. I was sure there wasn't nothing left for me in life. Waste of time to talk about it. I went to jump, but just as my feet shoved off the rock Lucius was there. He must of flown through the air, I don't know. Anyway, he grabbed me around the waist and I passed out. Next thing I knew, I woke up a long ways from here. I was in a round house and that pretty girl, Kaitlyn, was putting a washcloth on my forehead."

I held up my hand. "So the helpers, they've been here for a long time? I mean—the same ones?"

Jack chuckled. "I suppose so. Time don't seem to work the same way for them. They're everywhere. All over the world, as I understand it. Lucius recently told me things are speeding up out there in the world. I knew that, but only from a distance. He said his work is getting more and more important as the Big Shift gets going. These helpers have always been around, but now they're making contact with people who are ready."

"That's what Lucius told me when we first met," I said, "I still don't know how they picked me. Why was I more ready than anybody else?"

"No way for me to know that," Jack said. "I imagine you were a lot closer to the end of your rope than you thought. Seems like that's when these helpers show up, when things are about at the end."

"That's what I mean, Jack. I didn't think I was at the end of anything. Sure, I was stressed out, but when Lucius showed up I was busy being successful. I was playing the game as hard as I could."

"Well, you got lucky then. You didn't have to have a heart attack or get in some horrible car wreck. You didn't have to have a near-death experience. It goes back to what Lucius says about the momentum changing. Most humans ain't prepared. The helpers gotta take action and wake some people up. Sorry if I bust your bubble, but this is going on all over the world. You are definitely not the only one."

"Lucius mentioned that," I said, "Are the others forced to leave everything and go through the sort of experiences I have?"

"It ain't cut and dry, everybody's different. Some people don't change much on the outside. They keep going about their lives. Others sort of crack wide open. Radical stuff happens. The big thing is that people who wake up move into a new...um...consciousness.

They can't think about themselves and other people the same way ever again. I mean, will you go back home and pop right back into all your old ways like nothing happened?"

My old ways. My life. How will it look from this point forward? I wondered.

"See what I'm saying?" he said.

"Yes, I do. Is that why people aren't ready?"

"How do you mean?"

"You know," I moved my hands around, searching for the shape of the idea inside me, "the shiny wrapper. Life. What we call life back there in the 'real world' is moving so fast, it's so pervasive we think it's all there is. We get so immersed in the game that we forget it's a game. It's not that we aren't willing to wake up to a new way, really. It just doesn't seem like there is one.

"We're in a speeding train and the scenery outside is a blur now. It's been going faster and faster for a long time. We can barely stay on the tracks as it is, but we think we have to find ways to keep going even faster. The only reality we can imagine is what's happening inside the bubble of the train."

Jack nodded and grinned at me. "You're getting the idea. Try to picture the horrible surprise people will be in for if the train goes off the track. Real sudden-like, they go from a hundred miles an hour to a dead stop. Their comfortable, air-conditioned lives get wrecked, as best as they can tell."

"Are you saying that humanity is going to have a terrible apocalypse?"

"Well, you probably know that one meaning of that word 'apocalypse' is revelation or unveiling. In that sense, yeah, humanity is in for one of them. It could be terrible, but it doesn't have to be. That's why you and a bunch of others are gettin' this wake up call."

"Does this have to do with the whole 2012 thing?" I said, "It's all over the place. Books, TV programs...I think they even made some big movies about it."

"Oh, that," he said, "Well, I've read lots of old books. Stuff about the Mayans and Nostradamus. 'Course, I've read the Bible prophecies, old Hopi writings, Hindu scriptures, all kinds of things. I can't deny the patterns. Seems like the dots are getting connected in ways that point to some major changes real soon now."

"Do you think the world will end on December twenty-first in the year twenty-twelve?"

"What I think don't matter. We can't know exactly what the Mayans saw or even what they meant. Sure, it seems ominous. What do you think will happen to all those people who're sure everything's gonna end—when they wake up in the morning on the twenty-second of December—and we're all still here?"

"They'll be devastated. Blown away. They won't know what to believe next. Are you saying you don't believe the Mayan prophecies are real?"

Jack sighed. "It ain't that simple. It's not a matter of what I believe or don't believe. What's going to happen is what's going to happen. You're going to get a glimpse of some possibilities while you're up here. But you need to get this next part really good, listen to me.—All the focus and attention people give that kinda thing is a waste of time."

"What do you mean by that?" I asked, "If people can know what's coming and get prepared, wouldn't that be a good thing?"

"Well maybe, but they ain't getting prepared. They're just talking about it. That's human nature. Talk and talk and talk. It's entertainment. It's a huge distraction."

"A distraction from what?"

"A distraction from the real business people should be about right now. Instead of speculating on how the government is plotting this or that, people should be learning about themselves. They need to go within. They need to find out who they really are…"

I held up my hand. "That's what Lucius keeps saying, Who You Really Are. Almost seems like a code, a secret password. What do you mean when you say it?"

"Probably mean it the same as Lucius. Actually, let's go back to my story for a minute. That might help."

Chapter Twenty Four

Jack stuck his fingers under the beret and scratched his head. The eagle feather bobbed up and down. His keen old eyes looked past me as he filtered through his memories.

"As I said, I woke up a long way from here. I didn't see Lucius for days. Not sure what happened to me, but I couldn't move a muscle. I slept and drank the special tea Kaitlyn brought me. Whenever I opened my eyes, my mind started chewing on the hopeless mess of my life. I was still a young guy, but it felt like I didn't have any juice left. Maybe there was something extra in the tea, because I could only work myself up a little before I'd get exhausted and go back to sleep.

"Anyway, I can't say for sure how long I did this. Could've been a couple of days, or it might have been a month. One morning, I woke up and there was Lucius sitting on the end of my bed just watching me—you know how he does. I felt different. I wasn't ready to go tackle the lions again, but there was new life running through my body.

"Lucius held out his hand and helped me get up. I put my feet on the floor and stood up. I would've collapsed right away, 'cause I was so weak, but he caught me. He took me outside. The air was warm that day and I smelled the earth coming back to life. Something new was afoot, but I couldn't imagine what it would be."

Jack stopped to roll one of his cigarettes. I waited while he lit it. The smoke floated around us.

He cleared his throat and continued. "Well, there's more to the story and we don't have time to go through it all right now. I'll say that the next few months got intense. You've had some similar experiences to what Lucius put me through, but mine took a longer. He didn't seem to be in much of a hurry. I lived with him and learned my lessons a little at a time."

"Did you have the big circle of helpers with the altar and the peace pipe?" I asked.

Jack looked sideways at me, "What? Oh, probably not the same exact way you did. See, I already had my stuff burned up in real life. You got the special treatment because Lucius needs to make his point in ways that get your attention. Life was different back then for me. It was a lot more raw. We didn't have it easy and tidy. You modern guys in the civilized world have leapfrogged over yourselves time and time again."

"What do you mean?" I said.

"Back when I was first with Lucius, technology and all the stuff that you just take for granted in life was just getting started. Think about it. We're talking late fifties, early sixties. Yes, there were factories and airplanes and such, but get your head around where the world has gone since then."

He's right, I thought, *It's like we're living on a different planet.*

"Sure, I'm right," he said, answering my thoughts again, "I may not be in the middle of it like you are, but I keep up on things."

"Are you saying that technology is bad? Are you telling me that we need to go back to the time before the Internet?"

Jack sighed, shook his head and dragged on his cigarette. "No. It's not about bad or good. Actually, it's interesting, the science and miracles in technology are kind of leading humanity in a full circle."

"How do you mean?" I said.

"Well, take one example, in ancient times people had ways to communicate that modern man has pretty much lost. Stuff like telepathy was very common. You go visit primitive tribes—some of the Aborigines in Australia and other places like that. They don't have the stuff you have, but they still know about energy and invisible powers. They can talk to each other in a kinda intuitive way that people in America and Europe would think was voodoo."

"How is science leading us back to that?" I said.

"Oh, it ain't a straight line, but the more your wizards of science learn, the more they realize they're just harnessing mysterious powers that they can't understand. They're finding out that the principles they tapped into are much bigger than anything they've invented so far."

"What are you trying to tell me here?" I said.

Jack got up and searched around under the fallen leaves that lay thick beneath the huge oak tree and returned holding a stick. He cleaned a spot on the ground with his boot and sat back down.

"Look," he gestured with his chin to the dirt he was drawing in with the sharp end of the stick. I watched. He was making what appeared to be an inverted pyramid. After a few seconds, he looked up at me and pointed to the triangle.

"Imagine this is you—Who You Really Are," he said, "Up here at the top, where the triangle is wide, that's the place where your consciousness is connected to All That Is, or God, or the Universe. Whatever you want to use for its name. Call it 'Sally' for all I care. This is spirit and pure consciousness."

"Okay," I said.

He traced a line across the pyramid. "As we come down toward the point, we start to enter what some thinkers call the individuation."

"You mean a separate personality, that sort of thing?" I said.

"Yeah, but don't rush this. Even though I'm drawing lines to tell my story, there ain't clear places where one part stops and another starts. We move into deep things like emotions here. These can be sort of rationalized but they still are above what you'd call thought. Does that make sense so far?"

I got excited as the picture emerged. "Yes, go on."

"All right, you keep moving down and see how the walls close in? We're operating in a much more narrow range. This is where most of our thoughts come and go. This is all mixed in with personality and ego. Now, bring it to the very point here," he dug the stick into dirt at the tip of the pyramid, "That's your physical self." He poked me in the knee.

"You getting this?"

I sat there and took it all in for a moment. "This is amazing," I said.

"Isn't it?" he sat upright on his rock and grinned at me.

"So...wow! This opens up a lot to talk about, but how does this connect back to what you were saying about science?"

"Oh, yeah. Well, when science really took hold as a method for control of the physical world, people started leaning on it and ignoring what they couldn't measure or test. You agree?"

"I can't argue with that," I said.

He nodded, "Might as well not. It won't do you no good. Anyway, science is concerned with this junk down here at the smallest end of the scale—just what can be analyzed and proven. Do you know what the problem with that is?"

I took a deep breath and looked around at the sunny clearing. "Well, when I see it this way, it's obvious that we've ignored the whole bigger part of ourselves."

Jack punched the air overhead with both fists. "Yes! You got it. Down here, in the dense part of the vibration scale, that's where material stuff is. That's what we can see and touch and test. It's also where we believe we are separate from each other and from All That Is. Can you see where that leads?"

"If we think we're separate, then we fight for what we need. We try to keep other people from getting what's ours."

"Right! This is where ego lives. Down here is where the wars and scarcity and negative beliefs happen. You can call this the illusion if you like. The Hindus call it *maya*," he said.

"But it's not really just illusion, is it? I mean, you're sitting on a rock. We both ate food a little while ago."

"It's not that it ain't real. All of this is real," he drew a circle around the pyramid, "But the ego mind is so strong that it creates an illusion that this is the only reality. Reality is much more mysterious than we think. It can't be put in a test tube and broken down into some formula."

"But that's exactly what science has been trying to do!" I said, louder than I intended.

"Now you see what I mean, don't you?" he said.

"Yes! Yes, I do. And the further science goes..." I paused to formulate my thoughts.

"The more it brings us back to the big mystery," Jack finished the sentence for me.

"Wow," I said.

"Yep," he said, "That's what I been sayin' all these years up here alone in the mountains while I learned this stuff. Wow. Over and over again. Do something for me?"

I nodded.

"Get your book out, the one Lucius gave you. Copy this drawing and make some notes. You're going to need to remember this later. So much is happening, I'm afraid you'll forget."

I dug in my pack for *Emerson's Bible* and settled down to follow his instructions. Jack wandered off into the woods.

Chapter Twenty Five

Late afternoon. The great oak tree cast its shadow all the way across the open circle in the forest. Jack had been gone hours and a chilly breeze blew through the surrounding firs and aspens.

I wasn't exactly worried, I just wasn't certain what to do next.

The relative warmth of the sunny afternoon had seduced me into a state of contemplative stupor. After writing in *Emerson's Bible*, I reclined on the dry grass with my knapsack under my head. Although I didn't intend to take a nap, sleep crept over me. I dreamed a series of disjointed visions that left me disoriented when I blinked awake with blue sky bright in my eyes.

I stood and stretched my muscles. I was quite alone. The woods were quiet except for the sound of the wind in the trees. I was hungry and dug in the pack for food. There wasn't much inside: a few apples, a canteen of water and a big slice of cornbread wrapped in a handkerchief. I drank some water and settled back down on the rock to eat an apple.

A cold gust of wind made me shiver and I looked for my coat. *Must have left that back at Jack's,* I thought. After a few more minutes, a cloud blew across the sun and the world turned gray. *Decision time.*

I could try to find my way back to Jack's house, or I could just stay put and hope he would show up soon. The first option was problematic because I had no idea how to retrace our steps, but the wait-and-see plan made me anxious since the old mountaineer was not predictable in his comings and goings.

Fire. I can make a fire, I thought.

A side pocket in the backpack yielded a box of matches and I began scraping away leaves under the big oak tree to make a clean spot. It only took a few minutes to gather an armload of dry branches and I mentally marked a few large fallen limbs to drag in after the fire was going well.

Before long I was hunkered down beside a crackling blaze with smoke swirling around my head. It felt good and I held out my hands to the warmth. My mind wandered over the last several days. *Hard to believe it's been less than a week since I joined Lucius for this crazy journey!* Or had it been? I was having trouble keeping track of time.

Wonder what Jenn and the kids are doing right now? I thought. *Wonder what's going on with my business?* These thoughts brought with them mixed pangs of love and anxiety. I sat there and allowed myself to consider the load of implications unpacking in my consciousness. My path had seemed so predictable a few weeks ago, but now...?

The flames quickly chewed through the first small branches. I left the circle of warmth to fetch more substantial fuel. Nightfall was coming fast. Jack was nowhere to be seen and I felt it wise to prepare for another night alone in the forest.

I found heavy branches in the shadowy underbrush. They were too long and tangled in the thickets to be dragged back whole. I made a tremendous noise as I jumped on them with both feet to break them into manageable pieces.

Sweat ran down my face and trickled down my spine from the exertion of hauling two of the limbs back to my fireside. At the edge of the clearing, I stopped to wipe my forehead and catch my breath. I peered through the branches of a fir tree to see what had become of my fledgling fire.

My heart froze when I saw the figure of a man seated beside the campfire with his back to me. *It's not Jack*, I thought. In the glowing circle of light I could see that he was tall and sat very straight. *That isn't Lucius either.*

There was no way he could have avoided hearing the racket I made in the brush, but he didn't turn to look in my direction. I stood and watched him for a long moment until I realized that I was holding my breath.

"Come," he said without turning his head. His voice was deep and startling in the quiet. I didn't move. He put his hand up and beckoned. I tightened my grip on the small logs and pushed through the fir branches. A few steps brought me even with this new stranger—although I was careful to position myself with the fire between us. I let the wood slide from under my arms and thud to the ground.

The man turned toward me and I gasped audibly before I could control my reaction. His face—what was left of it—was a twisted mask of scar tissue. One eye was missing entirely: the socket was dark and vacant. The other bulged behind a torn upper eyelid. He appeared to be African, but the terrible devastation of his features made it hard to be sure.

"Did I frighten you?" His voice rumbled like musical thunder.

I hunched my shoulders but couldn't form any words.

He chuckled. "I can see how I might alarm you—showing up like this. Here, let's get some wood on your fire." He bent and pulled the butt end of a log into the blaze with one hand. Sparks flew into the darkness. The man stood and spread his arms out.

The robes he wore hung in rags. I saw that his right arm had been hacked off above the elbow. A light wind stirred the fire and smoke wrapped itself around him like the shroud of a ghost.

"My name is Gamaliel," he said, "Are you surprised by my appearance?"

I nodded and my knees felt weak.

"Be seated," he said, "You have nothing to fear." He gestured to one of the rocks with his good arm. I sat. Like Lucius, this man carried a powerful presence but the energy was different: not malevolent, but emanating a foreboding sensation.

"Are you one of—them?" I said in a whisper.

"I am." He smiled and his teeth flashed white behind lips distorted by a deep scar bisecting his face.

A fleeting vision rose in my mind. Rough soldiers were holding the man who called himself Gamaliel. Dust and noise filled the air. I saw a soldier's upraised arm holding a sword slash down. Gamaliel's face became a mask of blood. I blinked and the image vanished.

The words Lucius spoke came back to me then:

> "...If you wander alone and follow the advice of strangers you meet at this stage, you could easily lose your way. If for some reason, you find yourself alone and someone approaches you, it's critical that you determine whether or not they are a friend. If they appeal to your vanity or try to use your fear to manipulate you, run. Get away. Listen to your own inner voice, you'll know if they are a messenger of love and wisdom—or just an impostor who could lead you astray."

Gamaliel had seated himself and was studying the drawing Jack scratched in the dirt that afternoon. *Is he really a friend?* I wondered.

"Ah, I see you have been learning deep secrets today," he said, "This is good. It will help with what I have come to show you."

"Why do I feel so much fear right now? The other helpers led me to places of light. You frighten me."

"Do you remember your first meeting with Lucius? Did he not hint at revelations of things to come?"

"Yes he did, but the journey we have taken has been beautiful. I was afraid at first, but he and the others pulled back the veil. They showed me glimpses of Who I Really Am. Your presence fills me with new, dark questions."

Gamaliel nodded slowly. "It is so. You have been given glimpses of All That Is so you could know the truth of your own being. Had I been your first visitor, you would have been plunged into the illusion of despair. This did not serve our purpose. Time is short. We have much to show you still. That can wait a little. First tell me what you have learned about Who You Really Are."

I closed my eyes and drew a deep breath. Gamaliel's hand touched the back of my neck. A sudden radiance filled my body and I was caught up again in the glowing wonder of the realms that had been revealed over the last several days.

Eyes still closed, I began to speak: "I am part of the loving light of the Universal Being. The same Energy that gives birth to all the universes mysteriously flows through me, too. I am at once human and Spirit. The human senses cannot begin to comprehend the possibilities that are always present in the levels of consciousness that lie just beyond my Earth-experience. I am a beam of radiant light of God in this world."

Gamaliel removed his hand and I opened my eyes. My body was shaking.

His one eye held my gaze and somehow his wrecked visage was transformed. He became beautiful and full of the captivating power that illuminated all the other helpers. My internal vibration was raised by his presence; we glowed together in harmonics that transcended sight and sound.

"Do you see now?" he said. I nodded. The moment faded and his disfigured human form reappeared.

"What does this tell you?"

"I don't know a good way to put it in words," I said, "but thank you for helping me to see through your...well, your ugliness."

"Yes, that is my mission with you. When you agreed to accept the summons from Lucius, we rejoiced. It is no easy matter for a man of the world to look beyond the constructs of all he has known as life. We had to be careful with you. There is a fine line between awakening to higher consciousness and madness. Do you know what I mean by this?"

I shuddered. "Yes, I do. If what happened to me here in the mountains had occurred during my normal life, I'd think I was insane. In fact, I'm afraid that when I return to the regular world, it will be impossible to reconcile what I learned here with that reality."

He waved the stump of his right arm and said, "The world you inhabit is both very beautiful and ugly. As you have learned, it is a space of duality. Most people are so engrossed by the game—with all its competition and judgments—that they can't see the larger truths."

"Well, I've had an unfair advantage," I said, "Being up here, I've seen things in ways that I never would have in any other setting."

Gamaliel stood without warning, his tattered garments fluttering around his emaciated body. He walked over to the giant oak tree, placed his hand on it and looked back at me. "Come here," he said.

I joined him near the powerful trunk and looked up to follow his gaze. The night sky was black; the early stars were shining bright through the lace of interwoven branches.

"Jack told you about this tree?" he asked.

"He told me his story. How he tried to hang himself."

"But not the rest of it?"

"I guess not. Oh, wait, he did act like it was something special after I told him about my night here. He didn't explain anything else, though."

"Ah, well, I will spare a few moments for that now. Sit with me and I will tell you the legend." He sat cross-legged between the roots and waited until I was situated before he began.

Chapter Twenty Six

Gamaliel closed his good eye and held out his hand for me to hold.

"Join me. Let us take a breath together."

I clasped his hand between both of mine and we inhaled deeply. His words began as a gentle murmur:

"As with all things on the material plane, this tree is merely a shadow—a symbol that demonstrates the creative power that flows from the Great One. The mystery of All That Is contains both Father and Mother. The mystery is inseparable, yet always dancing and procreating in its own image. I give you this legend for the purpose of illustrating larger truths. Do not become entangled in the form of the story. Simply allow the words to germinate and grow toward your further enlightenment.

"In the times before time, a seed was planted here by Father in the womb of Mother Earth. The life force within it cracked open the shell and tiny roots reached forth into the rocky soil. So was born the Tree of Life on this planet. Imagine if you can, that this was the beginning of a new expression of All That Is—seeking to experience Itself in every way possible.

"The roots grew below the surface for years, deeper and deeper into the fathomless darkness beyond human understanding. Rains fell, sun shined upon the soil. At last came a moment when the slender sprout that lay curled in sleep awakened. It stretched itself and pressed upward into the light of day. When the first green shoot appeared, all the shining hosts in the realms of Spirit danced for joy. They are forever in worship of the Creator and the created, you see.

"Within this one newborn stalk was written the everlasting code of truth and life. All that stands upon the Earth is represented by its growth. The rise and fall of nations, the birth and death of tribes, the evolution of knowledge—all are present herein.

"The tiny tree grew. Living energy compelled it to reach up and dig down. For many ages of human time, the inhabitants of Earth were simple. They were only connected to the central trunk as it rose higher from the ground.

"Then Life pressed outward through the bark and to branches. Some were quickly broken but others became sturdy limbs—full of sap and energy. Can you say what these might represent?"

I sat silent, lost in the images of Gamaliel's story. He twitched his fingers that I still clutched between my palms. Startled, I found my focus and considered his question.

"I can imagine that they would be movements of humanity? Maybe channels of thought?"

"Very good," he said, "Yes, for the purposes of this lesson, picture the limbs as great nations or religions. They are all part of the Tree but they have pushed out in different directions from the main trunk.

"As I said, some of these grew into mighty limbs. The humans who were the fibers within them often mistook these off-shoots for the Tree itself. They cannot be faulted for this perception—it was all they had ever known. Their consciousness made the stuff of each limb. Still the Tree grew up and out and down. The powerful surge of Source energy within it always creates new expressions of itself.

Now look around us here on the ground beneath the Tree. What do you see?"

I released Gamaliel's hand and opened my eyes to examine the surroundings.

"I see rocks and grass…"

"Look more closely," he said.

I peered through the shadows dancing in the light from our campfire.

"I see some dead branches and old rotten limbs."

"There it is!" he said, "Do you understand?"

"Not really. What do they mean?"

"They tell us that even the great limbs that encompass many generations of human understanding will someday die and fall to the ground." He pointed to a decomposing log that had almost completely returned to the soil.

"Do you see? What once was vibrant and strong has now fallen. Its usefulness is just a distant memory. It will soon break down to nourish the Tree of Life with its essential nutrients. Nothing is wasted. Go back into the ancient teachings of Egypt, research every long-dead religion. You will find their threads still woven into the consciousness of humanity today.

Now look above you. Some of the limbs that are part of the Tree are still attached but will soon drop. The sap recedes and moves into new little sprouts that may also someday become mighty branches."

I felt excited as the picture formed. "What do the twigs and leaves represent?"

"Oh, many things, as you might imagine. We are keeping simple with this tale. The leaves can represent the individual beliefs born in the springtime, that shine in the summer sun and fall again to earth each autumn. The massive systems, such as a world religion—say Christianity—are no different. Beliefs grow and change with the seasons. Can you see how this is true?"

"Yes! I studied church history years ago and that was striking to me at the time. Things are always changing even among the denominations of Christianity."

"It is so," he said, "Now let's consider how it feels to be one of the humans within a limb that is passing away."

"It's frightening. It feels like life as we know it is ending. We don't know what to believe or even who we are anymore," I said.

"That is good. People cling even more tightly to what they've always known. They are terrified by the winds of change that rattle and crack their branches."

"I know exactly how that is," I said.

"Yes, you do. You are part of a mighty limb of the Tree that is being pounded by storms. In fact, the flow of essential sap is blocked and that particular limb is very brittle."

I held up a hand and said, "Wait. Gamaliel, are you talking about the limb of Christianity or the limb of America, or…what?"

"All of that. All of that and more. I am showing you the powerful myths that have served humanity for so long are dying. Entire world views will pass away before this great shift has run its course."

I shuddered and felt my face tighten as fear caught in my throat. Gamaliel regarded me with an expression of immaculate compassion shining through the terrible scars on his face.

"I understand your fright," he said, "I am challenging you to see a possible end to life as you know it in your world."

"Are you saying that's what will be? The end?" I heard my own voice quavering.

"We have talked enough for this time. You and I have much to see. Before we go, I will complete the circle.

"Let us return to the thought of the central trunk of the Tree. Imagine a storm ripping across these mountain peaks and sweeping through this very place. Imagine it is so fierce that every one of the limbs you see above is torn from the trunk and flung to the earth. What do you suppose would become of the Tree itself?"

I allowed my eyes to wander up the tree's massive torso and climb through the spreading branches to the topmost leaves. I tried to picture a raging wind that could strip away everything except the trunk. When I looked back at Gamaliel, his gaze was steady.

"I suppose the tree would survive. It would heal itself and new life would grow in time," I said.

Gamaliel rose straight up and stood. The stump of his amputated right arm pointed toward the sky. His eye blazed with intensity and his deep voice boomed, "Yes! You see it. That is good. Know this truth even as the Tree knows it: the great Life that flows within never dies. The Tree is always growing; always becoming more Itself. When a leaf or branch or limb is no longer vital, it falls to the ground and again becomes earth. The Tree does not fear. It simply draws more Life from the bottomless depths and from the sky above. To the Tree, nothing is the end of the world—not even what appears to be most certainly the end of everything."

I sat still, immersed in the power of Gamaliel's words. Suddenly, I felt the courage to ask a question. It had been lurking since my first contact with Lucius—a question I hadn't even been able to formulate before this moment.

Gamaliel nodded before I could speak. "Ask," he said, "It is a problem that has rested heavy in your soul for many years."

"You know my question?" I said.

"I do, but it is important that you speak it aloud."

"All right, since you seem to know how I got here, you probably know that I grew up inside a very rigid religion. I left that behind but have never resolved the question of what to do with this being called Jesus Christ. His claims—at least the way they were interpreted for me as a child—don't leave any ambiguity. He said, 'I am the Way, the Truth and the Life. No man comes to the Father but by me.' Your story about the Tree feels true, but it seems to suggest that he was just another religious teacher—that what he came to do will one day pass away like any other system of belief."

"Do you have a question in there?" he asked gently.

I grimaced and felt my face flush. "Well…yes. Is he who he said he was? And if so, how do I reconcile that with the picture you painted about the Tree?"

Gamaliel turned to face me. "Do you know who I am? Have you ever heard my name?"

"That has been bothering me. Your name is familiar, but only vaguely. You were well-known in the early Christian church, weren't you?"

"I was a friend of Nicodemus—who was said to visit Jesus in secret. I sat with this man known as the Christ. I listened to his words. I was one of those who became a follower of his teachings. My life was forever changed. In fact, I became a teacher from within the Jewish religious establishment. After I passed through physical death, I rejoined the Master and had the answers to my own questions resolved. Do you wish to know what I learned?"

I nodded.

He looked at the oak tree and then back at me. "The Christ is the embodiment of the Light and Life that has forever flowed. The man Jesus real-ized—that is, made real in human form—the truth of All That Is. He is a pre-eminent example of the possibility that is the birthright of all people. In other words, he showed the way for everyone. We are all part of the Great Everything. He walked the path through the pain and forgetfulness of the human condition in a manner that no other had done before."

"But that sounds to me like there *is* only one way to the Father after all," I said.

"This is a great mystery—one that mystics and enlightened masters have explored since the beginning of time. You will only understand part of it now. More will open itself to you as you live the question. What you were brought up to believe was only a shadow, a story *about* Jesus Christ. What he made manifest is the true story *of* the Christ. He was a focal point of all the revealed light. Other beings—

Buddha, Krishna and many others—also pulled back the veil. Each of them discovered the Way that lies within the myriad paths to God. You see, there seem to be many paths, but there is at last only the one Way."

"My head hurts trying to take it all in, but my heart wants to say yes," I responded.

"You were brought to this place to taste of the sublime truths that cannot be contained in only one vessel," he said. "Can you see why the other helpers burned your Bible?"

"It's clearer now, I think, but will you please explain?"

"Your heart knows the answer, but I will make it a little easier for your head. Humanity is being asked to move beyond its own rigid notions. Imagine that everyone—including you—could really grasp the story of this Tree of Life. What would become of religions and myths that have controlled the history of life on this planet?"

"Oh," I shook my head and chuckled, "That's not possible of course, but if it were, we would probably abandon our differences. We'd quit fighting over who's right or wrong. We would understand that the life which flowing through all the branches is the same life. We would love and respect each other. We would..."

Gamaliel held up his hand to stop me. "You see? The other helpers brought you here to reveal that truths cannot be shackled inside the old prisons humans built for them. The Bible isn't wrong—but it was never meant to be worshiped as the only expression of God. You grew up in a belief system that would wrap chains around the living Spirit that suffuses All.

"Your particular sect is an extreme case, but most who call themselves Christians hold a similar view—that their truth is the only truth. You are being called to see beyond one form and appreciate the vital Truth that flows through all. One day you will return to the dead ashes of your old Bible and discover new meaning. It will become an entirely different book for you. For now, trust that your journey afield will not leave you lost and abandoned."

I sat thinking about Gamaliel's words. A cloud passed in front of the moon and the flames of our fire subsided. Only the dim glow from the coals illuminated the roots of the tree. Gamaliel's left hand suddenly appeared before me.

He said bluntly, "Get up now. You have more to witness before this night is over."

Chapter Twenty Seven

"This way," he said over his shoulder. Gamaliel was already walking into the dark forest, following a faint trail that led up into the hills.

Night's breath was sweet with the smell of sage and mountain laurel. Smoke from the campfire followed us as we climbed the steep path. I could hear Gamaliel's footsteps ahead of me but he was scarcely visible in the deep shadows. The trail was narrow and brush pressed in on both sides. Twigs plucked at my clothes like bony fingers and I struggled to keep pace with my guide.

We reached the top of the hill where the path followed the ridgeline. The moon shone clear and bright overhead. Gamaliel was silent and swift leading the way. We journeyed under the shining web of stars woven across the black fabric of space. I grew weary but we walked on for hours, intent upon reaching some destination that my guide had not yet revealed. Just when I was sure that I couldn't take another step, the path disappeared around a sharp bend. Gamaliel halted and looked back at me.

"Come here," he motioned, "We're very close now. Walk beside me awhile."

My exhaustion must have shown because when I came alongside him, he put his arm around my shoulders and lifted just a little. In an instant, I stood up straight and felt my strength return.

"How much farther?" I asked.

"Look there," he pointed with his chin. Just ahead, the path vanished into the side of the mountain. Moonlight revealed a cave that yawned wide like the mouth of a toothless skull. It was black. Fear stifled my breath for reasons I couldn't put in words. I tried to take a step back but he held me still.

"We have to go—in there?"

"Yes," he said in a low urgent voice, "It is necessary. Your time with us grows short and you have yet to learn some things."

"I'm afraid. Can we wait until daylight? I think I'll be ready then."

His arm around my shoulders tightened, he was silent for awhile. Finally, he sighed and said, "No, the time has come for you to enter the shadow. It is a place of mystery and your fear is natural."

"But everything I've learned—all the things you and the others taught me are so full of light. Why pay any attention to the dark? What place can it have?"

"You will find answers to these questions, but not by talking about them out here under the stars. Will you trust me when I say you must experience this place?"

My body was throbbing with electric alarm signals. I wasn't just the fact that I couldn't see inside the cave, more than that. There was something essentially terrifying about it that went beyond mere darkness. The cave seemed to mock me with silent hollow laughter that echoed in the pit of my stomach and sapped the strength from my legs. I sagged and Gamaliel's arm tightened beneath my shoulder blades again.

He leaned close to my ear and said, "What is the one word you've learned to guide you through the lessons thus far?"

It was there in my mind in an instant. No hesitation, "Surrender," I said.

"Yes. That's the one. Will you?"

I drew a ragged breath. "I will, but…to what?"

"To what? To the unknown. To what you cannot see. To walk in faith through the doorway of the cave and trust that the darkness cannot snuff you out."

I nodded my assent. We moved toward the entrance, stones rattled underfoot like the dry neck bones of a skeleton. We stopped where the path disappeared into solid black. The pressure of Gamaliel's reassuring arm vanished from my back and vertigo swirled through my body. I turned to him but he was fading like a smoke-wraith in the wind.

"You're coming with me, aren't you?" my voice sounded loud and shaky. I heard my question echo deep within the cave, but Gamaliel was gone. I was alone, one foot across the cavern's threshold—but too terrified to take the next step.

I looked around, even the moon had disappeared. The moment stretched itself while crazy thoughts raced inside my head. I was within a breath of turning back—of trying to retrace the long trail back to the campfire and the oak tree on my own.

Why am I here? No good can come from plunging into darkness, can it? The helpers can find another way. I've already learned so much.

A harsh sound nearby shattered my internal dialogue. *Caw, Caw…Caw!*

Raven! That was my last startled thought. I leapt into the open mouth of the cave.

Chapter Twenty Eight

How long? Minutes? Hours? Days? It just as easily could have been years.

I had no way of knowing how much time slipped through my fingers in the cave. Galvanized by the raven's cry, I had plummeted impetuously into the absolute dark and lost all sense of time and space.

Terrible numbness pressed in on me and filled my lungs with murky, viscous fluid that threatened to drown my very breath. I alternated between choking panic and apathetic sadness. I was sure my heart would stop beating simply for lack of reason to continue.

Surely it's been days at least, I thought. I had given up trying to create a frame of reference. The blackness was so complete that I couldn't take a single step for fear of falling into some hideous, unseen pit. I had screamed through cupped hands to try finding the walls by echo, but my own voice was swallowed without a whisper in return.

"Why am I here?" I said, the words falling flat around me as soon as they left my lips.

It was as if that question—finally spoken out loud, had pushed a magic button in the cave's nether regions. From nowhere, from everywhere, visions emerged out of the dark. So vivid, it seemed that I was thrust into a 3-D movie, where I was both an actor and observer on the set.

Without warning, I was standing on a sidewalk in Times Square. It was like being dropped onto the floor of a shiny glass-and-steel canyon. The iconic facades of tall buildings pushed up to block the sky. Throngs of dark-suited men and women stampeded past me. Sweat stained their expensive collars and panic stretched the skin of their faces. Faces, their empty faces rushed by. I looked more closely, with a shock of horror I realized that most of the people jostling me had no eyes or ears. They were running and stumbling full-tilt ahead. Clutching the clothes of their mob-fellows in a blind attempt to find their way out. To get out—at any cost.

What does this mean? What's happening here? The questions had no sooner entered my mind and I was caught in the invisible flash-flood of terror that raged through the crowd. I was swept out into the middle of the street when the traffic light changed. Horns screamed, tires barked on the pavement. Then the shock of hands on my shoulders. Strong fingers dug in hard, towing me back to the sidewalk.

A sweating male face close to mine, "You wanna die, man?" he yelled. Spittle sprayed my cheeks.

I leaned back and almost fell. He shook me again. "Are you all right?"

I tried to speak but the crowd's din drowned the words. He bent his ear close to my mouth. "Huh?" he yelled.

"What's the matter with these people?" I yelled back, "What's going on?"

"Oh, them…" he shook his head, forehead furrowed, "Look." He pointed down the street. The giant screens above Times Square usually flickered with glamorous images. I had seen them hundreds of times in movies and coffee-table book pictures. They usually flashed neon-bright with sexy models wearing designer clothes and super-star performers advertising luxury brands. All the material prizes to which modern culture aspired. My mouth fell open as I watched. The massive displays were filled with nightmares. Newscasters wide-eyed and gesticulating as footage of destruction rolled behind them.

I turned to my rescuer, but he had already walked away. I took a few sprinting, panting steps and caught him by the arm. "Hey! Stop! What's going on?" I screamed at him above the noise.

He shook off my hand and kept striding against the tide of blind and deaf business people. I caught the back of his shirt and held on, trying to keep up. Scowling, he looked back over his shoulder and shook his head fiercely.

"I'm not letting go," I yelled, "You have to tell me what to do!"

"Over there," he pointed to a doorway alcove cut into one of the buildings, "Let's go."

We needed to cross only ten feet of sidewalk, but it felt like swimming across a vicious riptide. Dark-suited men snarled and crushed against us. Women screamed in our faces, red lipstick stained their teeth like blood. They kicked me, elbowed me and I almost lost my footing. The stranger grabbed my collar and hauled me to safety out of the grinding tangle of sharp heels.

In the doorway, we both slumped against stone pillars and sucked air into our burning lungs. After a few seconds, I glanced at my reluctant friend.

"This is insane, right? Can you tell me about...this?" I gestured at the stampeding mass of humans.

He swiped his sleeve across his sweat-streaked face and shook his head. "It's over, man. Over."

"What's over? What do you mean?"

"This is all...done for," he gasped suddenly and doubled up as if he'd been knifed in the gut. He began to sob. "The world...has...it's over. I can't...believe it."

I leaned over with my face close to his, "What are you saying?"

He squinted at me in disbelief, tears rolling down the side of his nose, "What? Where you been? You don't know nothing 'bout what's going on?"

I shook my head. "No. I've been...away. Tell me, please."

He sniffed, cleared his throat a couple of times and covered his face with both hands. More sobs. Finally he caught his breath and said, "Over night. Ten, fifteen planes... Poof! Blew up. Midair. Everybody's dead. Hundreds of people. All over the world. Some American. Some British. A couple Indian jets. At least one from Israel. All gone."

"That's—that's horrible! Who did it?"

"Not sure. Some wackos from somewhere. Doesn't matter. Soon as it happened the markets fell apart. I mean bad. Never seen anything like it. Stocks, bonds, currency. Crash. Everything opened up this morning like an earthquake cracked the world in half. Some of the big global currency players cashed in their chips, too. The dollar, the pound, the yen—all destroyed. You can't imagine..."

"They closed the markets, right? We'll get a chance to take a breath and figure out what to do?"

He waved his hands as if swatting at a squadron of black flies. "Sure, trading's stopped but the damage is done. It ain't just one thing this time. It's everything. A chain reaction. Like somebody threw a match into a warehouse full of dynamite barrels. Boom. We already got food problems. Inside of hours the borders clamped tight shut. Nothing going anywhere. There's fighting starting up in places all over the world. The ant pile got kicked to shit this time for real. A whole lot of countries declared martial law this morning. What's next? Who knows." he shrugged.

"And all these people? What are they doing?" I waved at the frantic mob on the sidewalks.

"Freaking out. Going home. Going to the bar. Going to jump off a bridge...this thing's so big I think people are running just to run.

Keep your legs moving an' maybe you'll stay ahead of the monster, you know?"

"But, even with all this happening, things will settle down. I mean, they always do. Remember 9/11?" I asked, almost pleading.

"Yeah. It'll settle down, but this hurricane still hasn't run its course. I don't think it's even started all the way yet. We're all connected. The whole world isn't like it used to be. More and more, we can't stand on our own these days. What just happened upsets the whole apple cart. Food supply. Financial systems. Energy. Boom. Like I said, the barrel of dynamite finally got lit."

Realization began to materialize. He was right. All the pent-up tensions of people around the globe were about to explode in dangerous, unpredictable ways. The gods of chaos had finally shaken their restraining chains and were now roaming the Earth in sadistic joy.

He continued as if he could read my thoughts, "But now it's all real-time. It's the stuff that economists, politicians and conspiracy nuts worry might happen someday. Well, the fuse is lit and now it's all happening at once. You unravel people this bad, there's nothing left to hold back the serious crazies around the world. They're gonna do what they've been itching to do all along. Won't take much for the nutjobs with nukes to figure this is as good a time as any to fire them off."

I shook my head. "Can we stop this? I mean...what happens next?"

He looked away and didn't answer. The moving pictures on the screens showed more worried government officials talking to news anchors. A general, festooned with gold braid and colorful medals, leaned into the camera. His face was flushed and twisted. He pounded his fist to make an emphatic point. I couldn't hear his words. I didn't need to. The situation was clear enough. The world was cracking up and humans were reacting from the limbic, fight-or-flight reptilian part of their brains. *Fight or flight.* Fight or flight, wars and killing, the story of humanity's worst moments since time began.

I recalled the words from a book I read once, *"Fight or flight is a sucker's choice. There's always at least one other option to employ, but the primitive, prehistoric part of our brain doesn't know that when we're faced with sudden dire circumstances. We tend to react immediately by running away or trying to smash whatever threatens us."*

"A third option," I said aloud.

My companion turned to look at me, "What did you say?"

"We need a third option. We know better than this."

"What're you talking about?"

"This is it. This is the big test. For thousands of years we keep coming to this point and failing. You know, fight or flight? I mean..." I paused, feeling certain that my words were a hopeless jumble, "I mean, humans keep building things up and learning more about everything, but just when we get close to taking the big leap... Just when we get close to making life good for everyone this happens. Smack! We hit a big bump and go back to running and fighting and killing each other. I think we know enough to do things different this time. We can write a different kind of story."

"You think that's gonna work? Wade out in the middle of the street and try an' tell that to the mob. Think they'll listen? You're crazy, man. This is how it's always been. Nothing's going to stop this madness until the fire burns itself out — and who knows what'll be left when that's done. We're on the edge of total destruction this time," he said.

Just then, a tremendous explosion shredded the already turbulent scene. A giant fist pounded the Earth. I was lifted off my feet by the shockwave and thrown into the air, twisting like a broken doll in a tornado. It was too much, I welcomed the sharp-fanged blackness. Its gaping mouth swallowed me whole.

I woke floating in darkness. The bright moon shining silver on my weightless body. I blinked, where on Earth was I? That thought rolled me over. *Earth.* Far, far below the silent Earth turned on its axis. It looked the way you see it in satellite pictures. The oceans glowed placid blue. The continents were mottled brown with wrinkled skin, furred in patches by some green fungus. Motionless white clouds curled themselves along the jetstream currents.

Am I dead now? I thought, *Is this what it's like?* Where was the shattered city and churning mobs of blind-deaf people? How much time had passed since the thundering Thor's-hammer crash hurled me into black oblivion?

Like a balloon's tether being yanked hard, I was irresistibly pulled downward in a sickening plunge. Down... down... I fell, regaining sensation with each fathom of empty space that whooshed past my body. Ice-clouds stung my skin and a few seconds later, the humid vapor of Earth's firmament engulfed me. I'm sure I screamed. I must have screamed. This waking nightmare vision of the Earth rushing toward me became all too real.

I slammed into the grip of giant invisible hands. Helpless, prone and quivering, the hands took me speeding face-down over the landscape below. A wailing howl assaulted my ears—I was sure it must be the wind. The sound keened on and on, pregnant with unbearable fear and sorrow. *Not the wind,* I thought, *but what?* In answer to my silent question, the soul-piercing cry intensified. It vibrated and undulated like a mother in wordless shattering sorrow for her dying baby.

Sounds like the Earth itself is weeping, I thought, *what has broken her heart like this?*

Unseen hands held me close so I could see the cause of Great Mother's grief. All around the globe, flashes of battles, scenes of starvation and desperate, terrified people appeared. The entire world was afire. I tried to hide my eyes—to turn away—but the implacable grip forced me to see all that transpired below.

Time stood still but the world turned quickly. I saw days...weeks...and months pass. Hatred and fighting erupted like raging volcanoes. The gaunt twin demons, Hunger and Disease, prowled among the nations leaving mass graves of broken bones in their wake.

I wept. Wept for all the raped mothers and their tender, broken children. Wept for the men and boys flung into mindless battle. Wept for the destruction of mankind's noblest ambitions. Wept for hope and joy now lost forever in the savage flames.

Will this ever end? I thought, *Can they wake up from this insane dream and remember Who They Really Are?*

Through my blurring tears, I thought I saw bright beings at the four corners of the Earth. They stood aside while the furies did their worst below. I thought I saw them holding space with their heads bowed and wings covering their faces.

Helpers? Angels? Why don't they stop this? Why didn't they prevent it? What purpose can this destruction serve?

Chapter Twenty Nine

And still weeping, I awoke inside the cave. Hot tears ran down my cheeks soaking my shirt. Sobs choked my breath as the visions faded. All but one.

The darkness was still thick and stifling, but a mysterious, slender glow pooled on the dirt and stone where I sat. I blinked and squinted, trying to find the source of the unexpected light. I couldn't imagine where it could possibly come from. My head cleared and I became aware of a raging thirst. My salty tongue rattled in my mouth like a sun-dried lizard carcass and my throat burned with desert breath.

I reached out with my hands and the luminous circle grew larger around me. A few yards away, something gleamed mirror-bright in the gloom. *Water? Thank all the gods and goddesses!* I thought and scraped forward. Sharp-edged pebbles stabbed my palms and knees but I could only keep crawling toward the promise of fresh water.

It took many slow minutes to drag my parched, shaking body to the edge of the pool. I found it at last and knelt, panting, with my hands in the cold water. I dug them into the sand and gravel bottom and rested. The light had followed me and was brighter now. Urgent thirst denied my curiosity. I leaned forward to plunge my face in the water and drink but stopped halfway.

A stranger's reflection appeared on the pool's flickering surface. I didn't recognize the bony, bearded man who looked back into my eyes. His lips were blistered and his cheekbones pushed out sharp against the weathered skin of his face. I blinked. He blinked. I smiled. His lips drew back, too. Stranger still, this man glowed with an inner light that sparkled on the tiny ripples in the pool. I shook my head. The man mirrored me, dark shaggy hair falling down over his face.

He looks like a pilgrim, a traveler from a different time and place, I thought, *can this be me? When did this happen?*

Thirsty. So terribly thirsty. I closed my eyes to block the image of the gaunt, glowing wanderer and plunged my mouth into the pool. *Drink, drink, drink now...* Three, four, five enormous gulps of cold liquid heaven cascaded down my throat to fill my trembling belly. I gasped and stopped to catch my breath.

I opened my eyes and watched the ripples fade. The pool smoothed itself to a mirror again. My dripping lips nearly touched its surface. In frozen horror, I saw that I was not alone in the cave. Reflected in the gleaming water were shadow figures watching. At least a dozen of them—maybe more. All with twisted, terrifying features—they leaned in close behind my back.

I choked and tried to scream but no sound came. The dark creatures pressed closer. Spider-fingers clawed my back and neck. Electrified I whirled, flailing my fists and grunting strangled growls. Immediately they vanished into the black crevices of the dungeon cave.

Then the light went out and I sat shaking...sobbing...gasping with garbled prayers and curses.

Moments or days later, who can tell, a familiar whisper echoed in my mind. *"Breathe...surrender..."* she said.

I resisted the gentle advice that had served me well over and over since my journey in this strange universe began. With every nerve and muscle, I wanted to run, to fight. But where to run? Whom to fight? The light was out, I couldn't move. Straining to hear, yet no sound came. Staring with ferocious intensity, but seeing nothing.

Exhausted and despairing, I closed my eyes and drew a long, ragged breath. *I'll die here. I know it,* I thought. *Breathe in...breathe out...*a small calm nestled in my chest. *Breathe in...breathe out...*the tight muscles of my neck relaxed. *Breathe in...breathe out...*warmth crept up my spine and melted the ice-hard terror.

More time passed but I lost all sense of tracking it. Thoughts dissolved. Without opening my eyes I felt the light returning, filling my body and replacing the dread. My hands fell loose in my lap. I blinked down at them. Nothing moved, but the glow around me was stronger. I sat up straight and looked for the shadow dwellers.

Hiding, I thought, *but why? Can't they see that I'm alone here. They must know how much I fear them.*

"Come out here," I said out loud, surprising myself with fresh courage, "Let me see you."

A few bat-wing rustles came from the shadows, a pebble rattled. I could not see beyond the little circle of my light.

I stood and held out my arms, "Who are you? Come, tell me your names. Or if you want to destroy me, then get on with it. You can see I'm not armed. If you come in peace, show yourselves. You have nothing to fear from me."

A ghostly whisper came from behind me, "You hate us. You want nothing to do with us. All your life you pretended that we don't exist. We are less than nothing."

"But I don't know you," I said, "I can't see you."

I heard a chorus of hollow, mocking laughter. "Oh, you know us," the invisible spokesman said, "You can't see us because you despise us. You ran away and fought us off all your life. You pushed us into this cave and closed up the opening nice and tight. We know how happy you are keeping us trapped in darkness."

"I know you? I trapped you? Let me be the judge of that. Come here into the light where I can see you."

"Judge? You be the judge? That's what you've always been. Judge, jury and jailer. Why should we expose ourselves to more of your judgment? We've had quite enough of that," he said and I heard a rippled mutter of agreement from the rest.

I sighed and sat back down. "Listen, I have no choice but to believe you. I'm alone in the cave with you now. There must be some reason we're here together. If you'll come talk with me, I promise to listen. I have no power over you anymore. See?" I held my hands up, empty, "I have no keys to lock you away. If I was afraid of you, it's because you showed up out of nowhere and startled me."

"No, you fear us because of how we look to you. Here, see if that's true." Feet scuffed in the gravel and a crooked, looming figure appeared at the edge of the light circle. He paused, his face still in shadow.

"I'm here," he said, "Look at me."

"Who are you? I can't see your face."

"You don't want to. You never did."

I shook my head, frustrated. "You're probably right. Come closer and sit with me. I know it's time for us to talk."

He hesitated in the gloom. I sensed him trying to decide whether to accept my invitation or vanish back into hiding.

"Please," I spread my hands, palms up in welcome, "I mean it. You're safe."

He surprised me by kneeling down on all fours and creeping forward, head bent. Halfway out of the shadows, he stopped and slowly raised his face so I could see him. From two feet away, he stank. Stale body odor, cigarette smoke and other nameless funks rose from his clothing. I started to recoil, then caught myself and smiled.

"Hello, I'm Jacob," He scooted forward and sat cross-legged. I held out my hand. We shook. His palm was dry and covered with grime.

We sat for a long silent minute looking at each other. *He's homeless,* I thought. His face was a crumpled brown map of wrinkles. Sunken lips told their story of missing teeth. He kept blinking—trying to meet my gaze but failing. His hair was white, wild and yellow-stained from sleeping under bridges and smoking cigarettes. Patches of sunburned scalp showed through the thin patches.

I reached out and touched the knee of his ragged jeans. "What's your name? Tell me about yourself. I want to know."

He hacked a rattling, painful cough into his shirt sleeve and wiped his nose. "I'm Tim," he said.

I took a long breath and smiled again. "Hi, Tim. I'm glad to meet you. Can you tell me about yourself?"

"Not much to tell," he said, "I'm...well, you can see what I am. Homeless. Got nothin' really. I live wherever I land and get by askin' folks for money. A bum, I guess you'd call me. By the way, you don't got an extra smoke, do you? I'm running a little short right now."

I patted my pockets, shrugged and shook my head. "No, I don't have much of anything with me. Look at me. I'm pretty ragged myself."

He grinned, then started to chuckle until a coughing fit cut him off. "I can see that. I guess we ain't so different at the moment, are we?"

"No, we aren't. So why did you think I'd hate you so much?"

"Oh, I've seen you in town lots of times. You never noticed me, not really. Couple times outside Walmart you tossed a buck in my cup, but I know you didn't want to look at me."

I searched my memory but couldn't remember seeing him before. It must have showed on my face because he nodded.

"Yeah. Don't worry about it. I'm everything you wouldn't want to be. You're a sharp, rich business guy. No reason you'd pay attention to a drifter—some loser who made all the wrong turns in life. I know what I am. Too late to change that now."

Shame flushed my cheeks and I felt tears sting my eyes. *He's right.*

He waved a hand before I could reply. "Don't worry 'bout it. Wait a minute. We can talk some more, but first you should meet my friends. I think they'll want in on this chat, too." So saying, he turned and crawled back into the shadows. I noticed that the light-circle had grown larger and brighter since our conversation began.

The shadow people gathered behind Tim as he shuffled back to join me, but they stopped short of the light. I heard nervous mutters and a whimper or two from the small crowd of bent figures in the dark.

Tim took his seat near me again and shook his head. "Looks like you're gonna have to call them in yourself. They didn't believe me when I told them it's safe to show themselves."

I stood and held out my hands. "Please. All of you. Come join Tim and I."

One at a time, they cringingly came forward and seated themselves. Light expanded to encompass the whole gathering as they took their places in a semi-circle before me.

I was stunned. Tim looked like someone who might live in a cave. Most of his companions did not. One of them—a beautiful woman—stared at me, her dark eyes bold and seductive. She pushed her breasts out and when she crossed her legs, her short skirt rode up high to reveal firm gleaming thighs...and just...a little... forbidden bit more. Still watching me, she turned her face and raised an eyebrow. She smiled slowly and desire squeezed its hot fingers tight around my throat. Blood rushed to my head. I covered my face with both hands and sat there, panting.

"See," I heard her say, "I knew it. You want me but you hate me, too. You men are all the same."

"But I've never seen you before. What do you mean, I hate you?"

"Never seen me? Oh, you've seen me," she said, anger hardening her voice, "I've caught you watching me at the mall and in restaurants. Remember that Las Vegas hotel lobby? I was there and so were you. You always look for me, but when I show up, you pretend I'm invisible. Like right now. You can't stand who I am, can you?"

From behind my hands I asked, "Who are you?" But I knew already.

She laughed, loud and harsh. "I'm a whore, that's who I am. I'll take your money and blow your mind."

I heard her move and felt the soft heat of her face near mine. She whispered in my ear, "I'll do it now, right here." Her fingers fumbled with my belt buckle. *Yes...yes...yes,* thoughts screamed in my head.

"No!" I grabbed her wrists, "Stop...I can't." My heart beat fast, sweat prickled my scalp.

She tore her hands away from mine. After a long moment, I opened my eyes. She was sitting as before—only now her face was in her hands and she was sobbing.

Sadness replaced lust. I held my hands together to stop their shaking. Tears ran down my face, too.

"I'm sorry," I said, "I mean...I'm so confused. I shouldn't want you, but I do."

"I'm horrible," she sobbed, "Horrible. It's not your fault. It's mine. I didn't start out this way. It just sort of...happened, you know?"

"How?" I asked, "How did it happen? I've always wondered."

She glanced up and must have seen a new expression in my eyes. Compassion? "Oh, you know. I was a pretty young thing. Big dreams, places to go. Along the way, things got tough. No money but I had this body—the kind men dream about. I found out I could pay the bills if I gave it up. Just favors back and forth at first, then a little more. Pretty soon I called them clients and pretended I wasn't selling my soul."

I nodded.

She sniffed and glared at me, "I know. I'm a cliché, right? Weak and miserable and shallow and dirty?"

"No, no. I wasn't thinking that. Just..."

"Just what?"

"Just that I understand. At least, I think I do. I hope you'll sit with me while I meet these others. Please don't leave."

She held my gaze for a long time and finally nodded.

Intense, I thought, *not sure how much more of this I can handle.* I turned to look at the other silent watchers who crouched around me.

A little boy huddled nearby, cradling a broken toy. Some secret fear twisted his face. My heart broke imagining the injustice that had stained his innocence. I longed to take him in my arms and whisper "everything's all right. You're safe."

On the other side, a tall man stared at me with the cruel eyes of a dictator. I was repelled by his implicit control and lack of mercy. Without smiling, he shook his head at me. *I'm wasting his time,* I thought, *he has no use for me. Well, it's mutual...what an arrogant ass.*

One by one, I made acquaintance with the shadow folk. In the light at last, they were real. Some pitiful, some angry, some disturbed. No matter. Now that I could see their faces and listen to their words, they didn't appear as cave demons any longer. They were real and I was real—and the light surrounded us all.

The light, I thought, *it's so bright I can barely see their faces.*

At that moment, from somewhere deep inside the cave, a gong crashed. *Boomshee!*

Vibrations shook the air and a whirlwind lifted me from the floor. Around and around I spun while the vision of my visitors faded. Just before they disappeared, each one of them flashed before my eyes. Something strange—a curious trick of light, perhaps—transformed their features. The bum, the whore, the wounded child, the dictator and the rest—they all were wearing my face.

Chapter Thirty

The meadow was warm with sunshine. I stood, arms outstretched, face upturned to the light—a human cross. The breeze blew and I swayed in its currents. Like a tree rooted in the mountain soil, I drank the air and basked in the nature of being.

A sound behind me cracked the silent moment. Thoughts filtered through the fissures in my stillness. *Where am I now? Where's the cave...how come I'm standing in daylight?*

A familiar voice that seemed to speak from a great distance gently said, "Come back now. Come back to Earth, you traveler."

Lucius? I forced my eyes open and stared, looking hard for him. I saw only trees, grass and sunlight. A crow swooped and landed at the meadow's edge.

Behind me, I heard my friend chuckle. "You didn't think I'd be away forever, did you?"

I tried to turn my head but couldn't move. Lucius put his hands on my shoulders, my arms descended from their cross position and hung limp at my sides. My knees shook and began to fold. Lucius caught me around the chest and helped me to sit. He sat in front of me shaking his head. Smiling with his eyes.

"You," he said, "You crazy, bold little man. So here we are again."

I blinked and tried to speak. My voice croaked. I cleared my throat and tried again. "What...why...how did I get here? The cave? The end of the world? Those people?"

He waved his hand. "Shh, I'll explain in a minute. First, let's ask the other helpers to join us."

He reached for the drum he carried by a leather thong over his shoulder. Handing it to me he said, "Here, you call them. You know how." I took it and looked at him. He nodded.

"Go ahead."

I closed my eyes and touched the drum's taut leather head. *Pum...* it said. Strength ran up my spine. I breathed deep and struck the drum again, harder. *Pum...* I peeked at Lucius. His eyes were closed and he had put his hands together as if in prayer.

Pum, pum, pum... I tapped the drum. A warm breeze embraced me then came closer to kiss my face.

I laughed loudly and beat the drum with palm and knuckles. *PUM pum pum pum, Pum pum pum pum, PUM pum pum pum.*

I was on my feet, dancing, swaying, laughing and crying. The music went on and on. I moved with eyes closed, yet I saw lights and figures gathering near me. Time paused in its constant ticking. I whirled and stomped, bent and jumped.

My laughter became a song without words. It flowed from an inner fountain, an inner source. The drum beat itself and other voices joined mine. Wild and free, I never wanted to stop.

At that moment, a raven called out in the symphony's midst. Still dancing, I looked up and the old monk appeared. He beamed and clapped his hands in time with me. Lucius still sat silent, but his face glowed.

One by one, the other helpers materialized: the medicine man, the Aborigine woman, Kaitlyn, Gamaliel and the rest. They took their places and my drumming dance slowed. I bowed to my friends. They looked at me and each of them bowed in return. Exhausted at last, I was ready to sit.

We sat in deep reverence a long time. I closed my eyes and saw myself at the hub of a wheel—one made of love and acceptance.

Lucius clapped his hands and spoke. "Brothers and sisters, welcome to this place. The time has come for our young student to return to the world of men, but first we owe him some explanation of what he has seen."

I looked around. The helpers sat, waiting for him to continue.

His face grew thoughtful and he regarded me without speaking for a while.

Finally he said, "So, what questions do you have before we send you home?"

"Do I have to go?" Tears stung my eyes. "Can't I stay here? I still have so much to learn."

He sighed and shook his head. "Your purpose on Earth is not completed. You have a mission, remember?"

"You haven't told me what it is and anyway, I'm not ready yet."

"We have gathered here—in fact you called us—to reveal your task. Be patient, we'll get to it. First, I know you have other questions begging for answers. What are they?"

I wiped my eyes. "You left me with Jack. He taught me so much. Where is he now?"

Lucius smiled, "He's being Jack somewhere. You might see him again...or you might not."

The cave appeared in my mind. *What was that all about?* I thought.

Lucius said, "Yes. That's your question, isn't it? We'll let this one explain." He motioned to Gamaliel.

I turned toward my scar-faced guide, he inclined his head and raised his good hand in greeting. "What do you wish to know?" he said.

"The end of the world. Did I see what will be? Is that how things turn out? Who were those blind, deaf people?"

"Ah, so many questions. How did that vision make you feel, young man?"

"It was terrifying. Horrible. Like scenes from the Book of Revelations, Armageddon and tribulation. But I'm confused, too."

He nodded. "As well you should be. Welcome to the world of the prophets, my son."

"Prophets? Are you saying that the world must end in fire? That's the only way it can go for us?"

He stood up, sunlight came shining through the holes in his clothes. "Humans have forgotten their birthright. What you saw was born of millennia spent creating darkness, greed, scarcity and love of control," he spread his arms wide. "You stand upon the Earth like sorcerers dressed in robes of white and black. In one hand, you hold the power to build a world of peace, a place of joy and light. In the other, a world of hate and evil. Which will it be?"

"So, we have a choice? The end I saw isn't certain?"

He shook his head. "Certain? Nothing is ever certain in the way you mean it."

"But what I saw made sense. It could happen that way at any second. The Third World War, you know? The end of life as we know it..."

"It could. Yes, it could. That's the key. Could is a fulcrum—a place of choice. The planet is like a seesaw. Energy has built up on the destructive side for so long that the tipping point is near."

"You're saying that we have a choice, but what can be done to change the momentum?"

Gamaliel nodded at Lucius, "He'll tell you more." He took his seat again with the others.

Lucius was silent, looking off into the sky. "As within, so without," he murmured after a few seconds.

I squinted at him. "What?"

"Law of the universe."

"Yes, but what does it mean?"

"You had a second vision in the cave. It was related to the first. Do you know how?"

"Oh, the shadow people?"

"Yes, those."

"It felt important, but I can't think how it helps me understand the first vision. It shook me up but didn't clarify anything."

"What did you see?"

I told him the story as best I could—about the bum and the whore, the crying child and the dictator, about my glimpses of thieves and murders further back in the darkness...about the twisted shadow creatures who crawled into the light.

"...and in the end, they all became me," I said.

"What do you suppose that means?"

I thought about this. The circle of helpers was silent around me.

"Lucius, I'm at a loss," I said, "It's a symbol, I imagine—a lesson I needed to learn?"

"The world is a reflection of you. You want to see only positive, happy things—and so does the world. You have ignored your shadow-self your entire life. You've suppressed dark thoughts and refused to know the ugly parts of yourself. So has the world. Does it all go away just because you won't look at it?"

"Well, probably not, but where does it go?"

"It builds up and becomes powerful. It seeks to express itself in ugly ways. You can't worship your light and lock your shadow in a dungeon forever. Yet that's exactly what you've tried to do all your life—and so has most of the world."

"This is confusing. Everything else you've showed me has carried me to places where love and light are everything. How does this fit together?" He leaned forward and placed his hands on my shoulders. "Your Earth is a classroom. It's a place of illusion—a dream within a dream. You see light and darkness as separate from each other."

"But they are!" I said, interrupting him, "I know the difference."

"Do you?" he said, "Do you really?"

"How can they be the same? One is light and one . . . isn't."

"You used the magic word without even knowing it."

"Which magic word?"

"One," he said, "There is only One. One light, one mind, one consciousness that cannot be divided."

"But the darkness?"

"It's only light that has not yet awakened into consciousness. It is only sleeping light. In your vision, what happened when those creatures came out of the shadows?"

"The light got brighter."

"Exactly."

Silence filled the meadow. All the helpers held me with their presence. The vast sky pressed close, the air's breath a potpourri of dry grass and pine needles.

Lucius did something with his eyes that roused my mind to questions again.

"I feel the truth," I said, "It's right here, sitting with us, isn't it?"

He nodded without moving his head. *How does he do that?* I thought.

"You're sending me back. What happens next?"

"We have spoken of great things here. You've seen deep truths and answers to ancient riddles. The time has come for you to go back and bring with you all you've learned."

"But, Lucius," I said, "These things make sense in your world. How can I possibly translate them so people who haven't been here will understand? I barely understand myself."

"Live," he said, "Walk the path. Be the path. Weave your awakening into the fabric of every day."

"Doesn't sound to me like that will change the world. You said before we're running out of time on the planet. Shouldn't I get on TV? Wake people up...warn them?"

"You could," he said, "but that would just set you up as another guru. Some people would hate you, others would flock to you. You'd get caught in that story. The last thing the world needs is another guru trying to convince them of something."

"But if we don't hurry, won't it all fall apart? What does it matter if I see the truth and humanity destroys itself?"

"Be careful now," he said, "You've seen truths but don't ever allow yourself to believe that you've found *the* Truth. As soon as you do that, you confine All That Is inside a box," he made a square with his hands, "here are the sides and here's the top. Then a new religion is born and the same old story goes on. See?"

"I do see. Thank you. But, what about the end of the world? What if time runs out and people don't change course? What if we destroy ourselves? Doesn't that shut down the classroom forever?"

He smiled and shook his head. The other helpers smiled, too. "You humans worry too much. You think you're so important. Listen to me, All of Life Itself is never done. It's always becoming more of What Is. Life finds a way.—Always."

"Then, why do anything? Why try?"

"You're stalling, aren't you," he said and laughed. "You know that we could spend years of your time with these questions. On and on, then you wouldn't ever have to leave. Let me make it simple for you."

He fished behind him and brought out a bottle of water and a piece of bread. "Here, eat. Take a drink."

It surprised me to notice I was extremely hungry and thirsty. I gulped water until it ran down my chin. Once I was chewing a mouthful of bread, he continued.

"Don't argue with what is. You've experienced your light...your eternal self, but you have a body and you live on Earth. The purpose of life is to experience Itself. God becomes more God by waking up through you—and the trees, the birds, even the rocks. From the highest to the lowest, all are part of the grand process."

I wanted to say something but my mouth was still full. He went on,

"All over the world, people like you are waking up to Who They Really Are. Pure freedom comes from knowing yourself fully. This is an eternal path with no beginning and no end. If the Earth you inhabit can't regain its balance—if it destroys itself—Life will seek out other forms of expression. Do you remember Gamaliel's story of the tree?"

I nodded.

"Your mission is simple. Not easy of course, but simple. Go back. Remember what you've learned. See the world through new eyes. Then, when you feel the truths you know in your body, tell others about it. This is important. You are a messenger of love. You don't need a pulpit or a radio show, but it's all right if you decide to use something like that. Maybe you can write a book if it will help get the story out. You humans love your stories."

I brushed crumbs off my shirt and said, "How will I know what to say back there? Who will listen?"

Lucius looked over at Kaitlyn and motioned with his head. She came forward and sat close to me. I smiled. She sparkled like fresh champagne.

"Hello," she said, "I'm glad to see you again before you leave."

"Oh, me too!"

She smiled and said earnestly, "You don't remember agreeing to go to Earth, but you did it on purpose. You have a lot of family here—people you haven't met yet. You all got together and arranged to come here at this specific time. Of course, once you arrived you forgot. Now, you're beginning to remember Who You Really Are. The lights are on. You're going to start finding your family. Don't worry how, just know that it will happen."

"So..."

"So," she continued, "you don't need to figure out what to say or who will listen. Everything you need will unfold perfectly. It won't always feel that way. You'll still worry about paying your bills and you'll wonder how to get your life on track."

I frowned, "I'd rather go back with a plan. Isn't that part of the deal?"

The helpers all burst into laughter around me. Lucius ho ～u and rocked back and forth. After some time they finally settled down. Kaitlyn wiped her eyes and sighed.

"A plan, well," and then she giggled some more, "Um...the plan is that you live your life. Shine your light. Let go of anything that feels old and heavy. This won't be easy, but do it anyway."

I looked at Lucius. "You know, I feel tricked or something. When we first met, you told me there was some big important mission. That I had to leave my old life and follow you...all of that stuff. This sounds too simplistic, too basic."

He shook his head. "Just wait 'til you get back to where you've been. You don't feel the drama with us, but once you're there again it'll all come rushing back to you. You're going to feel like a hero from the old myths struggling with supernatural powers. Your life will change. People won't recognize you. You're going to feel the pressure of the world at war with itself and wonder how any of this..." he spread his hands, "works down there."

I shrugged, "but..."

He held up his hand, "But that's the point. It doesn't work down there. Not yet. That's the job for you and all the others waking up right now. Your mission is to bring Heaven and Earth together. One breath at a time. One courageous act of love at a time. That's how you change your world. Even when everything seems completely wrong, when all you know comes crashing down...and most things will. The old structures—governments, nations, economies, anything built on fear and darkness—all of it will have to crumble before a new way is revealed. This will be frightening for a time. Not just for you. Everyone will feel it. You, and those like you, have experiences so you'll know there is a better way—so you can tell the others about it."

Kaitlyn leaned in and said, "Have you ever walked into a basement, one that's completely dark?"

I nodded.

"And if you lit a match down there, what would happen? Can the darkness alone put out the little flame?"

"Of course not."

"No. It can't. You can never out-dark the light. Even the smallest candle is more powerful than the deepest night."

Lucius said, "And so it is in your world. All over the planet, people are bursting into flame. Imagine that. Old stories are fading, ancient lies are losing their power. The light grows brighter."

From the circle, the old medicine man spoke, "You go light your own fire. Wait for those who are ready to join you beside it."

I turned to look at him. He nodded gravely.

Lucius said, "Yes, as it is true that when the student is ready the teacher will appear, it's also true that when the teacher is ready the student will appear. You're a crusader by nature. You'll have to learn to sit on the sidelines and wait. This won't be easy. Many will call you to join their crusades. You'll want to start some of your own.—Don't. Crusaders get killed or they destroy other people along the way. Walk softly and cherish solitude. Learn from everything, teach by living. The world is your mirror and your classroom."

Kaitlyn smiled and said, "It's also your playground. Laugh a lot, mostly at yourself. Love your wife. Play with your children. Feed people." She leaned forward to tweak my nose, "and lighten up!"

Lucius sprang to his feet. "Come on. It's time."

The helpers came forward as a group, dry grass rustling under their feet. They lifted me up and started singing a song with no words. Drums thumped and arms held me. I turned my face to the sky. A pair of turkey vultures soared above, black and silver against deep blue.

Around and around we danced. I felt Kaitlyn's face near mine. "It's time to go," she whispered, "remember what to do?"

I looked at her and smiled while tears ran down my cheeks. Then I nodded and closed my eyes. *Breathe... surrender...*

Epilogue

A warm wind stirs the leaves of a maple tree. It stands a few yards from the rental house where my family and I live now. Sitting alone on the front porch, I have retreated to this vantage point to survey the unfamiliar landscape of my life. Very little makes sense and I can't muster the energy to sort it out just yet. Questions float through my mind like ghost shadows of passing clouds across the sun: How did it all happen? What does it all mean? Where do I go from here?

Something shiny on the concrete steps catches my eye. I squint, bend down and scoop it up. The sun is bright so I blink a couple of times, trying to focus. It turns out to be an inexpensive silver charm bracelet that I gave my wife a few weeks ago. I saw it in the clearance bin at a discount store and bought it for her. Only three dollars, just a little way to say I love you. Holding it up, I notice its clasp is broken. The dangling ornament is still intact and inscribed with one word,

"Believe."

"Believe." Yes. I love that word. It bothers me though. Believe in what, exactly? From where I sit, the world looks topsy-turvy. Everything I once believed so fervently has been burned to ashes and blown away on the wind. It's as if a Divine Arsonist appeared in the night and set fire to all my most sacred illusions. Religion, career, ambitions, possessions...all gone. What now? What's real and what can I still call my own?

A splintered kaleidoscope of pain, sounds and light forced me into consciousness. My breath burned like fire in my throat. Electric tributaries of anguished nerve endings tormented the left side of my body. I felt my eyelids flutter open and daylight stabbed long unused retinas. The focus blurred and my eyes seemed to roll sideways, then backward into darkness again.

"Shh... It's okay. I'm here. Oh, my God, I think he's waking up!"

Jennifer? The voice sounded like my wife. *Where am I? What on Earth?*

Eyes blinking. Head swimming. Trying to focus. Soft fingertips stroked my forehead.

"Don't try to move. It's okay." Fog evaporated from my vision and I saw my wife's eyes. Very close.

What's going on?

A croaking sound rasped from between my teeth. "You? Where am I?" I tried to say around a hard plastic respirator tube in my mouth. She leaned over me. Her fingers traced down my face and gently covered my lips.

"Don't talk now. Just rest. You're safe. Oh, I'm so..." Her eyes filled with tears. I felt a large warm drop land on the left side of my nose and trickle down my cheek. She sniffed and covered her eyes, then buried her face in the sheets covering my chest. I felt her shaking with sobs.

"You're back," her words were muffled against me, "I knew you'd come back."

After a parade of doctors and nurses trailed in and out of the room with their bright lights, beeping instruments and professional mutters, she told me what had happened.

"I got a call late in the evening after you left. It was your state trooper friend, David. He was on patrol up Highway 21 and found you by the turnoff. You know, right there at Grimes Creek? Someone smashed into you. A hit and run, we think. It knocked your car completely off the road. Everything caught fire. No one was around to see what actually happened but it's a miracle that you got out alive.

We can't imagine how you did it. Your seatbelt—what was left of it—was still fastened. It's almost like someone was there to pull you out at the last second.

David found you lying unconscious, badly burned and completely naked in the creek. He was sure that you were dead at first. All your hair was singed off. We still don't know how you got out of your clothes and escaped from the car. You even took off your watch and shoes. Everything was destroyed."

I blinked and tried to say something, Jennifer waved a warning finger to stop me and continued.

"Thank God for David and for that creek. They said the cold water probably saved your life. David called in a Lifeflight helicopter and covered you with a blanket. He stayed with you the whole time. They got you down here to St. Luke's but you were in a coma by then. That was four months ago. Four months. The doctors are shocked that you made it at all. You were a mess. The whole left side of your body was shattered, ribs, arm, pelvis. The burns were bad but they were more worried about the skull fracture. They kept testing you for brain wave activity and every time they were amazed by the results. Even though you were deep in a coma, they said it was like you were living a parallel life somewhere else."

The feeding tube and all the wires taped to my head prevented me from nodding but I smiled inside when she said that. *A parallel life…oh, if only you knew!*

Later that evening—after the doctors had removed the feeding tube from my nose—my children came into the room bursting with love and life. They hugged me carefully and stood there beaming. As we talked, they exchanged private glances that I found hard to understand, but I was so filled with joy that I didn't pay much attention.

A few days passed and I was able to sit up and drink meals through a straw. My recovery was rapid after I returned to normal consciousness. Other visitors and well-wishers came and went in a steady stream. So many friends but the conversations were awkward. After a few minutes, they'd shuffle their feet, glance around the room, squeeze my hand and mumble something encouraging then leave. No one knew what to do with the person lying helpless under the sheets. This was not the man they had always known. I had become an enigma to them—or a cautionary tale, perhaps.

Conspicuously absent were my business partners. After several days, I asked Jennifer about it. She twisted her face into a thoughtful mask and looked away for several moments. When she met my eyes again, her expression was full of apprehension.

"I don't know how to tell you this part. Things have changed."

"What do you mean?" I said.

She took a deep breath, leaned over to kiss me on the lips and suddenly burst into tears. After a moment, she regained composure and took my face between her hands. Her eyes were full of pain but she moved close and whispered, "I want you to know that I love you more than ever. I still can't believe what's happened but it doesn't change how I feel about you."

Dread was heavy in my chest. *What now?*

She wiped her eyes and said, "After you'd been here for a couple of weeks, I started picking up the pieces—trying to sort out bills, keep the kids in some kind of routine. Before long, I realized that we were out of money. I talked with your partners to see what could be done . . . . That conversation went badly. It turned out that your business was far more precarious than I could've imagined. You never really brought it up that often. Anyway, they tried to shield me but I knew something big was going on. Apparently things had been coming to a head—you must have been aware of some of it. Well, after you left and had the accident everything accelerated. Your sales team fell apart within the first couple of weeks and no revenue was coming in any more.

But we can talk about it later. Right now, I just want you to rest and get well. Don't worry. We'll be all right."

My face felt frozen. "So, the retirement account? Our credit?"

She shook her head. "While you were in a coma, the stock market crashed. I called your financial guy and withdrew what I could from the IRA's, but there wasn't much left. The credit cards were loaded up already and I missed a payment or two in the craziness after your accident. Because of what's going on in the financial markets, the card companies cancelled our accounts. I called and tried to work something out, but they wouldn't do anything—especially after I let it slip that you were out of the picture."

I closed my eyes. The bottom dropped out of my stomach. "I suppose the house...?"

"Well, it hasn't happened yet, but we're going to lose it. I found a foreclosure notice stapled to the front door three days ago."

What was the advice that my helpers had repeated over and over when I was facing my deepest fears? Breathe...surrender... I drew in a slow breath, released it and opened my eyes. Jennifer squeezed my hand.

"You know we're going to be all right, don't you? I never cared about all the stuff very much."

"But, your house..." I said, "You loved it."

She sighed, "Yes. I hate to lose it, but right now, I'm just so happy to have you back that nothing else matters. We're going to be okay. Really."

"Do you mean that, or are you trying to be brave so I won't worry?"

"There are good days and bad. Sometimes I feel sick to my stomach but I keep being reminded that 'this too shall pass.' The sun will rise again."

Wise, wise woman, I thought but that didn't stop the swimming in my head. *What's next for us?*

After awhile she kissed me, then left so I could sleep.

I lay there a long time in the shadowy room and tried to remember my way back to the circle of helpers—back to the glowing transcendent love. Their faces were distant and ephemeral. I wondered if everything I experienced was the product of injury-induced hallucinations.

Weeks passed. I eventually saw myself in a mirror and was shocked by my reflection. My hair was growing back slowly but the burn trauma down the side of my face was red and angry. I didn't recognize myself. I had lost more than sixty pounds. My eyes stared out of a gaunt, shrunken shadow of who I had been. "You're a lucky man," the doctors said over and over, "Your bones will heal and your burns will fade. No one will know the difference in a couple of months." *Oh, but I will. I'll never be the same,* I thought.

The day came when they wheeled me down to the elevator and out through the shiny hospital lobby where my wife waited to pick me up. The kids were in school, so it was just the two of us riding in the van on our way home. January. Clouds hung low like a heavy gray ceiling over the valley and the roads were icy. A few houses still had their Christmas lights up and for the first time I realized that I had missed my favorite holiday with the family.

"You've been quiet for the last few days," Jennifer said, keeping her eyes on the road.

I glanced over at her, "Yeah?"

"Mmhmm. I come in the room and find you staring at the ceiling like you can see into a different world. You doing okay?"

"I don't know how I'm doing. It's like the universe turned itself inside out. Which way is up? What do I do next, I just don't know."

She drove in silence for awhile before saying, "So, I've been wondering about something. I mean, you didn't just go up to the mountains and have a car wreck. You were on a mission. You were answering a call. Before you left, you told me that you were afraid whatever you discovered might make you change your life. Well, here we are. Everything's changed. If all this had happened before, we wouldn't have thought much of it. It's life. People get in accidents. This is different, isn't it?"

"Yes. It's different. I haven't made sense of anything yet. Not sure I ever will. While I was away I saw . . . things. It was like a door opened so that I could see life in a whole new way. But now, I'm back to what I always thought was reality and it's hard to reconcile this with that, you know?"

She turned her eyes to me and nodded. "I wondered about that. Maybe you can tell me the story sometime?"

"I hope so."

~ ~ ~

So here I am, more than a year after it all began. It's summertime and the sun is warm on my skin. The shiny bracelet glitters in my palm. "Believe" it says. I stand up and tuck it in the pocket of my shorts. Maybe a walk will do me good. It's my day off from the part-time job so I have time on my hands. I finally got work to help pay the bills after a few months of convalescence from my injuries. I'm easily tired now—gone are my days of working like a madman, surviving on three or four hours of sleep each night. I often long for the energy and enthusiasm that once drove me. Where did those familiar taskmasters go? At times I miss the chase—the challenge of running in pursuit of a dream—but my life is on foot now and walking slowly.

Down the sidewalk, bright sunshine on my back casts shadows on my path. I look back at the modest house we rented after the foreclosure. It's comfortable. I'm amazed at how little it really mattered when all was said and done. A smaller home, fewer possessions, lower social status—somehow the trade-off for a simple lifestyle with much less stress seems heavily skewed to our advantage.

We live in an older neighborhood, close to schools and a few blocks from the grocery store. There's a coffee shop on the corner. It's too hot today for coffee but I turn my steps toward the shop anyway. I've spent many hours there over the last several months, reading, thinking and talking with the people who come and go.

I've settled into a routine of sorts. It seems good on the surface, but lately my sleep has been disturbed by dreams that carry me back into the mountains—back to the company of supernatural helpers and visions. It's all so vivid that I wake up shaking in my bed. I remember the mission I was given, but in the light of day it fades into shadow realms of myth and mystery. I've tried to tell a few friends about my experiences but the conversation falters when the skepticism on their faces mirrors my own doubts. Was it all just a fantastic journey of consciousness that resembles the other stories of near death experiences I've read? How can I possibly understand it myself—much less tell a tale that will be helpful to other people?

One indisputable truth remains: I see life through different eyes now. My fear of failure has dissipated—as has my desperate search for approval. I catch myself reveling in the magic of a golden sunset. My children are wise, radiant creatures who bathe me with love. Life before the accident was one long rush of action, but now I find treasure in the quiet pauses. Squirrels, birds and breeze-ruffled leaves speak directly to me in a poetic language that was once only background noise. Perhaps this is enough. Maybe my numinous adventure wasn't real. Now I must go on living, even when that confusing, urgent message stirs inside me during moments of contemplation.

I approach the street corner. Cars race past. A gray-haired homeless man is standing there, leaning against the light pole. On the ground beside him is a sign that reads "Just passing through. Anything helps. God bless you." I dig in my pocket and come up with a handful of coins and the broken silver bracelet. Moving up beside him I touch his shoulder.

"Here," I say, "it's not much." Without turning his head, he holds out his hand and accepts my offering.

"Thank you," he says. Then he reaches into his vest and pulls out a package wrapped in newspaper, tied with string. "Here, I'm supposed to give you this." He holds it up for me over his shoulder, still without turning around.

Stunned, I take it in my hands and stare. What is this? *It's heavy in my hands and feels like it might be a book. I shake my head and turn to ask him questions but he's already across the street. Just before he reaches the other side, I see him put a hat on his head. It's a rusty black beret with an eagle feather sticking out of it. The breath snags in my throat and he turns to look at me over his shoulder.* Jack? *He winks and grins—showing his toothless gums—and then shuffles away from me. Through the noise of traffic I imagine that I can hear tiny brass bells tinkling as he moves.*

I stand there, trying to catch my breath and realize tears are streaming down my cheeks. The dizzy Earth seesaws beneath me. I squeeze the package hard in both hands, trying to keep my balance. I look back across the street, wanting to run after the crazy old mountain man, but he's gone. If it weren't for the gift he left behind, I'd doubt that he was anything other than a trick of my imagination—some psychological artifact. But it's here. Right here in my hands. It's as solid and real as anything else we might touch or feel in our everyday world.

Taking a deep breath, I look around. Cars buzz past. A bicyclist swerves to avoid me on the sidewalk. I need to sit before I unwrap the package. Coffee shop, *I think,* I'll go there.

It's half a block away and I move toward it like a swimmer through the summer air. Walkers pass me, traffic flows down the avenue, but I'm lost in the waves of my eddying thoughts. The blacktop parking lot smells of melting tar. I cross it and tug open the door. A gush of cool, coffee-infused air greets me from the dim interior of the shop. The barista nods at me and smiles. I'm a regular here. I wave at her and look around for a quiet corner. I'm in luck, no one else is in today.

I find a leather chair—my favorite one beside a window where I can see the foothills—and sit. I feel the weight of Jack's gift on my lap. I haven't looked at it until now. Seeing him again and holding tangible evidence of my adventures has suddenly thrown my internal equation out of balance.

Now, I pick up the package and turn it over in my hands. Wrapped in newspaper, tied up with rough twine. I tug at the string, but the knots are tight. I fiddle in my pockets for my fingernail clippers and just snip it. The newspaper catches my eye. It's from the Statesman. *Carefully, I pull it open and squint at the headlines. It's the front page from over a year ago. I'm startled to see a picture of myself as I used to look underneath a story banner:* "Boise Businessman Narrowly Escapes Death," *it screams. Momentarily forgetting the gift inside, I read the short article. Phrases jump off the wrinkled paper:*

...a devastating hit-and-run accident on Highway 21...the Boise man was rescued by a State Trooper and transported by Life-Flight helicopter to St. Luke's for emergency treatment of multiple compound fractures and third-degree burns...he remains in critical condition...local law enforcement is searching for evidence that might lead to the arrest of the perpetrator, but they hold out little hope due to lack of evidence. *Bald facts of my close-encounter with death read like any other attention-grabbing story. The stock in trade for newspapers everywhere, "If it bleeds, it leads."*

I close my eyes for a moment and take a breath. Nervous. I pull the paper off and drop it on the floor. There, like a long-lost friend's face appearing suddenly in a crowd, Emerson's Bible, *stares up at me.*

"So, here you are again," I say out loud. Across the shop, the barista looks up and raises her eyebrows attentively. I shake my head and wave her off. More quietly, I say, "Here you are again. You're real after all." My chest is trembling and I press my fingers on the soft cover, lingering to feel the embossed symbols and stroke its edges.

I flutter the pages, my own scrawled notes fill the lines. All there, I think. *The book falls open near the end, to the page where I've copied Jack's stick drawing of the inverted pyramid. A folded sheet of paper stands up from the binding crease.* A note?

Flattening it open in my hands, I read one word written large across the page: Remember. *That's all it says.* Remember.

"Remember what?" *I wonder.*

Inside my head, the gong crashes and reverberates through my body. Boomsheee! *As the vibrations fade, a smaller sound—a prickling intuition of another presence standing close to me, makes me whip my head around. No one else is near.* "Shh...listen," *my invisible helper says,* "Remember everything. Remember the lessons. Remember the mission you were given, but most of all remember Who You Really Are."

Author's Postscript

This book tells the story of a journey. Like all stories and all journeys it has a beginning and an ending. At the end of something is the birth of something else—in this case, more life.

Alfred Korzybski famously said, "...the map is not the territory". During and since the writing of this book, I have been invited by life to continue re-seeing, re-experiencing and re-learning. With each new step along the path, I find myself less dependent on old maps and much more interested in the journey itself.

So, I recommend that you burn this book and set out upon your own expedition of inner discovery. Perhaps we'll meet somewhere in the field of all possibilities and compare notes of our adventures beyond the map's edge.

About the Author

Jacob Nordby is an author, speaker, and personal transformation coach.

He is published with Jack Canfield in <u>Pearls of Wisdom: 30 Inspirational Ideas to Live Your Best Life Now</u> with Dr. Bernie M. Siegel in <u>The Thought That Changed My Life</u>, and is currently writing another novel, <u>The Cosmic Compass: An Adventure of Inner Guidance</u>.

Mr. Nordby is the founder and publisher of the popular e-magazine site, www.YourAwakenedSelf.com.

You are invited to visit this site to download a complimentary copy of his short e-book, <u>ReMapping Your Life: Get Unstuck, Chart New Paths & Follow Your Purpose.</u>

Scan this code or visit the site to download your complimentary ebook & MP3